This Broken Beautiful Thing

Book #1 in the Broken Beautiful Series

Sophie Summers

Work by Sophie Summers
FairyTale's Don't Exist Series

Alexia Eden (#1)

Angel Blackwood (#2 – To be released 2014)

Broken Beautiful Series

This Broken Beautiful Thing (#1)

A Broken Beautiful Beginning (#1.5)

This Broken Beautiful Beast (#2 – To be released 2014/2015)

<u>To the Little People…</u>

I'd like to thank my family and friends for all their help and support through this little adventure of mine. I'd like to thank all of you who helped get the word out and all of you who made the effort to read my book.
Charmaine, you are an absolutely star! You don't know how much your encouragement and enthusiasm to get my books out there has helped and I will forever be grateful.
Lisa, you don't need to do shit… you're just awesome standing there looking pretty, well… thank you for looking pretty while eagerly reading my work.
To my sexy Bumble Bee and all your tattoo clad beauty, my true love and soul mate… Thank you for being there for me and inspiring me through this journey.

I Love You!

Contents

<u>Chapter 1</u>

"Harley! Please tell me you're ready? We're going to be late!" Ashley, my best friend knocks on the bathroom door.

I look in the mirror at my reflection. I've left my light blond hair down naturally so it hangs in waves down my back. I've done my makeup heavy and smokey, I even went through the effort of placing on fake lashes and boy did that take me a while to figure out. It was worth it though because now my dark blue eyes stand out. I don't usually go through such effort with my appearance, I'm a less is more type of girl, but since tonight is a special night I wanted to look good for him.

Him, being my boyfriend Caleb, we've been best friends for as long as I can remember. I was the nerd and he was the jock. Cliché I know but that's exactly how it was; we are total opposites in every aspect. He never treated me like the rest did, he never looked down on me when I was a nobody and since we've been exclusive I'm a somebody. He was always there for me when I needed him…and I needed him most of the time.

He comes from a large wealthy family, with both parents in the picture and three brothers; one older than him and twins two years younger than us. My home life doesn't exactly include a picture perfect family. My mother is a party-holic whom never married my father; her life revolves around hanging out with friends and acting like an eighteen year old. When she met my father she was working at a strip club, the same club she works for now no less.

They weren't an official couple when she fell pregnant but he still wanted my mother to move near him so he could support us. Momma being the stubborn woman she is couldn't leave the life she led, so she just refused to leave the little town we called home.

Daddy, who goes by the name of Grant, wanted to take me home with him as soon as I was born and that *was* the plan…until I was born. Momma was selfish and kept me even though she knew she wouldn't be able to raise me right and look after me the way Daddy could. When I would ask her why she didn't leave me with Daddy, she'd say that she didn't want me to live with a bunch of dangerous men.

Oh! Did I forget to mention my father is the president of a Motorcycle Club called Devils Grimm? Yeah...well... he is and his road name is Grimm, for obvious reasons...reasons I sure as hell don't want to know. He also had an old lady waiting for him back home while he was shacking up with my momma. Daddy introduced me to his wife Annalie, on my fifth birthday. He had come to see me and found me home alone. Momma had forgotten it was my birthday and was on one of her drinking binges again.

He threatened her with taking custody and decided that after keeping me a secret for five years it was time to take me home for the weekend so I could meet his family...his club.

My father and Annalie were never able to have children so she welcomed me with open arms, as did the members of his club. I felt more at home with all of them than I ever did with my own mother.

My father is a huge man, he has dark black hair that comes just above his shoulders and is always messy. I get my eyes from my father but my body size and figure from my mother, she is short and skinny with light blond hair but she has brown eyes.

Annalie desperately wanted me to live with them and if it wasn't for Caleb I most probably would have. As the years flew by, my feelings grew stronger toward him; I was hopelessly crushing on my best friend even though in the back of my mind I assumed he would only ever see me as his dorky best friend.

Soon Annalie became a mother to me and I called her mom just like she asked. I'll never forget the smile she threw my way the first time I called her that. I was able to talk to her about boys knowing she would never betray my trust and tell my father. We both knew how possessive men from the club were over their woman. Dad never let me stick around long enough at the club house to actually get to know the families that were part of it. I spent every moment I could with my father and new mom at their lake house.

Caleb knows about my home life but I never did tell him about who my father was and what he does. It wasn't that I was ashamed or anything...I mean...my mother is a stripper for goodness sake. My father is a biker and I live in a Trailer so it couldn't get any worse. I knew if Caleb met my father though, my dad may scare him away and I didn't want to take that chance.

When we both started High School the relationship between Caleb and I changed. Even though I was still a total dork, I hit puberty and my skin cleared, my braces came off, breasts grew and curves formed. Guys started to take notice and Caleb didn't like that, he started looking at me in a way I'd never seen before.

Caleb is the captain of the football team; he is tall, muscular with jet black hair and bright green eyes. Evidently he always had girls hovering around him but he would never pay attention to them.

At the end of eighth grade, Caleb finally confessed his feelings for me. He told me he was in love with me, how he only ever wanted me and how he couldn't stand the fact that other guys wanted what was his. I told him how much I loved him and how I never thought he would see me as anything besides the nerd I am.

We started dating and soon all his friends, the same ones that didn't know I existed became my closest friends. The boys from the football team became protective over me and the bitchy cheerleaders knew to stay away.

I turned sixteen on the night of our grade school formal. I was in total shock when I found out that Caleb was a virgin. Of course he'd done other things with girls but he had never had sex and obviously me being me... I was still a virgin. I mean c'mon Caleb was my first kiss after all... That night we lost our virginity and it was the best night of my life.

Caleb is perfect; I knew how lucky I was to have him and I tell him that every day. Girls still try their luck with him not bothering that we were in fact together, but he only ever did have eyes for me and I trust him with all of my heart. As we got older, Caleb and I experimented and shared a lot of other firsts. Our sex life is amazing and that's probably why I'm sitting in this predicament at the moment.

We graduated today and it's our 4th year anniversary too. Ashley, Caleb and I are all going to the same college a few hours away. Caleb and I had found an apartment while Ashley decided that it would be more fun in the dorms.

Caleb has been asking me to marry him every month since I turned eighteen. Of course I've said yes but he says he's going to propose officially as soon as he can afford to buy me a ring with his own money, as he doesn't want to spend his parent's money. I know Caleb won't turn me away once I tell him the news tonight, that's the reason why tonight is so special because tonight I tell him... I'm pregnant.

"Jesus Harley! Answer me!" Ash yells through the door pushing me out of my thoughts.

I open the door to look at my gorgeous best friend. She is tall and skinny with black shoulder length straight hair. Ashley comes from a very wealthy family too. Both of her parents are doctors, her mother's a Gynecologist and her father a plastic surgeon. Her parents have also basically adopted me, welcoming me into their family when I wasn't at Caleb's house.

Before we were friends, her reputation was the main topic through the high school grape vine. I didn't really pay attention because I wasn't all that interested in trash talking other people. I didn't enjoy other people trash talking about our fellow class mates, so if I wasn't with Caleb or his friends I usually just kept to myself.

One day I was sitting in the library and Ashley was doing detention for PDA in the boy's locker room. As her punishment she had to help put away books in the library the entire week after school. She wasn't sure how to place the books so I showed her. Even though I knew she was *friendly* with most of the guys, I found I enjoyed her company *and* her crudeness. We became friends, I ignored the remarks the boys made about her and the warnings they gave me. We got along great and we were soon as close as sisters, and just like with Caleb, Ash and I were total opposites. She is the type of girl that guys like Caleb *should* be dating. She is hot, she knows it and she uses it to her advantage.

"Wow, you look gorgeous girl!" she whistles as she opens the door.

I'm wearing black ankle boot heels with a curve hugging tight mid-thigh black dress; it has a corset type front and is something I would never usually be seen in.

"You should see what I have underneath…" I wink at her. "…and besides I'm not going to have this figure for too long… so I guess I'll enjoy it while I can." I giggle and wink at her. "You look amazing Ash!" I look her over.

She's wearing a bright red dress that's impossibly shorter than mine. If she bends over I could probably see her ass but because she is skinny and tall, the outfit looks good on her. She has black stilettos that only make her already long legs lengthier.

"Yeah babe, who knew you had all those curves hidden under those hideous clothes you wear." She teases. I playfully smack her ass as she bends to look in the mirror fluffing her hair and she squeals. "Hey!" she laughs then her face turns serious. "You nervous about tonight?" she asks.

Ash and her mother are the only people that know about the baby so she knows how important tonight is for me and Caleb. I needed to find the right time to tell him and since we were writing exams and he was focused on his football, there never was a right time to tell him the news.

A few months ago I wasn't feeling too well and explained my symptoms to Ash's mother Lynn. The thought that I could possibly be pregnant didn't even occur to me, I've been on the pill since we started having sex. No one explained that when you take antibiotics it cancels out the birth control pill.

"Nah I know he will be happy, you know how Caleb is…I just want to go see him already, I miss him I've hardly seen him all day…Let's get out of here Ash." We make our way out of her house and to our graduation party that the footballers are throwing at one of their parent's cabins.

Since I can't drink I'm the designated driver. I make my way to my white Ford Fiesta that dad bought me when I passed my drivers and we head to the party. As we get closer to the cabin where the party is being held we turn onto a dust road and wooded area. Obviously they chose this place for a good reason, there's not many houses around to argue about the loud noise and since there will be a lot of underage drinking going on, no one will bug us.

I park the car and we head up to the massive log cabin, I told Caleb we would be here at nine and it's already ten thirty.

"Little Miss Harley Ryder! Is that you?" I look over to Brent, who is Caleb's best friend. He's eyeing me up and down in a way he's done one too many times before. I try reaching for Ash to help me out of this one but she's nowhere to be found in the crowded house. Brent is just like Caleb looks wise;

He is tall and muscular but has blonde hair and blue eyes. He is like a brother to me so him looking at me the way he is right now is making me feel *really* uncomfortable.

"Hey Brent, yeah it's me." I give him a shy smile as I finally respond to him.

"Damn babe! You look hot! Looks like Caleb and I will be spending the evening fighting the boys off you." He teases and gives me a tight hug. He isn't drunk yet but I can smell the beer on him and it grosses me out.

"Speaking of Caleb, have you seen him?" I ask Brent trying to change the subject.

"Yeah, saw him earlier chatting with some of the guys, kept asking if you've arrived yet but we didn't see you come in. Do you want me to help you look for him? Let's get a drink for you in the meantime." He says and walks off but I grab his arm and say, "No thanks Brent, I'm going to go find the bathroom. I'll be back, but if you spot him keep him with you and I'll come find you okay?"

"Sure thing babe." He says as he walks off backwards smiling at me.

I turn to find my way to the bathroom and I notice a couple of guys looking at me the same way Brent just did…with lust in their eyes and a few even wink.

Argh… Really boys?

I desperately need a pee so I walk a little faster trying to find my way to the bathroom. I spot stairs and walk up them. I notice the party is down stairs and no one is on the top floor, the bass from the speakers downstairs can be felt through the floor but it's a little quieter up here.

I make my way down the long hallway when I hear loud moaning coming from one of the rooms; I stop because the voice is familiar.

Seriously Ashley? We haven't even been here for fifteen minutes and she's already screwing someone. Shaking my head I turn to walk away when I hear another familiar voice.

"Shhh... Keep quiet, bend over!" Caleb says in a menacing tone, one he's never used on me before. I back away against the wall opposite the door where the noises are coming from. The pain in my heart hurts so bad, my trembling hand rests over my heart feeling it beat wildly as I stand leaning against the wall that's keeping me from collapsing. I stand there frozen, I try to move, try to get away but my legs won't budge. I knew it was too good to be true, how could he ever be satisfied with me? Ash is the perfect girl for him...she's everything... I'm not.

I continue to stand there listening to her moans and his grunting. I feel the tears tumbling down my face and the make-up I did so perfectly to please him running, all ruined.

"Whoa... Harlz? What's wrong? You okay?" Brent comes skidding to a halt beside me, I wasn't even aware he came upstairs. He looks at me then turns and looks at the door, he does this three more times before his eyes widen and he whispers almost out of breath.

"No...It's not...It can't be..." he too can hear the sounds from the room. I nod my head and his face reddens with fury as he tenses his jaw holding back the anger. He goes for the door but I stop him and whisper, "Don't ...just wait..." he nods and pulls me in for a hug while I hear the door open from behind him.

I peak around Brent's shoulder. I find a distraught looking Caleb looking at the floor; he hasn't even noticed me yet. When a sob breaks out of my mouth I cover it quick with my hand and he whips his face up to look at me. His once tan skin is pale as a sheet with his mouth hanging open, he looks at what I'm wearing and a look of need forms on his face. It disgusts me as much as it did when the other boys looked at me that way, as if I'm a piece of meat.

Brent turns around in a protective stance forcing me to stand behind him and I appreciate the distance he's putting between us more than he will ever know.

Ashley bumps into Caleb while paying attention to fixing her dress. She looks up and gasps. A couple more people have now made their way upstairs and are watching the scene unfold while they whisper to one another.

"You guys have fun? All finished now? Sure you don't want to have a quickie in the next room?" I say sarcastically pointing my finger to the door behind me. I'm wiping away the tears from my face but it's no use, they keep betraying the brave façade I'm trying to portray.

"Harlz it's not...I mean ...I can explain...she meant nothing. I only love you! I've never done this before... Fuck." He runs his hands over his face then looks up and takes a step toward me but Brent pushes his hands up to Caleb's chest.

"I swear! I'm so sorry ...Please... Harley? Say something!" Caleb rambles on looking around Brent at me. He comes closer but I match his steps with my own as I step away.

"Don't touch me. It meant nothing to you? Nothing at all? Well it means *something* to me!" I shout at him. "If you didn't want to be with me, why not just tell me? Why cheat Caleb? Why?" I yell as the tears begin to fall again.

"No Baby I wanna be with you, I love you Harlz you know that! This was a mistake! My head isn't clear, I've got so much going on right now...fuck I don't know what I was thinking." He looks up at me, confused and terrified.

"I'm going to marry you remember? Let's just get out of here so we can talk in private, let me explain...Please Harley." He's pleading as I watch the tears fall down his regret filled face. I've never seen Caleb cry before, he always shows this brave exterior, especially whenever he's around his male friends but right now he's weeping like a baby.

I look to Ashley, she has her hands covering her mouth with the same look of regret on her own face.

"Harley, I don't know what I was thinking! I didn't really think he would take me up on my offer. I'm so sorry, you're my sister, my best friend; it wasn't supposed to happen this way. Please don't hate me, Please!" she squeals as she bursts into tears.

I look at the people around me, their faces show the sadness and sorrow they feel for me. Most know the history between Caleb and I, I see the disgusted looks and head shakes the audience is giving both Caleb and Ashley.

I turn my head in disgust over to her, the slut that I see in front of me. "You know how many times I defended you when people would talk shit behind your back saying what a whore you were? Well Ashley *that* was a mistake... because you *are* a fucking whore."

I look over at Caleb again and see the tears continue to make their way down his beautiful face, he's trying to get closer to me but Brent won't allow him and I can see it's making Caleb angry.

I look down at my trembling hands as I say the following words because if I have to look at his perfect face I might just cave in and forgive his cheating ass.

"Guess you and Ashley don't have to hide anymore now that I'm out of the picture. You guys can shack up in your little apartment and live happily ever after... without me..." the tears fall. I look up to Caleb as realization hits. My whole future, the one I was planning not even an hour before has just crumbled before me.

"You can't leave me Harley! I don't want to live with her, I want you! I love you!" Caleb roars pushing against Brent's chest to get to me. A few more of the guys from the team are now helping Brent hold Caleb back.

"Well… she's all you have right now because I don't want you! I can't even look at you… you both disgust me. I hate you right now! You were the *one*… good thing… I had and now? I don't want anything to do with you…both of you! Just stay away from me and I'll stay away from you." I back away and when Caleb breaks free from the boys hold, I run. I push through the crowds making my way out the house and towards my car. I can hear Caleb calling me even through the loud speakers; hopefully the guys can hold him off for a while, just until I make my escape.

Chapter 2

I jump in my car and speed off down the dust road, the wooded area clears as I head towards the main street of our town. The streets are empty and all the shops are closed, *this town is so dead.* I stop at the red light and burst out in tears. My whole body is trembling as I touch my tummy protectively and whisper…

"Guess it's just you and me baby."

I look in the mirror and wince as I rip off my fake lashes. I use my black cardigan that lies on the seat next to me and remove the makeup that's running down my cheeks.

I don't understand how Ashley could do this to me, she knew how important tonight was and how much I love Caleb. I was betrayed by the two people that I never thought would hurt me like this. I wonder if she will tell him about the baby. *Most probably not, she knows he'll want to be a part of his child's life and she's too selfish to share him with his own kid.*

The light turn green; I'm not even two meters away when I see a set of lights on the side of my window, I hear the tires screeching but it's too late. The sound of the glass shattering hits my ears as the airbag knocks the air out of my lungs. I can hear the scratching and grinding of metal as the car rolls. It all happens so quickly but I feel like time has frozen as I watch the glass fall around me. The car rolls a couple times then slams against the tree on the side of the road.

My head hurts as I come to. I'm hanging to my side and my seat belt holds my body in place tightly. Without thinking I unlatch it and drop to the floor with a loud thud, crying out in pain as I hit the broken glass beneath me. I hear the metal door above open and feel the presence of someone as they pop their head in.

I must have died because this guy looks like an Angel; a dark Angel. The most beautiful creature I have ever seen asks me in a gruff voice, "Darlin' are you okay? I'm so sorry, here… please take my hand." he leans down into the car and reaches out his hand for me to take.

I place my small hand in his large ring covered rough ones and I gently stand and squeeze my way through the buckled seats. He lifts me up and out of the car and carries me to the back of the tree, sitting down and leaning against it with me still in his lap. My eyes are beginning to clear but my head still hurts. I take a closer look at his face; he has beautiful blue eyes with black hair just like Caleb's, although this guy's hair is much longer. It covers the side if his face almost in an "emo" kind of way but it just comes off messy and sexy. He has light stubble on his jawline, maybe a day old. He's wearing a tight black shirt with a biker leather jacket, and on it a patch I instantly recognize.

"So Raven huh? " I smile and look up at him as he types on his phone. He seems shocked that I was able to read his badge.

"Hmm Devils Grimm too…" The adrenaline must be running through my body because I feel giddy and my heart is beating really fast. I look at the emblem on the side of the jacket above his name.

"How do you know all this? You are too pretty and innocent to have any business with bikers…" he chuckles and takes a tissue from his pocket and places it against my throbbing head where I hit the window. I take it from him and look down at the blood covered napkin and place it back on my head feeling the adrenaline slowly leave my body, replaced by panic.

"Grimm's my daddy…" I say. I feel him suddenly tense underneath me.

"Fuck, you're Harley? Your daddy's gonna kill me." he says. I can sense the fear coming from him. I suppose I would also be afraid of my father too if I was in his position.

"Nah…don't worry about him, I'll tell him it's not your fault. It's okay…" I mumble worried that my father might hurt him for causing this accident.

"No it's not okay! I shouldn't have skipped the red light; I was in such a hurry. I'm so sorry Harley. I've called for help; the ambulance should be here soon, are you okay?" He says looking my face over, obviously assessing the damage.

"This night couldn't get any better." I mumble sarcastically then notice him wince.

"Oh, I'm talking about the shit I had to deal with tonight…" he looks at me waiting for me to continue.

I groan then explain, "I caught my boyfriend hooking up with my best friend…on our fourth year anniversary. So I guess it can only get better right? When you hit rock bottom, there's only one way out… right? Up." I bend to take my heels off but he stops my hand and takes them off for me.

"I'm sorry babe, no one deserves that, give me his name and address and your father and I will pay him and the whore a visit." He gives me a breathtaking smile obviously trying to lighten the mood; I notice he seems older than me but not nearly as old as my father. Even though in this moment I hate Caleb for what he's done to me, I would never ever want to see him hurt and I don't think I'd ever be able to forgive myself or my father if he did ever hurt him.

"No Raven you can't tell him about that; I'll keep your secret if you keep this one. Please!" I beg him, "Daddy will kill him." I say softly.

He runs his hand through his hair and lets out a deep breath. "Okay Darlin', but do me a favor… my real names Jace, a pretty girl like you don't need to call me by my road name." He flirts making me laugh at his cocky attitude.

"Jace, how old are you?" The adrenaline continues to leave my body, the pain from all the cuts as well as the impact from the seatbelt against my chest and rolling in the car is starting to take its toll on me.

"Just turned twenty five baby." He winks again then his phone starts vibrating in his pocket beneath me. I move and he helps me off him, I slowly stand as he answers his phone. My body is aching and I try to stretch my muscles. My head hurts really bad as well as my ribs.

I look at the wreckage and notice his large black SUV has only a small amount of damaged by the front metal bars. *That's why he only had a few small scratches.* My car on the other hand is a total write-off, there's glass all over the road and the front of my car is now smoking. I hear Jace talking on the phone but I'm too busy looking at the damage around us; usually the police are quick around here but I can't hear any sirens. I know the ambulance might take a while because the nearest hospital is half an hour away.

As I walk back to the spot we were sitting, I feel cramps in my stomach then an excruciating sharp pain in my lower stomach. It makes me hunch over and hold my belly while using the streetlight post for support as I cry out.

"Oh baby, please be okay." I say as the tears fall. Jace does a double take when he sees me, then races in my direction telling me my father is on his way. I feel warm liquid running down my bare legs, I look down and see blood.

"Oh no…" I say crying harder. Jace holds me against his chest tight preventing me from falling on my feet.

"W….what's happening? Fuck…you're bleeding!" Jace panics when he notices the blood. He pushes me away from him, still holding my arms tight looking me over to see where the blood is coming from. I am relieved when I hear the sirens coming over the hill.

"Jace I think…I think I' m miscarrying…" I say dejectedly as look up into his beautiful eyes and feel the tears escape mine.

"Shit…you're pregnant? Why didn't you tell me when I got you out of the car? This is my fault! I'm so sorry Harley." he says filled with sorrow as he pulls me closer into his chest and kisses my forehead.

"It's …it's…" I don't even know what to say? Should I say it's okay and make him feel better about the situation when all I really want to do is scream and shout at him and tell him this is all his fault. I do neither and opt for a different approach.

"When they take me… don't leave me alone… please." I beg as I cry into his warm chest.

"I won't leave you baby…I promise…I'll be by your side the whole time." He promises as he picks me up and sits us back against the tree with me tight against his chest, taking my hand and holding it tight on my lap.

I hear sirens closer now then I hear tires skidding and doors opening and closing.

I hear Caleb shout out, "Harley! Babe please be okay... Please." I hear footsteps then I hear someone jumping up onto the car and climbing up over the metal and glass. I hear Brent shout, "She's not here! Where's the other driver?"

They obviously can't see us behind the car and tree. Jace tries to move from beneath me but I tell him I don't want to see Caleb right now and his body becomes rigid.

"That's the fucker who cheated on you?" Jace whispers angrily into my ear.

"Please Jace, let's just wait for the ambulance, I can't deal with him right now." I say as I clutch my stomach twisting in pain.

"It hurts so much Jace...they need to hurry. I can't lose my baby too...I can't." I start crying into his chest. He places his hand on my belly over my dress and rubs me gently, he is so big and manly, this little gesture seems so unlike something someone like him would do. It gives me tingles throughout my body and I cuddle closer into him. We hear the sirens head in our direction and Jace picks me up slowly, careful not to hurt me.

"Come on, the ambulance is here baby, let's get you some help." He starts walking me to the ambulance quickly as I lay in his arms cradled to his chest.

"Don't let him near me please...don't let any of them near me, promise me." I whisper into his chest.

"Okay Harley, I promise." He says as he kisses my head.

"And don't tell anyone about the baby, okay?"

"Wait...doesn't Caleb know?" he asks in confusion.

"Only my best friend knew, I was going to tell him tonight, just don't say anything okay." I whisper yell and he nods tensing his jaw.

"I'm feeling...really...tired Jace, I'm going...to...close my eyes....just for a little bit. Don't leave...me alone....okay?" I feel my eyes grow heavy and my body growing weaker. I close my eyes and fall into a deep sleep as I hear Jace shouting at the paramedics and warning me not to sleep.

I wake up lying on the soft grass with a woman's hand on my chest performing CPR, "We got her! She's breathing!" the lady says looking at the guy that was removing the breathing apparatus from my mouth. "Harley we need to get you to the hospital but you need to stay awake okay sweetie? You've lost a lot of blood and you're in shock." the lady says and I nod my head.

I look to my side and see Caleb calling for me as the cops keep him away. Jace is whispering comforting words to me holding my hand and rubbing my hair with the other. I look to my right when I hear the rumble of motorbikes and see my dad leading what looks to be the entire club. He parks his bike and comes running to my side.

"Harley! Are you okay? What happened?" he says kneeling down kissing my forehead.

"Daddy, it's okay I'm feeling better now. I wasn't looking and I skipped the light; it was all my fault I'm sorry." I say as the tears fall and the salt from them burn the cuts on the side of my face making me wince. I feel Jace squeeze my hand knowing I lied to save him from my father's wrath.

"It's okay baby girl, we'll sort everything out, luckily I was in town when it happened. I love you Harley. We will see you at the hospital okay? I just have a few things to clear up here quick." he says and I nod.

He stands up then turns to Jace. "Thanks for looking after her brother, take care of her, I need to have a word with the police but I'll meet you at the hospital. The boys will follow the ambulance." Jace nods and my dad saunters off in the direction of the police officers.

"Sorry sir, you can't come with us if you aren't family. You need to get checked out too, there's another ambulance on its way for you." The male paramedic says.

"There's no fucking way I'm leaving her alone, I'm her man let me go with you. I promised I wouldn't leave her alone." Jace says, anger dripping from his voice. The lady paramedic tells the male that it's okay and lets him into the ambulance with me.

I smile when Jace says he's my *man*, he's too perfect to be mine… I thought Caleb was perfect and look how that turned out? Jace winks at me as he enters the ambulance and takes my hand.

As the ambulance drives away I hear the roar of all the motorcycles escorting us to the hospital. I turn to the lady paramedic, "I'm pregnant…but I think something is wrong with the baby." Tears roll down my face as she nods, gives me a sad look and pats my hand.

She rushes to the radio and speaks to someone on the other end explaining my condition to them. My eyes are heavy again and I try really hard to stay awake but I'm too exhausted…emotionally and physically.

Chapter 3

CALEB POV

"What the fuck is wrong with you!?" Brent shoves my chest as Harley runs down the stairs and out of my life. I keep screaming for her to come back but she doesn't, Brent and some boys from the team hold me back, I turn around and rush off to the bathroom.

I slam the door and punch the wall. I fucked up so badly, how could I do that to her? What the fuck is wrong with me? I've only ever been with Harley, I was going to propose to her tonight... I saved for the ring and finally got it this morning. *What the fuck have I done?*

I came home today to find my father fucking his assistant so I came to the party and headed straight for a room. I was sitting in one of the bedrooms trying to clear my head with a bottle of jack when that fucking slut walked in. She offered to take my mind off everything for a few minutes, I didn't think she would strip and pull out a condom. I don't know what I was thinking, I couldn't even finish; however she on the other hand was quick to fucking climax, I was so disgusted in her and what I was doing, I stormed out the room.

She is supposed to be Harley's best friend; she knew my plan to propose tonight, but instead of taking my mind off what my father was doing I ended up doing the same thing to my beautiful Harley.

When I walked out of the room and saw my stunning girl standing there all dressed up with tears and make up running down her face, I knew I had fucked up a beautiful thing. My heart broke as she looked at me with such hatred, she is so perfect....she is too good for me and I was trying really hard to be good enough for her but I was bound to fuck up...and I did just that.

When she said she didn't want me anymore I knew it was true, but I also know that I will spend every day of my life trying to make it up to her. I need her; she makes my life brighter and happier. As I watched her walk away I knew I lost my most precious treasure...her.

"Dude, what is wrong with you? You fucked up a real good thing! Dammit dude, what the fuck?" Brent says as he follows me into the bathroom shaking his head, he leans against the counter and he watches me with the same disgusted look. I'm sitting on the end of the bath with my head in my hands, tears falling down my face.

"I know Brent, I fucked up...I know."

"Harley is perfect man; you ruined all that to hook up with *fucking Ashley?* What were you thinking? Do you realize how many guys have wanted Harley; you know how hard they've tried to get with her too? *Really damn hard* but she turned every. Single. One. Down, that girl was so in love with you man. You're my best friend and you know you are like a brother to me but man….you don't deserve her…she deserves way better." Brent says.

I want to yell at him right now but I know every word out his mouth is true. I can't tell you how many times the guys from the team have told me how lucky I am to have Harley and here I am fucking everything up.

"Don't you think I know that Brent? I fucked up okay! Are you going to sit there or are you going to help me find her?" I say, as I get up then head out the door to find my girl not waiting for his reply.

Brent decides to drive since he's only had one beer, we see ambulance lights and two police cars overtake us; I have this bad feeling in the pit of my stomach. We are heading toward the main street when I spot a large Black SUV with the front damaged, I follow the glass and rubble lying all over the road and I see Harley's little white car lying on its side against a tree all banged up. Brent races his car towards where her car lies and skids to a stop forgetting that the cops are already assessing the scene by the black car. I run out and look through the front window but can't see anything, Brent climbs on the car and looks inside and tells me she's not there. I start to panic, this is all my fault…

The cops are asking us questions when I spot a tall big guy coming out from behind the tree where Harley's car is, he's holding Harley's little body in his arms. Her legs have blood running down them and the side of her face is covered in blood and scratches. I move in her direction, calling her name out but the cops stop me. The guy cradling my girl to his chest looks over at me and gives me an obnoxious glare then pulls Harley closer to his chest and kisses her head with his eyes still on me.

I want to rip his fucking head off for touching my girl. I see the paramedics rush over to her and they place her on the soft grass; she's not conscious.

The big guy heads in my direction with a determined look on his face, standing just behind the police officer that was restraining me, "Don't you dare go near her, do you understand me?" he says.

"Who the hell do you think you are? She's *my* girlfriend; *you* better stay the hell away from her! I should be there with her *not* you!" I yell at the arrogant asshole.

"Your girlfriend?" He scoffs, "I don't think so buddy, especially after she caught you fucking her best friend. I guess your loss is my gain because *I'm* the one that's going to look after that beautiful girl and *I'm* going to treat her the way you *should have* treated her." He shouts back at me, filled with that cocky attitude. Okay so he might be bigger and a little taller than me but he doesn't scare me at all. I'm not going to let this dude take what's mine and Harley *is* mine.

"That's never going to happen, we've known each other all our lives, she belongs with me…she's mine!" I bellow as I move toward him until Brent stops me.

The guy doesn't even flinch, he stands there looking at me with a cocky smirk, "Nah…you got that wrong again *kid*…she's mine now. You better stay away from her because if you don't…I will come after you, and I will be more…hands on." he says as he grins at the cop, winks at me then backs away. This guy makes my blood boil. *Who the hell does he think he is?*

He has balls threatening me in front of the officer like that but the officer doesn't do anything, he ignores the comments the guy made. These damn bikers think they're high and mighty and the police accept it. The bikers tend to run the towns around here because most of them have inside contacts in the police force, most cops are afraid to go against the biker clubs; these clubs are known for their brutality.

I turn my attention to the paramedics who are now performing CPR on Harley. My heart hurts as I see them pounding on her chest and pumping oxygen into her.

"Please be okay Harlz…please." I whisper as I continue to watch them try and save my girl. Brent watches too and puts his hand on my shoulder showing that he's there for me. We see them stop with the CPR and her eyes are open, that *guy* kneels down next to her and holds her hand while he runs his hands through her hair. She lets him do it and it pains me to see it, I can't even imagine how she must have felt to find me having sex with Ashley. *Oh God, what the fuck have I done…?*

We hear the rumble of motorbikes as about a dozen or so bikers approach the scene. The huge guy that was leading the troop stops and jumps off his shiny bike and runs to where Harley is lying on the grass. He kisses her forehead, "Who the fuck is he?" I say out loud and the cop decides now is the time to speak up.

"That's Grimm, don't let him hear you talk like that 'bout him, he'll kill you on the spot." The old guy says as he turns back to look at *"Grimm"* who's now talking to my girl with a soft expression on his face. Grimm starts walking toward us, he stands in front of the cop and I can see they know each other well.

The cop asks him, "How's she doing? Did you find out what happened? We wanted to wait for you to get here before we wrote it up."

"Yeah my baby girl is okay, just a lot of bleeding .They're taking her to the hospital now, my guys will help escort her there. She says she skipped the red light when she hit Raven's SUV. Raven isn't pressing any charges but if there's any damaged to property you know where to send the bill." Grimm says to the cop using an authority not even the police officer could have pulled off if he tried. This guy is massive, he towers over the cop and he doesn't look to be too old, maybe in his late thirty's early forties. I can see he's packing beneath his leather jacket, his gun handle sticks out. He must be Harley's father, no wonder she always kept quiet when it came to him.

They continue to talk about some meeting Grimm was at in town while the paramedics take Harley away. I turn to Brent and we make our way to his car. We notice a couple other cars pull up. I see Ashley come out of one of them and start running towards us, heels clicking on the tar road.

"Is it Harley? Is she okay? Where is she?" she says frantically as she comes up to me and touches my forearm.

"Don't touch me! No, she's not okay; they've taken her to hospital." I say bluntly, walking to the car but she stops me again saying, "This is entirely our fault; she shouldn't have had to find out that way!" She wails, and her voice only irritates me more. I don't know how the fuck I managed to go through with hooking up with her.

"No I shouldn't have laid a hand on you, you're fucking disgusting! I can't believe I did that to Harley." I shout. She looks at me with disbelief.

"You wanted it just as much as I did! Don't act like you didn't feel the tension between us? It was bound to happen Caleb. Don't you see it's you and I who are *supposed* to be together! I love Harley yes but I can't stand the fact that she has you. You and I come from the same life, don't you get it? We are meant to be together Caleb. I don't want to hurt Harley in the process but... now everything works out, we can be together without hiding anything. We can stay in that apartment you guys got...it's going to be perfect babe." Her smile infuriates me.

"You are delusional! I fucking *hate* you Ashley, do you honestly think I would choose you over Harley? You've fucked the whole school, you're so fake and you irritate the living shit outta me. You planned all this? Well guess it didn't work out all that well did it? Because you and I are *never* going to be together! I made a mistake sleeping with you, a *huge fucking* mistake and I regretted it as soon as it happened. I belong with Harley and not only did you fuck our relationship up but you ruined the only true friendship you ever had. She was the only real friend you had and she stood up for you when no one else would, even when the boys and I warned her to stay away from your no good slutty ass. You lost *that* Ashley! And for what? To be with me? Well *that* was one big fucking mistake! Stay the fuck away from me Ashley." I yell, as I walk away and jump into Brent's car.

I look at her through the window and see the realization of what she's just done hit her and I see regret...the same regret surging through me.

Chapter 4

I wake up and hear my father and Anna's voices, they don't notice I'm waking up so I keep my eyes closed as I listen to what they're saying.

"Anna baby, she's coming with us, I don't care what her mother says it's final. I'm not going to argue about this with you." My father says in a harsh tone.

"Grant please… we should speak to her mother first and let her know what's happening to Harley. What if Harley doesn't even want to stay with us, it's the right thing to do!" Anna argues with him.

"I don't give a fuck what the *right* thing to do is, Harley is MY daughter and she should have been with us from the moment she was born. She could have fucking died, I'm not losing any more time with my baby because her mother is too selfish to let her go. Have you seen how skinny she is? I stopped at the house before I came to the hospital to tell Roxanne about the accident, the cupboards are all empty and the only thing in that fridge is beer! She won't let her live with me because of the club but I *will* at least be able to feed my child and look after her. Harley is eighteen, she can make her own decisions now, if she wants to I've with us then it's happening …whether her mother likes it or not!" My father lectures poor Anna and I don't hear a reply from her. There's no arguing with my father, he always gets his way.

Okay so I know there hasn't been food in the house for a while now but I really don't think I've lost that much weight. Caleb mentioned it to me and so did Ashley but I didn't really take notice. I've always been really skinny and I thought my curves were still there even if my clothes were a little looser than they were before… Luckily I'm skinny enough that the baby bump can hardly be seen through my loose clothes.

I attempt to loosen the tension in the room, "Daddy, I'll stay with you and Mom." I say with a rough dry voice.

I open my eyes to see my dad whip his head around and rush to my side along with Anna. My biological mother is known as Momma and Anna is Mom to me. Anna just smiles over at me.

"Baby girl, we were so worried about you! You've been out for a couple of hours, doc says the meds were pretty strong but didn't think they'd have you sleeping *this* long. How are you feeling?" my father says as he looks me over and kisses my forehead.

"I'm feeling better, how's Jace? " I ask them.

"Jace is fine sweetie; he just went downstairs to get us some coffee so he should be here soon. All your *friends* are out there waiting to hear if you're okay, want me to let them in?" Anna says. I know by the way she says *friends*, who exactly she is talking about….Caleb.

"No! Don't!" I blurt out and she raises her brow confused by my outburst. "I think you should just tell them I'm asleep, I'm guessing it's late and they should... um... go home. Tell them you'll let them know when I'm awake or something." I beg Anna giving her a pleading look; she nods, kisses my cheek and leaves the room.

My father then asks me, "You really want to stay with us?"

"Yeah daddy, I need to get away from here besides the college is just a Block away from you anyway. I don't think Momma really wants me around in any case, she won't even notice I'm gone." I say softly, saddened by the fact that my own mother wasn't here when I woke up.

My father tenses and I notice the frown lines on his forehead, I can tell he's pretty angry right now at her. "I swear I could kill that woman for treating you this way!" he says loudly as he runs his hands through his hair in frustration.

"Are you okay to stay with us? You know...since we live in the club house most of the time, the boys from the club are always around? It's usually rowdy and you may see things you won't like. I could buy you your own apartment if you'd prefer, anything you want baby girl, I will do it?" he says calmly as sits in the chair next to the hospital bed and places my small hands in his much larger ones.

"No Daddy, its fine...I really don't want to be alone. I don't mind all of that as long as you and Mom are around I'll be fine." I smile sweetly at him and he returns the smile.

"Of course we will be there, I'm so happy you decided to stay with us honey!" Anna says as she walks in the room and kisses me on the cheek happily.

"Thanks Mom, uh...did the doctor say anything to you guys while I was sleeping?" I ask nervously hoping the doctor hasn't mentioned anything about the baby. Thinking about the baby, I place my hand on my stomach praying that my little bundle is still safe inside me.

"No honey, I asked the nurse while I was in the hallway and she said she should be here shortly." Anna says concerned.

"Mom, will you and Daddy be able to go over to the trailer and fetch my things, I don't want to go back there." I say to both of them, then turn toward my father. "I need Mom to go with you because of all the girly stuff I need but I don't want her to go alone in case Momma's there and starts causing trouble... you're the only one that can talk to her Daddy."

"Okay baby girl, I'll call Jace to come sit with you while we're gone. You gonna be fine by yourself?" Daddy asks me. I nod and give him a small smile.

They each kiss and hug me gently, careful not to hurt me and leave just as Jace walks in the door. My father whispers something to him then leaves.

Jace walks up to me, smiles then kisses me on my forehead, the way he lets his lips linger against my skin is rather intimate. My head is spinning, why the hell is he acting like this and why do I feel a bond with him, like we just click? I've only met him a few hours ago but he's acting like we've known each other for years.

Guess when you're in a life or death situation it brings you closer to the person you're sharing it with….

"Harley, how are you feeling? You had me nervous there a couple times…" he says as he sits on the bed next to me and holds my hands.

"I'm…I don't know how I am… I just want to speak to a doctor and find out how my baby is doing…are you okay?" I ask him trying to find my voice. I feel so shy when it comes to him and it's probably due to the fact that he's gorgeous in a spank-me-and-whisper- dirty-things-to-me kinda way. He's certainly not the usual boy next door type that I'm usually around.

"Yeah baby I'm all good, just a couple scratches." Jace says as he looks down at my hands in his.

I hear the door open and I see Ashley's mom walk in. I straighten in the bed as she walks over to me, eyeing Jace who continues to hold my hand in his.

I cringe; even though she hasn't done anything I can't help but think of her slutty daughter who has ruined my life.

"How are you feeling honey?" She says as she looks over my chart.

"Been better, is the baby okay?" I ask quickly needing an answer.

"Yes honey the baby is fine, the impact from the steering wheel caused a slight tear in your placenta. You need to stay on bed rest for the next few days and take the medicine I prescribe you. Your father has emphasized that you will be living with him and he wants you out of here as soon as possible. So if everything goes as planned then he can take you home this afternoon but you need to take it easy. If you don't, you can put your baby's life in danger. You are really bruised around your stomach and ribs but I will prescribe medicine for the pain. I also wanted to speak to you about your weight. We did an ultrasound whilst you were under and it looks like you are fourteen weeks along now, but you aren't showing because you're so underweight. You really need to put on some more honey; the baby is taking all your nutrients and vitamins and you are already underweight as it is Harley. I will prescribe you vitamins that you need to take daily for you and your baby's health. Although your baby is getting nutrients, the concerns I have regarding your weight is not good for either of you long term." She says in a stern motherly tone, I can see this bothers Jace as he sits there glaring at her, he isn't aware of the fact that she is Ashley's mother.

I didn't occur to me that I could be that far along; that means I was pregnant longer than I realized. I am disappointed in myself that Lynn felt it necessary to lecture me on my weight; I would never want to cause my baby harm ever.

"Harley who is your...uh...friend here?" Lynn says in a snotty voice.

"He's um –"I say but I'm interrupted by Jace.

"I'm her man; why are you speaking to her so rudely?" Jace says as he turns around and stands up next to the bed opposite Lynn with an angry expression.

"Jace, wait. This is Ashley's mom, you know the best friend I told you about? I've known Lynn for a long time and she's like a mother to me. Calm down big man." I say as I reach out for his arm and pull him closer to me.

"Oh... Sorry Ma'am." He murmurs looking back and forth between us.

"Honey why did he say he's your *man*? Why isn't Caleb here with you?" she asks genuinely, looking back at me genuinely concerned.

"Me and Caleb aren't... I mean... he-" I say, but I'm interrupted by Jace yet again.

"That piece of shit isn't here because Harley caught him having sex with none other than...*your daughter*!" Jace sneers as his temper rises again; his face turning red. I hear Lynn gasp and cover her mouth in shock.

"What! Oh my goodness! I'm so sorry honey...I don't know what to do with her anymore." She walks back and forth scratching her head. "I don't understand how she could do that to you? You both are as close as sisters! She loves you as much as we do. I'm so sorry honey; don't you worry, when I see that girl her father and I *will* be having a few words, her behavior is so disappointing and unacceptable." She says in an angry tone. "What's going to happen to you and the baby? Where will you go? Have you told Caleb yet?" she rambles on nervously as her attention turns back to me.

"I'm going to be living with my father as you already know, but I still have to tell them about the baby. I was supposed to tell *him* tonight; you knew how special tonight was...but yeah... I am going to tell him, I just need a little space right now. I can't look at him in the face after what he's done...not for a while at least." I say, wiping the tears away from my face. Jace comes up to me and rubs my back, he smells good... manly.

"Of course honey...you call me if you need anything." She gives me a hug and leaves the room.

Jace and I sit in silence before he decides to speak up.

"Sorry about my temper...I kinda have a short fuse and I didn't like the way she was talking to you." Jace says as he moves his hands through his long messy hair and moving the hair that's falling into his face.

"Yeah I noticed. " I chuckle.

"You know... you didn't have to lie to your father about the accident. I deserved to get my ass beat by him for skipping that light." He sits on the chair next to my bed and gets comfortable leaning back with his arms behind his head, boots up right against my bed. His arms are covered with various tattoos and it only adds to his masculine beauty.

"I don't want there to be blood on my hands." I tease him and he chuckles. "Why did you skip the light?"

"I...ah...was on a job and was trying to get out of there quickly. I had someone on my tail but when I hit you, they drove past not wanting to be there when the cop's came. I wasn't focused on the road and I didn't even see your car until it was too late. I'm so sorry babe." He says; his voice is full of sorrow.

"A job?" I ask him.

"Um...yeah for your dad; club business. Please don't ask me what job because I really don't want you to think badly of me anymore than you already do." He lets out a small laugh but I know he's faking it, just trying to sway from the topic.

"C'mon just tell me? I give him a pleading look and I can see he's about to cave.

"Okay but you keep this between me and you and don't tell your daddy, he will kill me if he hears me telling his little girl all his club business. Ah man... I really don't want to tell you." he signs but continues.

"Okay, so Grimm sends me around for the money runs. Meaning, I collect the cash from the guys that owe him but...if they don't ...I ah....rough them up a little...just to get the point across that we don't expect tardiness on our payments. So that's what happened tonight, I had to get in and outta there quickly before anyone saw but a couple of their guys came after me. I swear I never saw you at the lights and I feel fucking terrible that I've put you through all of this." Jace says quietly and I see the regret all over his face.

I knew the club was dangerous and my dad was involved in illegal activities but I didn't know the extent of it all. I don't understand how the Jace I've met, the one who's treated me with such gentleness is basically a hit man for my father. I'm shocked by what he's telling me; even though he looks exactly like the dangerous type I should stay away from, I can't seem to get him out of my head.

We spend the rest of the morning chatting, I enjoy his company and spending time with him. My father and Anna come back and he looks angry, my mother was most probably at the house when he arrived. He doesn't mention anything to me but I notice the tension in the air.

My father then argued with Lynn when she said she wanted me to stay in hospital for a few more days. He was still in the dark about the baby so to him all I had wrong with me was a few scratches and bruises. After he informed her that he would make sure his doctor kept an eye on me she reluctantly agreed to let me leave that afternoon. Jace wheeled me out and I was thankful that Caleb and Ashley weren't outside waiting for me. Jace helped me into my father's SUV; Daddy's Harley sits on a trailer at the back of the car. Yeah that bike is Daddy's pride and joy, no one else is allowed to drive it.

I'm guessing you've realized how I ended up with the name I have...

My body is sore and stiff, the medicine I was prescribed definitely doing its magic. Jace sits in the back with me while Anna and Daddy are up front. We're escorted the whole three hours back to the club house. I wake up as Jace carries me into a room and places me on the bed. I know it's his room from the scent that surrounds me. He places a side light on and I sit up in bed wiping my eyes.

"Grimm told me to look after you; he hasn't had a chance to get your room ready. Guess you will be sleeping next to me so I can keep an eye on you if anything happens." Jace winks as he closes his room door and stalks over towards a desk where he throws his leather jacket over the chair. I notice him pull something out from the back of his jeans and put it in the drawer next to his bed, it lands with a loud thud. I look closer….a gun. My eyes widen with surprise and I'm a little scared. I've never seen one in real life.

I've only ever been around guys my own age and even then they were never really much to look at because Caleb was everything I wanted and more. Aside from my father, I've never been around guys like Jace, he is angry and mean looking but the way he talks to me and treats me is something else. I'm so in awe of him and even though my conscience is screaming and telling me not to go down this road I just can't keep my eyes off him.

He sits on the bed and takes his boots off, followed by his shirt. He's definitely something else. His chest has a tattoo of two large sparrows surrounded by beautiful red roses. His nipples are pierced too with small little studs in each. He suddenly stands and I watch his hands go to his black studded belt but suddenly he stops with his fingers on the zip of his jeans and he looks down at me.

"Um… Sweetness, you might want to turn around, I'm commando." His sexy grin appears and I know I've been caught staring. *Thank goodness I'm not drooling.* I quickly turn my head and hide it in his pillow covering my face as I lie down.

Oh god how am I going to get any sleep with all that next to me…Argh…

I feel the bed dip behind me and the covers are pulled, I move up to the other side of the bed as far away from him as possible. I take a sneak peak to see him getting comfortable leaning his hands behind his head.

I raise an eyebrow and point to the large thick blanket, "I swear Jace… you better not be naked underneath here."

He chuckles as he rests his head on his folded arm making the muscles stick out and flex. "Why don't you have a look and find out?" he gives me a naughty smile as he lifts the blanket slightly. I quickly turn my head and whine, "Jace…"

"Fuck…didn't think I'd get this response the first time I brought a girl to my bed." He says dramatically and I whip my head back to face him.

"What do you mean the first time you brought a girl to your bed?" I ask confused, surely he would have tons of girls lining up for him.

I don't know how but he reads my thoughts. "Oh baby I have plenty of girls waiting on me but I never bring them back here. I'd rather they not know where I stay so they don't hassle me after all is said and done. I don't want a relationship, I could never make one woman happy and I don't do well with commitment. I'm still young, I can worry about having an old lady in a couple years. You're the first girl to ever sleep here next to me." He says in a cocky tone as if it doesn't faze him.

What a player….

"That's disgusting…" I fold my arms over my chest, "…and why am I so special that that you allow me to grace your precious bed with *my* presence?" I say sarcastically causing him to chuckle.

"Yes you are very special…and…by that repulsed look you just gave me, I know your hands won't wonder in your sleep, besides all that? You're already pregnant…damage is already done." He trails off laughing, as if me being pregnant is a good enough reason for him allowing me in his bed.

His cockiness annoys me; I turn over and put the side lamp off. I don't climb under the blanket even though I am freezing my ass off, I curl up into a ball.

"Harley if you don't get under this blanket right now, I am going to make you." Jace says firmly through the silence of the dark room.

"Go to sleep Jace." I say with the same tone as I make my pillow comfortable.

"I'm wearing boxers for fuck sake just get under the blanket you stubborn woman." he rumbles.

"No." I say through gritted teeth.

"Fine…I warned you." I feel him leave the bed, and then I hear his heavy footsteps in the dark as he walks towards my side of the bed.

I won't lie…I'm kind of scared.

I see his shadow loom over me as he gently picks me up ignoring my squirms then pushes the blanket down and places me on the bed. He climbs in behind me and pushes me with his body towards the other side of the bed. I surrender and hold the blanket up to my chin enjoying the warmth from the spot that he was laying in moments before. I'm only wearing tight leggings and a long t-shirt that comes mid-thigh.

Jace doesn't stop there, he pulls me into his side so that my head is resting on his arm and his hand is over my stomach. The side of my body is pressed up against his front as he lies down facing me and I can feel his warm minty breath on my right temple. He slowly moves his hand over tummy and I flinch as his rough hands touch the bare skin under my belly button where my small baby bump is. Fact is I hardly know him and even though it feels like we know each other…we don't, not really. I attempt to move his hand away.

"Keep still baby, you don't want to know what I'll do next if you don't listen to me this time." He says against my head with a stern voice; I nod and sigh defeated and a little afraid. I don't know why the hell my father would let the guy that's beats up people for a living look after his daughter.

I feel him smile against the skin of my temple when my body relaxes against his.

"I like it when you listen to me babe. Are you warm now?" he says softly.

"Yeah. Thanks Jace." I whisper.

He starts rubbing my stomach now from hip to hip. His large rough hands leave tingles all over my body. Only Caleb has ever touched me and left that feeling. The way he brushes his rough hands against my belly is such a protective gesture. I do it all the time when I think or worry about the baby growing inside of me and what the future holds for us.

"I don't know what I would have done if your baby didn't make it." He lets out a deep breath and I can feel his chest rise and fall against me.

"I'm so sorry for putting you both through all of this." He whispers in rough voice and slows the rubbing on my belly, my heart melts at his sincerity and affection. Without realizing it I relax and snuggle closer to his warm bare chest. I can't see him in the dark but I can feel the ripples of the muscles in his stomach as well as the firmness of his chest and arms around me. I turn my face so that my cheek is now leaning against his warm chest and he snuggles closer to me breathing into my hair. His hand from the arm that I'm leaning on comes up pushing me impossibly closer against his chest as he softly runs his hand gently over my scalp and through my hair. In this moment I feel so safe and protected in his warm arms.

I guess that's what I'm going to miss most about Caleb, how I felt when he held me tight. A tear falls from my eye as I clear thoughts of Caleb from my mind. I breathe in Jace's minty scent and instantly fall asleep.

Chapter 5

A week has passed; the medicine Lynn has me on has made me rather drowsy so I've hardly been outta bed the entire week. My father and Anna have been in and out of the room but Jace is always here. Ready to wake me up to get food or walk me to the bathroom, he even threatened the doctor that Daddy sent to look at me. He told him about the pregnancy and that I didn't want my father to know about it just yet. I think the doctor was more afraid of keeping it from my father than the thought of what Jace might do to him if he let it slip. Even though we've only known each other for a week , I've grown quite attached to him.

I wake up unusually early this morning because my stomach is feeling rather weird. My face is resting on something hard and warm. I open my eyes to see that I'm lying on Jace's rock hard chest. The blanket has slid down to his hips revealing his very appealing muscular form, he has the perfect V-line disappearing into his boxers and I immediately want to run my hands down his rippled muscles. Of course Caleb had a six pack; I think that boy was born with one, he didn't have one ounce of fat on him but it was still a boy's body. Who knows, maybe when he's twenty five he'll look just as manly as Jace. I certainly wasn't this fascinated by Caleb's muscles but I want to touch Jace's *really* bad. It's probably because I haven't been this close to another guy....it has only ever been Caleb.

My thoughts vanish as soon as the familiar nauseous feeling takes hold. I quietly disentangle my body from his and tip toe out of his room toward the bathroom at the end of the hall. I make it just in time to empty my stomach in the toilet bowl. I sit there against the wall next to the toilet with my head in my hands for a couple more minutes waiting for the nausea to disappear. I eventually find the energy to get off the floor and wash my face. After using the toilet I quickly make my way back to Jace's room to collect clothes. I think if I have a shower I'll feel better.

I notice the entire building is quiet, I don't even hear a sound from the bar downstairs. Daddy has a house by the lake which only ever gets used when he and Anna need a break, most of the time they live in the club house. The club house is near the local college, so we are basically surrounded by Frat Houses and dormitories. It consists of an old apartment building, the upper two floors Daddy has converted into rooms with the furnishings a normal household would have where some of the guys stay. Beneath the living quarters is a bar. The bar is often crowded by the bikers themselves but also with the students from the college that are brave enough to enter a biker bar. At the back entrance of the building Daddy has recently opened a tattoo studio, it was his nineteenth wedding anniversary present to Anna who's a tattoo artist. There is also a work shop at the back of the apartment next to Anna's tattoo parlor near the parking area that my father owns as well; he works on various cars and bikes in his free time.

I visited my father regularly and that's how I know all about the club house but Daddy would always keep me to himself so I never got the chance to meet any of the guys from the club.

I walk back to Jace's room and sneak inside towards my bag on the floor. It's only seven in the morning and he's still out cold. He's cuddled up to the pillow I was using and its rather adorable seeing a man that raw curled into a ball holding a pillow tightly against his chest. I pick out my navy blue sundress that hides the baby bump easily with a pair of pumps. I have the same sundress in five different colours. Even though I have my tom boy ways, putting on a pretty dress always makes me feel better. I head to the bathroom, take a shower and wash my hair. I feel so much more awake now that I'm all cleaned up. I head down to the kitchen to see if I can find something to eat, I have such a craving for pancakes with syrup. My tummy rumbles just thinking about it.

I search through the cupboards and look for the ingredients and luckily they have everything I need. I decide to make everyone breakfast to thank them for all their help.

I let the bacon and eggs fry while I start on the pancakes. The kitchen in the house is massive, with all black and grey granite and stainless steel appliances. The food smells really good and I can't help but taste the pancakes as they come out the pan.

"Harley the food smells amazing! If I can wake up to that smell every morning, I will be in seventh heaven!" My father smiles as he sits on the stool opposite me watching. Anna soon follows rubbing her tummy.

"Hey! Don't act like I've never cooked breakfast for you." she says and I giggle. I know for a fact that both of them hate cooking and they usually get the cook from the bar to make food for them. This is probably the first time the kitchen is being used, I don't mind cooking though and I've been cooking for Momma since I was tall enough to reach the stove.

"I decided to make your guys breakfast, how many of the guys are here at the Club House?" I ask my father as a proud smile forms on his face.

"There's only about eight that stayed over honey, including us. I'll make the coffee, I know you don't drink the stuff." Anna answers for my father as he comes over to where I'm cooking and gives me a big hug and kisses my forehead.

"You're going to fit in perfectly here baby girl, the boys are going to love you." he says happily, I smile as he returns to his seat. Jace is the next to stumble down the stairs putting his shirt on with the pillow creases still imprinted on his face. His long messy hair is standing in all different directions.

"What is that smell? It's amazing! Never woken up this early in my life. Fucking worth it." he says as he inspects all the food I'm cooking. He grabs a piece of sausage and I smack his hand.

"Sit down Jace, I'll dish you a plate." I scold him. My father and Anna chuckle as Jace follows my instructions and hands me over a plate. I put a little bit of everything on and I'm pretty sure I can see him drooling. He sits at the end of the table next to my father and I watch my father eyeing Jace's plate.

"Our baby girl already has Raven wrapped around her little finger…" he says through laughs.

"Daddy I'll dish you and Mom up food now too while it's warm, there's also pancakes for after." I tell my father. They both excitedly nod; you would swear they were little kids waiting for cake on their birthday. My father and Anna are only thirty five, he had just turned eighteen when he knocked my mother up, my mother was twenty at the time. He had been married to Anna for a year at the time.

"Grimm, she has you wrapped around her finger too." Jace says with a mouthful of food. He smirks and my father chuckles saying, "Of course she does." Then winks at me.

I hear heavy footsteps as another rather tall bulky man trots down the stairs in the direction of the smell. He looks identical to Jace, just older but still very much as good looking as him. It has to be his father.

"Harley, this is Ryan, Jace's *old* man." My father says emphasizing the word old and laughs. Ryan pats my father on the back then comes over to me.

"It's good to finally meet you love. It's about time you packed your shit and came. Grimm won't shut his mouth bout you, talks about you all the time. He's very proud darling." He puts his arm over my shoulder then looks at my father.

"She's gorgeous Grimm." Ryan says as he pulls me into a big hug.

After Ryan releases me, I look at Jace who has stopped eating and is now glaring at his father whose hand is resting on my shoulder. My father looks at Jace and chuckles.

"Raven boy don't sweat, we know you've already staked your claim. Baby girl here is already taken, your old man knows to stay away from her." I'm rather confused at what my father is saying; I'm taken by who? Jace?

Ryan chuckles then whispers in my ear with a gravelly voice, "Seems my boy has taken quite an interest in you love. If he doesn't treat you right you call me, your daddy and I will teach him how to treat a lady."

I laugh, shaking my head as I dish him out a plate to eat. The rest of the guys dawdle down to the kitchen eventually and I dish all of them out food. I notice that most of the guys are young with the oldest guy looking around fifty at best.

When I finally finish cooking, I lean against the counter and smile as I watch everyone laughing and chatting around the big dining room table eating the food I prepared. The smell of the bacon has started to stir the nausea in my belly so I quickly excuse myself and run up the stairs toward the bathroom. As I'm leaning over the toilet throwing up I hear the door behind me open and close. I spot Jace's unlaced dirty black combat boots in the corner of my eye, he comes up behind me and holds my hair up with one of his hands and rubs my back with the other.

It shouldn't be Jace helping me through this … this is supposed to be Caleb. Caleb should be here helping me through this. I feel the emotion building up inside me and my tears are going to spill soon. He helps me up and I brush my teeth again. After I rinse my mouth and wipe my face on the towel, I hold the towel against my face as I start crying into it, muffling the sound of my cries with the barrier of the soft towel. I know he can see me crying but I don't want to see the pity in his eyes. He probably thinks I'm a tragic mess; I couldn't even keep my boyfriend satisfied and now I'm stuck being a single mother.

Instead of leaving me alone in the bathroom like I expect him too, he pulls me into him and tugs the towel away from my face. I wrap my arms around his waist and cry into his chest, my head resting under his chin.

He brings his lips to my ears as he whispers, "It's his loss babe, he lost out on such an amazing girl. You deserve so much more than what he has to offer you. You have all of us here that will support you through this; you just need to tell your father."

I pull away from him and look at up at his face. "Thank you for everything Jace. You've helped me so much even though you're not responsible for me and this baby. It should have been Caleb here to help me through all this and I appreciate everything you've done for me…I don't think I could ever repay you. I know I have to tell Daddy but I need to tell Caleb first and see where to go from there. I think I'll phone him today and get it over with, I just need to find the courage." I say, wiping the tears from my face.

He nods his head. "You need to eat and take those meds, you haven't eaten yet and you need to rest too." He brushes the hair away from my face and pulls me out of the bathroom holding my hand.

I look in the mirror before we exit the bathroom to see if there's signs that I've been crying but my face isn't too blotchy so I allow him to lead me out.

"I'm not eating the bacon and egg, the smell makes me want to gag." I tell him as we make our way down the stairs.

"Okay babe, go sit down, I'll get you some pancakes with some cinnamon and syrup. " Jace orders and I know not to argue with his determined stubborn personality.

I sit next to Anna by the table; she gives me half a hug. She frowns and mouths "Are you okay?" Not wanting my father to hear.

I smile at her and tell her I'm fine. She turns and faces me as she says. "I'm so glad you're staying with me now, you know I love you so much and you're my daughter right? Even if you don't see me the way I see you, I just wanted you to know that I love you Harley and that you can talk to me about anything. I'm happy that I have someone decent to hang out with now and I don't have to hang around those whores that run after the boys in the club." I laugh at her blunt attitude.

Anna is a little taller than me; she has long dark straight hair with a red streak down the one side. Her ears are full of piercings and her arms both have sleeved tattoos. She is quite the bad ass but she is so sweet and gentle when it comes to me, and she doesn't take shit from any of the guys or the "whores" from the club, from what Jace tells me. Even though she acts like a teenager she is more of a mother to me than my biological one ever was. She is one person I know I can always rely on. I can talk to her about anything and I trust her to keep it between us.

I see my dad eavesdropping but I don't mind him hearing what I'm about to say.

"Anna you know I see you as my mother, maybe even more so than my biological one. I love you too; I'm happy I have you and that I'm here with you. I felt so alone living with Momma because I knew she didn't want me around… but I feel like I'm wanted here and it makes me happy that I'm at least wanted somewhere." I let out a deep breath and look down at my hands. "I love you mom even if you aren't my biological one and I LOVE YOU TOO DADDY!" I emphasize the last words knowing he is listening in. I don't know why there are tears in my eyes but there are. My father whips his head around and smiles at me knowing I caught him eavesdropping.

"Harley you will *always* be wanted here. We love you so very much. You should've been here all along because you belong here…with us." My father says as he comes over and joins in on mine and Anna's hug.

Jace hands me a plate of pancakes and leans on the table watching me eat every little bit. He then hands me a glass of water and all the pills I need to take.

After taking my medicine I head back to Jace's room for a nap. I'm just about to doze off when I hear the door slowly open and close, I peek through my fallen hair and watch as Jace pulls the curtains closed. From the corner of my eyes I see him open the drawer by the desk and pull out a prescription bottle. He drops two pills into his palm and throws the bottle back in the drawer. He takes out a metal flask from his back pocket then downs the pills. He throws the flask in the drawer too. When he turns to face me I quickly close my eyes and even my breathing again. I feel his presence when he stands in front of my side of the bed; the bed sinks near my stomach as he sits down. I feel his body turn to face mine and I can feel his eyes on me. He gently leans over me and pushes the hair out of my face. He runs his hand gently through my hair; bringing his other hand up and softly rubbing my lips with his rough fingers. I so desperately want to stick my tongue out just a little to taste him. He leans down and runs his lips along mine. Not enough for an actual kiss but enough for me to feel his soft lips against mine and also enough to get a whiff of the whiskey on his breath.

He kisses me gently on my forehead near the cut and bruise; the spot is still a little tender and I try my hardest not to wince. After running his fingers one last time over my lips he leaves, shutting the door quietly behind him.

I lie in bed wonderstruck thinking about what the hell just happened. I'm curious about those pills and I really want to confront him about drinking so early in the morning but I don't know if I have the right. He's been kind about offering his bed to me even if I have to share it with him and I don't want to go invading his space more than I have already by snooping through his drawers for answers I'm not sure I'm ready to know. Thinking it over I realize not one second of the time I spend with Jace is taken thinking about Caleb, he totally takes my mind to a different place. I smile to myself as I cuddle into the pillow.

Anna wakes me up in the afternoon with a sandwich and more medicine. She apparently too has been sleeping the day away. I go with her downstairs to the bar; my father had to be at his shop because they are going to repair the damage on Jace's car. They told me my car was a write-off so he decided to sell it for scrap and get me a new one. Even though I told him he didn't need to, he still insisted.

We walk into the bar area and it looks like a tornado has hit.

"Fuck sakes, this is why we don't have any of the guys working at the bar. We leave this place for a week and see what happens? These people can't run a bar for shit." I laugh at her then immediately start picking up glasses and bottles lying around.

"No honey you don't have to do that —"she says but I interrupt.

"*Mom*, I'm staying here so I want to help out? I can't sleep all day, I need to do something." I smile at her.

She stands there looking around obviously realizing it would take her a while to clean this place on her own. "Okay honey let's get this place spotless." She starts picking up bottles.

After an hour of cleaning and chatting about the club and people I haven't met yet I decide to ask her what's been on my mind all week.

"Can I ask you a favor?" I say nervously.

"Yeah honey anything." She says eagerly as she stands closer to me.

"Can you please speak to Daddy for me? I need a job and I know if I ask him he will refuse and just give me money, but I want to work for the money he gives me. I know he doesn't like to hire people to work here so he makes you help him, but you guys are understaffed." I continue to clean tables and make my way around the bar as I speak.

"So… I was thinking maybe you could ask him if I could help out around here? You can manage the bar and all the alcohol and I will deal with any non-alcoholic beverages as well as the food. Then I can help with cleaning up as I go along? At least then when the nights over, you won't be stuck around cleaning for hours." I suggest. She smiles over at me.

"I think that's a great idea babe. I'm sure he will be cool with it; he will at least get to spend time with you. If you need money though, you know you could just ask right?" she says honestly.

"I know but I want to start working and earning my own money. I need to. It will also help me meet new people." I continue.

"Okay Harley, I'll have a chat with Grimm as soon as I see him. Tomorrow when we open up the bar I'll show you what's going on, sound good?" I smile and nod.

"I'm so excited; this is going to be great!" She says as she puts the music on and starts dancing with the broom. I stand there laughing hard, very close to peeing myself.

Chapter 6

We manage to clean the entire bar, luckily it's not too big, it's small yet cozy. It's the typical biker bar you'd expect but has more of a modern edge to it due to Anna's artistic ability. There's pictures scattered all over the walls of old bikes and the men that rode them. Above the bar on the wall, my father has a life size model of a hot pink Harley and on the gas tank is my name and date of birth.

The first time I saw it, which was when he brought me here on my fifth birthday, I told him one day I was going to get a real one like that. He gave me the biggest and proudest smile I'd ever seen.

The bar offers food too but nothing fancy. Daddy also doesn't open during normal restaurant hours either; the bar opens from four in the afternoon till late. It has its own kitchen at the back and one chef that comes in and rotates with another. My father doesn't trust people easily so he doesn't employ people he doesn't know. He usually gets the prospects from the club to help out around the bar but he prefers to only work with Anna behind the bar. They work hard with long hours; I don't know how they manage to do it since they both have the other shops to run during the day.

I'm busy wiping down bottles behind the bar when Daddy walks in and sits on one of the bar stools, covered in grease.

"Please can I get a whiskey on the rocks ma'am?" he winks and I giggle, I pour him his drink and hand it over to him as I continue to wipe all the dusty bottles.

"So you want to work for your old man huh?" He says taking a sip of his drink. I wet a new cloth and hand it to him to wipe his face and hands.

"Yeah, I just want to do something productive and it'll be a good way for me to meet new people around here. I don't really know anyone besides you guys." I lean on my elbows over the bar looking at him.

"Okay Harlz, anything you want my girl." He pats my hand, "Thank you for what you said to Anna today, she loves you very much and you must know how happy she is after that little heart to heart. Love you loads baby girl, I'm so happy you're here with us now. You even managed to impress the boys with the breakfast you made this morning, they were telling all the brothers in the shop. I think they're going to expect that every Sunday and we will probably have more joining us with the way they were ranting." He sniggers taking another sip.

"That's a good idea actually. We should have a big Sunday meal! I've always wanted to have a Sunday meal like all my friends did with their families. We could even make it an afternoon lunch instead of a breakfast. I could make a big roast with all those vegetables and side dishes? What do you say Daddy?" I say full of excitement. My friends always had them on Sundays so I was never able to come over during lunch time. Those were the days when my loneliness really crept in. I was left alone at home because Momma was at the club while all my friends were spending time with their families. I used to make roasts for us hoping one day she would be around long enough to sit down and have a meal with me but she never did. Eventually Caleb came to the rescue and I started spending Sunday with his family, it wasn't the same though; although they felt like family to me, they weren't.

I look up to see my father smiling at me. "That's a great idea baby girl. Maybe you can show Anna a thing or two about cooking." He teases and I laugh. "I know she hates cooking and I don't mind cooking now that I'm here, I enjoy it."

I finish cleaning around the bar area as my father sits there sipping on his drink watching me with a grin on his face. By the time we walk back up the stairs to the house it's already dark outside. Daddy tells me he has a meeting with some of the brothers in his office so I decide to lounge on the balcony and enjoy the cool fresh air. I bring my legs up to my chest with my head resting on them. I look down at the street and my surroundings then rest my head on the back of the chair staring up into the beautiful sky lit up with stars.

"What you doin' out here all on your lonesome?" Jace says as he sits next to me holding a beer in his hands.

"Thinking…" I say through a sigh.

"Bout?" he asks hesitantly.

"Everything…I need to tell him Jace. Its eating me up inside and I would never be able to hide this from him. Even though I don't want to hear his voice right now, I have to tell him. I just need to tell him and get it off my chest." I say.

"I know what you mean babe. Come." Jace says as he gestures for me to take his hand. I get up and place my small hand in his much larger one, he leads me up the stairs back to his room. He pulls me to the bed, tells me to sit and I oblige.

"Here, call the idiot now and get it over with." He says throwing me his phone. My phone was destroyed in the car accident so I'm in the process for getting a new one with the number transferred. I'm not sure having the same number is a good idea though.

"Jace, it's not as easy as you think, I'm scared!" I admit. He sits on the bed next to me and puts his muscular arm over my shoulder and pulls me to his chest as he speaks against my hair.

"Babe it is as easy as I think. Call him, tell him about the baby and say you will discuss details later. Just get that off your chest, you'll feel better. I promise." He says comforting and giving me the courage to take his phone and dial Caleb's number with my trembling hands.

I hear the dial tone and I wait a few minutes as I stare at Jace who's looking cautiously at me as he mouths, *"It's okay, everything will be fine."* I nod and give him a reassuring smile but it quickly vanishes when someone answers the line…and it's not Caleb.

"Ashley?" I ask as I hear her answer the phone cheerfully.

"Harley! Is that you? Oh my gosh! Hun I'm sorry! I didn't want to you to find out about us that way. I'm so sorry, you're my sister and I never should have betrayed you like that. How are you? How is the baby?" Ashley says in a caring tone but I'm not fooled at all.

My heart aches when she mentions that she didn't want me to find out about *them that way*. Obviously they've done it before. I ignore her questions and ask flatly.

"Where's Caleb?"

I hear her sigh, "He's not in at the moment. Please tell me you forgive me, I love you Harlz, you're my best friend. Just come back, you can even stay with us." It breaks my heart at the mention of them living in the apartment that was supposed to be Caleb's and mine.

A tear falls down my face and I look at Jace who is clutching the bedding in his fisted hand, his white knuckles on display.

He grunts , "Give me the phone, NOW!" in an angry tone but I shake my head and move away from him so I'm sitting in the middle of his bed with the phone against my ear.

"I need to speak to Caleb now, where is he?" I ask through a muffled voice as I sniff.

She lets out an irritated breath, "Harley, what do you need to speak to him about? The baby? You don't have to do that, I already told him about *it*." She says cunningly and it pisses me off how she calls the baby growing inside of me a… *it*.

I yell at her, "What the fuck Ashley? I don't care if you're together now, it wasn't your place to tell him! I was supposed to!"

Jace jumps at me trying to take the phone away but I quickly turn around so I'm holding the phone tightly against my head with my side pushed into the bed and my head in between the pillows in the middle of the bed as he hovers over me. I mouth *"just hang on!"* he gives me an angry look but stays hovering over me.

"Well too bad because I did and he doesn't want *it*." She says in a harsh tone. I gasp and suck in a deep breath as she breaks what little of my heart I had left completely with her words.

Jace snatches the phone from me and yells into the phone. "Slut, listen to me *very* carefully! If you ever come near Harley again or utter one word to her, I will pay you a visit and it won't be pretty!"

I turn my face into the pillow and hold it tight against my face as I cry into it. My whole body is shaking and I can't control the loud sobs and the tears that soak the pillow. I feel Jace hovering over me with both his legs on either side of me as his manly built body envelopes me. He leans over and wraps his one arm around me with the other brushing my hair gently.

He puts his mouth in my hair near my ear and whispers, "Shhh baby….I'm here…talk to me." He leans over and rests his head on the same pillow I'm hiding my face in and removes his body that was over mine. I instantly feel cold without him there, but he soon pulls me up so I'm snuggling into his chest.

"He…he doesn't want…the baby." I stutter as I cry and put my face into his neck and squeeze him tight. He squeezes me back and pulls me so that I'm now lying on top of him with our legs scissored between each other's and my head resting just under his chin. He starts rubbing my back softy trying to comfort me. My body is still trembling but my sobbing has stopped. I can hear and feel his beating heart beneath my ear and it strangely calms me.

There is nothing sexual about the way he holds me, it's definitely intimate but it's more of a protective manner than a sexual one and it's something I don't expect from an intensely sensual man.

He rolls me over so that I'm next to him with my head leaning on his arm, I'm still tucked tightly against his chest. I roll over so I'm lying on my back and take a deep breath. I feel his hands playing with the bottom of my dress before he reaches under, I tense under his touch not knowing what he's about to do.

"Trust me..." He says and I nod. His large warm hands reach under my dress and land on my stomach as he rubs me softly the same way he does each night.

"You don't need him. He doesn't deserve you, either of you." He says softly as he continues to run his palm against my stomach protectively.

"Thanks Jace." I clear my throat, my tears all dried up. "I don't know why I wasn't prepared for that, I just wasn't expecting him to be so harsh. I don't understand how he doesn't want this baby *we* made. I was already in love with the little person growing inside me the moment I found out. How can he be so cruel? I…I don't understand." I clear my throat again.

"Babe, you don't need him. You have us and we will help you through this. You have me Harley, I will be there for you and the baby. I won't let anyone hurt you ever again." Jace says as he kisses my forehead.

I reach up and kiss his cheek leaving him with a big grin.

I finally catch my breath and get off the bed to look at my face in the mirror. It's a little red and my eyes are still a bit swollen.

"How long am I going to be sleeping next to you?" I ask him. He looks up at me from the bed as if I've interrupted his thoughts.

"Forever?" he replies cheekily.

"No seriously, how long? Sooner or later you're going to get sick of me hovering around you and I'd rather give you your space before you get tired of me." I say leaning against his door frame.

"Babe that's not going to happen but either way, your bed or mine, you'll be sleeping next to me." He says matter of factly; I don't bother to argue with him because it won't get me anywhere. I shake my head and leave his room in search for Anna.

Chapter 7

I walk up to the fourth floor towards my father's bedroom. I knock on the door softly and hear Anna call for me to come in.

She's sitting on the bed working on her sketches; she seems shocked to see me in her room as she puts her sketch board down next to her on the bed.

"What's wrong, have you been crying?"

I ignore her questions and head over to where she's sitting.

"Can I ask you a question?" I sit down on the corner of the bed and cross my legs, playing with a loose cotton piece on the frill of my summer dress

"You have been crying! What happened? Was it Raven? Do I need to get the bat out?" she pulls me closer to her and holds me tight.

"When dad cheated on you with Momma, how did you get over it?" I ask her sadly.

"Oh no Hun, he didn't? That's why you didn't want to see him at the hospital?" she says in disbelief as I nod.

"I'm going to kill that boy; you two were so good together. I can't believe he fucked it up. Are you okay babes?" she says, holding my hand in hers.

"No I'm really not but that's why I'm here, I need to know how to get over it. Jace has been great and most of the time he takes my mind off it but I just can't stop the hurt that keeps creeping in. I don't want dad to know about this, and after this conversation I never want to speak about him again. I don't want to mention his name, hear about him or even think about him. I want to forget! How do I just... forget?" I say as I tremble and the tears begin to fall.

She pulls me in for a tight hug, trying to comfort me and it works.

"It's very hard my love, you believe you won't be able to trust men again but you will. I knew what I was getting in to when I married your father though. These biker boys are hard to handle but I love your father too much to not work on our relationship and make it work. When he had that drunken one night stand with your mother, your father and I were going through a rough patch especially as I'd just found out I couldn't have children; I felt useless and I pushed him away. You see babes, these men don't like being told what to do and they want a woman that'll submit to them. That's why so many of them have whores on the side but I wasn't willing to do that, it's not in my nature and your father knew that. He told me the next morning that he'd cheated and I didn't speak to him for about two weeks. I knew he felt terrible because he wouldn't stop apologizing to me and each and every apology was so incredibly sincere. It was so hard trying to ignore your father and eventually we talked it out. I made it known that if he ever so much as looked at another woman the wrong way I'd be gone without a second glance and I knew that scared him. About ten months later I knew something was up when he purchased that big pink Harley for the bar with your name and date of birth on it. I didn't ask or question him and I would always catch him staring at the handwriting with a fulfilled smile on his face. We both had secrets Harley and his biggest one was you. He was always away at club meetings but one day he came back with you at his side. The first time I saw you I knew you were his, I loved you from the very moment I saw your pretty blue eyes that matched your fathers. I only ever wished that I was your mother and that you were mine..." she says wiping away the tears from her face with her tattooed fingers. I sit on my knees and give her a hug as I tell her in her ear.

"You are my mom, I am yours ....and Daddy's." This makes her cry harder and squeeze me tighter. A few stray tears fall from my eyes, this is very unlike Anna, she doesn't show emotion easily.

"Anyway, I knew that even though your father cheated on me during one of his vulnerable moments I still loved him and wanted him, you just have to work it out. I swear it will get better. I know its hard babes but you are a strong girl. If you love each other enough, you will find your way back." She says wiping away all her tears.

"I guess you're right but that could never happen... he's with *her* now, she's living in the apartment that was supposed to be ours. I lost my boyfriend and best friend in one night. Crazy right?" I sadly look down at my nails trying to swallow down the tears and the sobs threatening to escape.

"Oh no...he's with *her*. He cheated on you with Ashley!" she asks sounding angry.

"Yeah, I mean...they're perfect for each other and I'd like to say that I hope they will be happy together but that would be a lie. I hope they betray each other the way they betrayed me, and get to feel the heartbreak they have put me through." As I say this I can feel the hatred surging through me.

"Yeah you're right! They don't deserve you babe. You are too good for them." she says seriously, making me smile.

"Let's go see what your dad's up to?" She pulls me out of the room and we stroll down the stairs toward the club. As we head into the bar, I notice a couple of girls I've never seen before wearing really skimpy outfits making me feel like a nun with my sun dress that hangs mid-thigh.

Anna puts her arm over my shoulders as she guides me towards the back of the bar area. We walk pass Jace who is surrounded my half naked woman; one goes to sit on his lap, she's got pitch black hair and her big boobs are held tightly up in a bikini with a small skirt and strappy heels on.

As soon as she sits down Jace tells her to get off making eye contact with me, I laugh at his rudeness towards the woman and he smiles back at me then winks. A couple of the girls turn around to look at who's caught his attention.

Anna pushes me towards a large door and knocks on it. A big man opens it, I only see his chest, I look up to see Ryan smiling down at me looking ever so handsome just like his son.

"Look who came to visit me, Prez." Ryan says as he puts his arm over my shoulder.

"I think she came to visit me actually, Buck." My dad chuckles waving me over.

"Come here baby girl, meet the rest of the guys."

I walk towards him through all the bulky men, the large room has about thirty people in it. There are men sitting around one long table as well as men standing around the room. I eventually make my way to my father who is sitting at the head of the table in a big leather chair. He gestures for me to sit on his lap so I move to sit on one of his legs.

"Boys, I want to officially introduce you to my baby girl, Harley." Dad says excitedly from behind me; all the men cheer, whistle and hoot. Anna and my father start laughing and I blush.

The noise softens. "She's strictly off limits to all of you!" he says in a stricter tone. I hear Ryan's deep laugh on the opposite side of the large room.

"Besides Raven… of course…" my dad snickers and I raise my eyebrow looking back at him.

"She's gorgeous Grimm… but she doesn't look like she belongs here." A guy standing to my right says and I hear my father laugh from behind me.

"I think she will fit in just fine." someone says through the crowd, I look over to him and do a double take….Raven.

I smile at him as he winks and I mouth, *"Thanks."*

"Boy's already whipped!" another guy says and a couple of them snicker. Jace brushes them off not caring.

"Okay, enough boys. Harley here will be working at the bar from tomorrow night, I expect you to keep an eye on her and not give her any shit." my father says.

I look at him and raise my eyebrows, "Really Daddy? I can look after myself you know, I don't need *any* men to *"keep an eye on me"* I say deepening my voice trying to mimic him, but not having the effect I would have liked. He just looks at me and smiles.

"Definitely Grimm's girl." An older man says as the crowd chuckles at my outburst.

"Harley, even if your father hadn't told us to keep an eye on you, we still would. You are part of our family now and an innocent girl like you has obviously never been around this type of life before." The same guy that said I was gorgeous speaks again.

He comes out from behind the crowd so I'm able to get a good look at him. He is a little taller than Jace and also really well built. He has shaven blond hair with brown eyes and dark thick lashes and eyebrows. He looks about Jace's age too. His face is striking with high cheek bones and slight stubble covering his jawline.

"Okay okay…" I say as I lift my hands up in defeat. The men chat for a few more minutes before everyone starts to filter out of the room leaving Anna, my father and I. I'm not sure where Jace has disappeared to. I need to tell my father and Anna about the baby but I don't want to do it alone.

"Uh guys…can I have a quick talk to you while we're here?" I ask them.

"Sure Harlz." My dad says as he sits in his seat again. Anna sits in the seat near him.

"I just need to get something quick, but wait here…I'll be right back." I yell as I quickly run out the room in search of Jace.

I spot him chatting to the blond guy who now has a baseball cap on. I quickly make my way to him and snake my hand around his arm, my head only just reaching his shoulder. He looks down at me tensing before he relaxes when he sees who it is. He wraps his arm around my shoulders and pulls me into his chest holding me close to him. The blond guy looks down at me and seems to be confused as to why Jace has his hands on me.

"Jace, I need you to come with me quick." I say looking up at him.

"Why, what's wrong?" he asks lifting the glass up to his lips. Before he can have a sip I take it from his hands and put it on the table near us.

"I need to talk to my dad soooo….I need-you-to-come-with me!" I repeat through gritted teeth nodding my head towards the back of the bar.

"Oh right! I'll be right back Hunter." Jace says to his friend and quickly leads me back to the office.

"Don't leave my side okay! And don't get angry if Daddy says horrible things to me, just sit there and hold my hand okay?" I say into his chest as I give him a quick hug before heading in.

He pulls my face up to look at him. "I told you I'd be here for you and I am but I won't let anybody disrespect you…not even your father." I nod as he opens the door and leads me inside.

My father and Anna are laughing about something when enter; I walk over to them and sit on the other side of my father, pulling Jace closer to my side. I need contact with him, I need the reassurance that he is there by my side because I know I'm not strong or brave enough to tell my father my secret on my own. I pull his hand and put it on my lap and hold onto it; he squeezes my hand giving me the assurance I need.

"What's wrong babes, why're you so nervous?" Anna says looking worried. My father leans onto the table, his hands together looking at me anxiously. I let go of Jace's hand and hold onto my father's rougher ones. Jace moves his hand to rest on the bare skin just above my knee, rubbing me softly as I continue to talk.

"Daddy I have to tell you something and…I just want you to know that I haven't ever wanted to disappoint you, but I know after I tell you this you won't look at me the way you have my whole life. If you don't want me around after I tell you this, I'll understand too…fully." I am softly failing at sounding confident and brave because right now I'm scared shitless of what my father might do.

"Just talk to us Harley." Daddy says frowning.

"I….I'm pregnant Daddy!" I say, looking down at my hands which are now being held in Jace's. I can't bear to look at the disappointment that is most probably covering his face. I look up to Anna and her face is drained of any colour.

"W…what….How? Who?" my father asks in shock.

"Daddy…I'm not going to explain the details, it just happened okay." I tell him.

"Who's the father and when am I going to meet him?" He says sitting straighter running his hands through his hair looking older than his age.

"He won't be in the picture. He doesn't want the baby …or me." I tell him sadly trying to keep the tears I feel building up from spilling; I'm done crying over Caleb. After tonight Caleb will no longer take up my thoughts.

"What?" My father asks in disbelief looking back and forth between us. "I'm going to fucking kill the bastard for doing this! Who is this kid? How long have you known him and why doesn't he want to be part of your child's life?" He yells, making me flinch as Jace tenses beside me, squeezing my hand a little tighter.

"You don't know him, I've known him most of my life but we dated for four years. He's found someone else, he's with her now and there isn't space for us; that's why he doesn't want this baby." I say wiping a few tears.

"Oh Harley, I'm so sorry." Anna runs to my side and pulls me into a hug.

She pulls away and I'm pulled into my father's strong arms.

"It's okay baby girl, you don't need him…I swear when I find out who he is though, I will be having a word with him about fatherhood. I'm not disappointed in you Harley; you're going to be an amazing mother. I love you baby girl." Daddy says holding me tight, talking into my hair.

"Thanks Daddy, you'll make an awesome granddaddy too." I look up to him then look to Anna at my side and say, "…and you'll be the coolest grandmother ever." she smiles and pulls me from my father's grip and hugs me again.

Chapter 8

To say I was surprised by my father's reaction is an understatement, I was at least expecting to get lectured or yelled at... even if he's never scolded me before. What I did not expect was how happy he looked at the thought of being a grandfather.

It was only ten o'clock at night when we left the office. Jace walked out with me while my father and Anna stayed behind obviously to talk about the situation privately.

Jace pulls me through the crowd and shields me from getting trampled on by the noisy crowd. Everyone at the club house is older than me, only club members are here as it isn't open to the public tonight so there aren't any college students around like there usually is.

"Jace, I think I'm just going to head off to bed...I'm really exhausted after today." I tell him covering my mouth to yawn.

He chuckles and brings me into his side again. "Let's go then gorgeous." He waves to his friends and leads me to the back stairs leading to the apartment above.

I flop myself onto his bed too exhausted to change. I watch him as he starts to take his shirt off.

"You can go back to your friends...you don't have to babysit me." I say leaning on my elbow watching him, he puts his arm back into his shirt and sits on the bed next to me.

"I don't mind *babysitting* you..." he says smiling at me as he lifts my feet to his lap and takes my shoes off.

"No really Jace, I'm fine by myself besides... it's early for you. I'll be here when you get back." I tell him sitting up.

"Okay babe, get changed so I can tuck you in." he says and I start giggling.

"Really Jace? Tuck me in? Do you tell all the girls that?" I tease him through chuckles as I lean into my bag and find something to sleep in.

"Only you Harley..." he mutters running his hands through his hair.

I take out a pair of pajama shorts and put them on under my dress, I turn to see Jace watching me running his eyes over my body.

"Jace turn around so I can put my shirt on." I don't want him to look at my body, a guy like him has definitely seen models naked and my body could never measure up to that. I'm not completely comfortable with my changing body at the moment and I would prefer if no one sees me naked.

He laughs, "C'mon... there's nothing I haven't seen before." He teases making me feel uncomfortable under his lustful gaze.

Jace is a gorgeous guy with sex appeal oozing from him; he must have hooked up with a whole harem of women. I don't think he realizes how inexperienced I really am... even if I am pregnant. There's only one guy that's seen me fully naked ever and I'm not the kind to strip in front of anyone.

"Of course you've seen it all but you haven't seen all of me, so turn Jace." I say raising my eye brow making him sigh and turn his head as I quickly drop my dress, pull my bra off and slip my shirt on.

I gently fold my clothes and place them neatly on the chair by his desk. I turn around to find Jace watching me intently, "Jace! Did you see? I told you not to watch!"

He smirks at me and pulls me onto the bed. "You should know by now, I do whatever I want and I wanted to watch." He says smiling down at me as he pulls open the covers.

"Of course you are used to getting your way amongst the ladies." I mutter to myself angrily as I get into bed folding my arms over my chest.

Of course he hears me...

"And why is that Harley?" he asks looking confused.

"Really? You *have* to ask? I mean, look at yourself Jace, you're hot and obviously girls follow your every command... but I think you confuse me for the type of girls that hang on your every word. I'm not like them, you should know that...so when I say don't look when I'm getting dressed, I mean it." I turn around to avoid looking at his face.

He jumps over me then lies on top of the blanket next to me, he places his head on the pillow so that we are on the same eye level as he says, "You're right...girls usually listen to what I say. I know you're not like them..." he lifts a piece of my hair and places it behind my ear.

"You are so much better baby, I know I should have listened but I don't know why you are so self-conscious about your body. You think I'm hot? Babe you're gorgeous...even with that little baby bump. I know you're a stubborn girl and you like getting your way just like I do but you need to know, as long as you stay here I will be the one that protects you. You need to get used to how the men of this club treat their women and how the women listen." I try to interrupt him but he placed his hand over my mouth.

"We just want what's best for you Harley. I know your father is wrapped around your little finger, he doesn't care whether you listen to him or not when your mind is set on something. That's why from now on while you are here, you *will* listen to me. Yes, I want my woman to do as I say, even though I've been sweet and kind to you, don't take that as who I am...because it's not! I do things how I want and when I want and I want you and that baby safe. If I want to look at you while you're getting changed, so be it, I will never hurt you and I will always want what's best for you. Ever since the accident, I have had this overwhelming need to keep you both safe and protected. You need to know I am a very possessive man that's why your father knows you are safe with me. I fucking rage when people don't do what they're told…you don't ever want to see me angry Harley." he says in a harsher tone.

I'm left speechless. I've only ever met the happy loving Jace, I've never seen him so uptight and serious and it scares me. This boldness was what I expected to come from Jace from the moment I saw him. This attitude fits him, he's a big masculine guy covered in tattoos, he's beautiful yet bad and it's fucking scary! I guess I just warmed up to him being a big cuddly teddy bear but I was wrong… really, really wrong.

"Do you understand what I just said?" he asks me, I nod and close my eyes. I'm not used to being told what to do by a man, I guess by no one really. My mother wasn't exactly the strict type and well… I wasn't around my father long enough for him to actually parent. It's not like I was a troubled mischievous child, so there wasn't really a need for me to be lectured. I don't appreciate the way Jace is belittling me but I'm too scared to say or do anything else besides act like he isn't there in the hope that he'll leave. Caleb and his friends used to make sure no one bothered me so I've kind of had a sheltered life up until now…guess that's all going to change.

Jace kisses my forehead and rubs my baby bump saying goodnight to the baby before he leaves the room turning off the light. I find it kind of cute apart from the fact that he went all alpha on me just minutes before.

I lay there for a few more minutes listening to the bass from the music playing in the bar below as it vibrates off the floor and windows. I find the sound comforting and fall into a deep sleep.

Chapter 9

I wake up a few hours later when someone's arm wraps around me pulling me into their warm bare chest. I immediately know its Jace when he places his warm hand on my belly under my shirt and rubs it gently. I hear him let out a deep breath as I place my hand over his, he gently laces our fingers together. If it was any other person I'd be very uncomfortable by this gesture but with Jace I feel content and safe.

"I'm sorry if I scared you." He says in a gruff voice against my ear sending chills down my spine, I can tell he's just got out of the shower by smelling his minty breath and his fresh body wash that still lingers on his skin. I don't respond just nod my head. *What am I supposed to say? It's okay? Because it wasn't okay! He scared me...*

"I want you and the baby safe... I know you haven't seen me so serious before but it's who I am, I'm not the sweet guy you think I am and I need you to know that even if you bring out the sweetness in me, I'm not that person and I never will be Harley. I will never hurt you intentionally but I am dangerous and if anyone fucks with what's mine I *will* destroy them. I get what I want and all I want is to keep you guys safe, so if scaring you into listening to me does the job, I'll do it. I apologize for watching you but I didn't think it was such a big deal. I've been thinking about how you looked under those clothes since I met you and I needed to see, I want you to trust me to look and not touch. I was just pissed off because I've never been chastised for wanting to look before and you caught me off guard." He explains.

I'm still stuck on the part where he said he's been thinking about how I looked under my clothes, eventually I respond, "I'm not as open with people looking at my body as other girls are, especially now that my body is... changing. Caleb is the only guy that's ever seen me naked, I trust you Jace but I don't feel comfortable with you looking..." I whisper.

I feel him move as he sits up and leans on his elbow looking down at me as he asks in shock, "You've only had sex with one guy?" I turn to look at him.

"Of course! I've been with him for four years. I haven't been single long enough to have sex with other guys...it's always been Caleb." I say looking at him. I can't see him fully in the dark but I can see his glistening eyes.

"Damn Harley you *are* just as innocent as you look, doing the same guy for four years? Doesn't it get boring?" he asks seriously and I start laughing.

"Jace!" I slap his arm. "Haven't you ever been in a relationship? Technically I wasn't *doing* him for four years, I lost my virginity to him at sixteen and no it wasn't boring. It was beautiful and exciting. Wouldn't you prefer to be with the same girl you know hasn't been around rather than sleep with random chicks that have already been taken by the whole club?" I cringe outwardly and he chuckles.

"Being intimate with one person isn't always boring, it's exhilarating and it makes you connect on a whole other level; you teach each other new things and show them what you like." I laugh and shake my head. "Okay.... I guess for you it's easy to pick up chicks but imagine not having to go through the effort of finding a girl to hook up with because you already have someone at home waiting for you and no one else?" I look at him as he watches me intently taking in what I'm saying. I can't believe I'm being this open with him, usually I'm too shy to talk about this stuff but he already knows my secrets and I feel comfortable opening up to him.

He laughs and falls back down on the bed resting his head on his folded arms as he looks up to the ceiling. I lie on my stomach and look at him as he talks.

"I've never really thought of it like that before. You are right though... I would rather be with someone that hasn't been with the entire fucking club and isn't sleeping with other guys while hooking up with me. Fuck... that just grosses me out! Now look what you've done, every time I look at those girls I'm going to wonder how many guys she's hooked up with." He lets out a deep breath then settles back into bed and continues. "I've never dated girls before, it's always been about sex and I'm clean I swear, I always get checked out. Yeah it's not really an effort for me to get the girls. I mean the sluts here so desperately want to be part of the club that they will do anything to get in; they don't realize that the guys will never make any of them their old lady. I get what you're saying though about coming home to someone waiting just for you, I guess that would be nice." He says softly as he smiles deep in thought. "I still can't believe you've only ever had sex with that asshole, aren't you the least bit interested in feeling how it is with someone else? You know everyone is different and has their own...techniques? Holy shit! Is he the only guy you've seen naked? You must have done other stuff with guys before him at least?" he asks excitedly as if hearing this from a girl is news to him.

I laugh, thankful the room is dark because I'm blushing so hard my cheeks are burning red.

"Gosh... I can't believe I'm talking about this with you Jace...Yes! He's the only guy I've seen naked and no I never touched anyone before Caleb. I never really thought about having sex with anyone else while I was with him but now... I suppose? I don't know!" I cover my face full of embarrassment. "I guess now that we're not together I wonder how it would be with someone else and maybe he felt the same. Maybe that's why he slept with Ashley, because he was thinking the same thing? I *was* the only girl he'd ever had sex with too. Shit...maybe he *was* bored with me, I never thought of that! Shit…argh…whatever…" I shake my head trying to get the images out of my mind.

"No, don't think like that, it's his loss remember that. He's missing out on a good thing babe. You are really innocent but that's good! I like that." he says as he pulls me closer to him and kisses my head, I wrap my arm over his ripped stomach and rest my head on his chest.

"Okay enough talk about me, how about you, how many chicks have you had sex with? How old were you your first time?" I say, swiftly changing the topic.

"My first time? Well I don't remember much because I was so pissed but I think I was about fifteen. I looked much older though and I had a fake ID, snuck into a club with my mates. I don't know her name but she was *much* older than me, could've been in her thirty's, late twenty's? Anyways it was in the back of her car. I don't think it was that great because I don't remember all the details and I can't even tell you how many chicks I've been with since because to be honest I've lost count." He chuckles as if this pleases him and I laugh.

"You hoe! You lost your virginity to an older woman in a car! How is that even possible?" I say shocked. When Caleb and I had sex it was always in a bed under the covers and that was because he liked it that way. Of course I knew people had sex all over the place but it had never happened to me.

"Baby? You've never had sex in a car? Have you ever done it in any other place besides a bed?" he asks amused by my lack of knowledge.

"This conversation is over! This is getting *way* too detailed." I quickly turn around and lie on the pillow out of his grasp too embarrassed by my inexperience to reply to his question.

"Fuck! You've only ever had sex in a bed?" he teases and chuckles as he leans his chin on my shoulder looking down at me. "What is wrong with that kid? You still have so much to learn babe." He says as he cuddles me.

"Yeah okay…I've only ever done it in a bed. He was always afraid people would catch a glimpse of me and he didn't want them to see me that way so we would always wait till we were home in a bed. Maybe I do still have a lot to experience and learn…I don't know, I really don't think anyone's going to want a single mother Jace so I don't think I will have much to worry about in that department." I laugh it off even though the thought of being alone the rest of my life hurts.

"Babe you are crazy! You're fucking beautiful and the fact that you're doing this all on your own just shows what an amazing person you are. There's going to be plenty of guys after for you." He whispers back rubbing my tummy.

"Thanks… Jace?"

"Yeah baby?" he says in that sexy deep voice.

"Remember earlier today you said you're going to be sleeping next to me even when I move to the other room?" I ask him thinking about it.

"Yeah and I am, you don't have a say in this Harley." He says with the same tone he used earlier on me.

"I know and I don't mind, I enjoy knowing you're next to me when I sleep but I wanted to know… why do you want to sleep next to me?" I ask him.

"Harley…when you are next to me I can sleep easy. The things I've done and the people I've hurt haunt me; before you came I was unable to sleep more than three hours without waking up from the nightmares. I see their faces in my sleep so I prefer not to sleep at all. I basically live on energy drinks and coffee because of the insomnia. That first night you were here, your father told me to keep you in my room because he didn't want any of the other guys trying it on with you before he'd introduced you to them. To be honest, I didn't want to sleep next to you but when Grimm tells you to do something - you do it, no questions asked. I was afraid I'd wake up during one of my nightmares and was worried I might frighten you; I didn't want you to see that. That night was the first night I've had a full night's sleep in years and I knew it was because I had you beside me. That's why I'm going to be sleeping next to you from now on. I don't want to have those nightmares Harley, I hate them." He says sadly with a muffled voice as if he's close to tears. I slowly turn around to face him and sure enough his eyes are shiny. Those dreams must be terrible if they affect him this way.

"Don't cry Jace, I would love to be your personal teddy bear and keep the nightmares away. Everyone needs a teddy at least once in their life and I'll be yours. You can sleep next to me as long as you want; I'll always be here for you. Kind of like that girlfriend I told you about, the one at home waiting for you? Yeah well I'll be that chick... but without the sex. Whenever you want a cuddle or to sleep…I'll be waiting for you and only you Jacey." I say as I wipe away the tears he's clearly trying to hide from me. I give both of his cheeks a kiss then pull him so that his head leans against my chest, wrapping my arm around his big body as I run my other hand through his damp silky long hair and rest it over the heavy arm resting over my stomach.

He wraps his arm tighter around me as I hear him let out a shaky breath. "Thank you for being my teddy babe. You're already my girl, you just don't know it yet but if you call me Jacey around the boys I will tickle you till you pee yourself and that goes for telling anyone I cried too. You're too perfect for someone like me." he mumbles.

"All your secrets are safe with me …you are better than you think you are." I whisper as I continue to run my hands through his hair.

"Baby if you knew the things I had done, you wouldn't think so. I'm a terrible person…" he says as he holds onto me tighter, snuggling into the crook of my neck with his forehead now leaning against my jawline. I kiss his forehead.

"Stop saying that. Go to sleep its late, we can chat in the morning." I say softly. A few minutes later I can already hear his deep breathing, his chest pushing against the side of my body. I smile to myself knowing he's sleeping peacefully and I'm the reason for it.

Chapter 10

I wake up with Jace's heavy legs wrapped over mine and I can feel his morning arousal pressed firmly against my ass and it's not small either. I also feel his large hand that he left on my stomach last night is now resting at the curve of my breast with his thumb nestled between my two breasts. Tingles course through me as he continues to hold me firmly against his body. I try wiggling away in an attempt to get him to shift but instead he pushes his body into mine and moans into my ear.

"Jace, wake up." I say softly.

"Mmmhmm…" he moans again.

"Jace…you…you're kinda…poking me…" I stutter.

He chuckles. "Yeah…I kinda am…" he says through his throaty morning voice, bringing his hand higher on my breast still not reaching my nipple. I let out a squeal as he squeezes gently and I flinch under his touch. I grab his hand to move it away but he won't budge.

"Teddy, remember what I said about getting what I want? I want to touch you and I'm going to. You feel too damn good not too. Your skin is so soft…" He purrs into my ear.

"Oh… is that my new nickname? Teddy? Aren't you original….Jacey. I honestly don't care how much you want to *touch me* right now, I'm nauseous and need the bathroom, so unless you want me to chunder on you….move!" I yell at him.

"Oh shit! Sorry Harley." He yells back as I run out the bedroom and toward the bathroom.

I've been leaning over the toilet for about twenty minutes when Jace eventually saunters in. I have no more food to throw up, my throat is raw and I have tears coming from my eyes; I'm once again reminded of the little person growing inside me and the person who helped put it there.

Jace kneels behind me and takes my hair from my hand. He uses his other hand to rub my back gently like he's done before. I know he's trying to help and it makes me cry harder over the toilet. Eventually the nausea subsides and he helps me up so I can brush my teeth. I wash my face and wipe it down with a towel. He leads me to his room and tucks me back in bed, climbing in the other side of me and wrapping his arms around me.

"You okay baby?" he asks sweetly.

"No Jace I'm not okay, how am I going to do this?" I let out a deep breath trying to calm myself from the panic attack I feel building up inside me.

"Baby I told you already, you have us; if you need anything just let us know and we will be there for you. You are part of this family whether you like it or not. You will never be alone my Harlz, I'll be here whenever you need me…sex is included in that offer, just say the word." Jace teases and winks. I scoff and smack his chest playfully.

"I suppose I can deal with you being touchy feely if you keep saying sweet things like that to me" I kiss his cheek.

While I'm sitting on the sofa in the lounge a few hours later, Anna strolls in.

"Morning babes! How are you feeling?" She asks as she sits down next to me on the couch with a cup of coffee.

"I'm all good, you?" I say smiling at her.

"I'm great babe. I wanted to ask you if you'd like to go shopping with me today, get stuff for your room?"

"Just us?" I ask excitedly. I never got to have shopping days with my mother like all the other girls did.

"Yep."

"Of course! That sounds fun. Will it be okay if we stop at the college? I want to speak to the student counselor, I need to find out if they'll be able to change my enrollment from full time to correspondence. I just think it'll be easier with the pregnancy, at least I can work as much as possible to pay for all the baby stuff." I explain.

"Harley you know we are going to help you financially? Your father wouldn't have it any other way… you know how he is when he's determined? This whole correspondence thing? Is it really because you are pregnant or is it because you don't want to run into a certain someone when college starts?" she asks me raising an eyebrow.

I sigh knowing she's caught me out. "Okay…I guess it's a little of both. The thing is I'm just not ready to see them together. I can only take so much. I won't be able to take seeing them all lovey dovey in their new relationship while I have to deal with what he left me when he threw our relationship down the drain. I know how my dad is when it comes to me but I need to pay my way, especially with the baby, I want to be the one to provide for him or her." I tell her sternly as she nods her head in acceptance.

"Speaking of the baby, is it okay if I make you an appointment with a doctor around here? I think it's best we introduced you to a Doctor in this area, you may even find out the sex of the baby during your next consult." she says enthusiastically.

"I can't wait. Thanks so much Mom" I squeal excitedly giving her a hug.

On the way to the college my nerves start to kick in as I think about running into either Ashley or Caleb while I'm there. I know everyone is still on break so hopefully they haven't moved up yet.

"Don't be nervous babes, I'll be here with you the whole time and if I see either of those two dipshits I will deal with them. Don't stress." She pats my hand soothing my nerves.

After speaking with the counselor, she gave me a variety of options. The management degree I wanted to take offers a correspondence course as well as night time classes three times a week due to it being popular amongst people that already work full time. I would only have to attend the night classes three times a week for a two hour session.

Anna said I could work the evenings that I don't have college; my schedule works out perfectly and it feels it like a weight has been lifted off my shoulders.

I spent the rest of the day shopping with Anna; she was determined to spoil me and bought me an entirely new wardrobe. She bought clothes that I would be able to wear to work; most of what she picked out was the type of suggestive clothes that she usually wears and even though it's not my taste, I'll wear it if it makes her happy. I pray my father doesn't have a heart attack when I dress for work tonight. The clothes are sexy; Anna said that I should enjoy my body while I can and since the baby bump isn't all that evident under loose clothes I decided to take her advice.

It's time for a change....

All the furniture for my room will be delivered tomorrow morning and I can't wait to finally have my own space. We arrive home an hour before the bar is about to open so I quickly get ready for work. I decide to wear a black loose, off the shoulder top, it hides the baby bump perfectly. I pair it with denim shorts, there not too short but I still feel naked with my bare legs sticking out. I look through my duffle bag and reach for the black mid-thigh socks. Looking myself over in Anna's long mirror, I already feel more confident in what I'm wearing. I pick out a comfortable pair of heeled ankle boots to finish the outfit off.

Whilst doing my hair in Anna's bathroom, she knocks on the door.

"Come in." I shout as I switch off the blow dryer and place it in the draw.

"Wow babes you look hot. Your father is going to kill me!" she says laughing.

I look her over, she has a tight black shirt on with her cleavage sticking out paired with short red hot pants and a pair of plain black heels. All her ink is on show. "You like?" she says twirling for me.

"Wow, Daddy's gonna have a fit!" I laugh with her.

"Here, let me do your makeup and hair." She says gesturing for me to take a seat on the tall stool.

She straightens my hair and it falls down my back flawlessly then she takes the front piece where my long fringe is and braids it down the side of my head so that no hair falls in my face. She does a dark smokey eye with red lipstick. I don't even recognize myself in the mirror, I look much older than my eighteen years and I love it.

She hands me a short bar apron that has the clubs bar logo on it, I wrap it around my waist and stick the notepad in. We head to the bar and I notice the entire house is unusually quiet with no one hanging around.

"Where is everybody?" I ask her as I start wiping down tables.

"The boys had business with another club they should be here later tonight. Mondays are usually our slow night so it's just you, me and Jesse out here tonight with Toby manning the kitchen." Anna says as she packs the bar with clean glasses.

"Jesse? Daddy actually allows you to work with another guy?" I ask her confused; I know how possessive and jealous my father can be.

"Honey, the only reason your father lets Jesse work with me is because he's gay. Well I got a feeling he's bi but I won't tell your father that, he thinks that Jesse flirts with the girls at the bar for better tips." she chuckles and I laugh with her.

She shows me how the bar and cash register works, when she shows me how to work the beer taps I ask her, "I can't hand out alcohol? I'm too young, what if someone catches me serving alcohol."

"Harley calm down, no one comes around here asking questions and when you dress up like that you look much older than your real age, besides I had this made for you..." she says digging in her back pocket, handing me a fake ID that says I'm twenty two.

I look at her in shock. "You are the coolest mom ever!" I giggle looking over at my fake ID.

She heads my way and hugs me, "I am, aren't I?" she says smiling. "Besides it's not as if you can drink anyways?" she says looking down at my belly.

"Does Daddy know about this?" I ask her tapping the ID.

"Of course...he got it made after I suggested it." she says flatly like it's just another thing parents do for their kids.

She continues to show me how to work everything and I catch on pretty quickly. I head to the back storeroom to fetch more glasses for the bar. I use my ass to push open the swing doors but as I push against the doors they open and I stumble.

"Whoa there tiny! Let me help you with that." I turn to look at who's the owner of the deep masculine voice to see a tall beautiful man...*must be Jesse*. He's wearing a tight black shirt that has the bar's logo on and straight cut jeans. The muscles in his broad chest can be clearly seen through the material, he's not as stocky as Jace and he has more of a lean body but nevertheless he has muscles in all the right places.

He has beautiful green eyes similar to Caleb's but lighter. He has brown curly hair and is definitely a "pretty boy". Jesse reminds me a lot of Caleb and the clean cut good looking boy he is. I quickly shut all thoughts of Caleb down and look back up at Jesse who's smiling at me now; he must have caught me staring. I hand him the glass trays and walk past him with my head down trying to hide my rosy cheeks, and then hold the door open for him to walk through.

He chuckles as he passes by and I follow him into the bar. I notice Anna has opened the bar and a couple of people are already seated by the bar and a few of the tables.

"So aren't you going to introduce me to the new girl?" Jesse says completely ignoring me whilst speaking to Anna as she pours drinks and places them on a tray for him.

"Jesse, this is my daughter Harley." Anna says proudly. I can tell she loves calling me her daughter and it makes me happy. I watch as Jesse's eyes widen with realization.

"You're Harley? *Thee* Harley?" he says pointing to the pink Harley model mounted on the wall holding my name.

"Yes, I'm *thee* Harley." I say mimicking his awe filled expression.

"Wow, so good to finally meet you babe. I'm Jesse and it looks like your daddy is going to be using that baseball bat tonight." He says pointing to the bat mounted under the bar.

"Fuck, I'm gonna have a hard time keeping these horny college boys away from you. " Jesse says as he takes the tray from Anna and walks away.

The night has been going smoothly so far and I've already got the hang of things. A few guys have flirted with me but luckily all of them have kept their hands to themselves. I've noticed both Jesse and Anna have been keeping a protective eye on me and apart from all the flirting that's been coming my way from drunk college guys ,I've been having a great night so far.

"Harley?" I jump at the sound of Jace's voice in my ear, turning to see him checking me out with wide eyes.

"Hey! Haven't seen you all day." I wait for him to respond but he continues to stare from my toes to my eyes, looking at me filled with surprise.

"Jace! Stop that…" I playfully push his arm and he chuckles and puts his heavy arm over my shoulder protectively.

"You boys all finished with that meeting?" I ask him removing myself from his arm before walking back to the bar with empty glasses. He follows me making sure to keep his eyes on me.

"What are you wearing? Annalie did this to you right?" he ignores my questions and walks up to me, takes the tray from my hands, places it on the bar nearby then corners me up against the wall with both of his hands on either side of my head.

"W…what are you doing? What's wrong with the way I'm dressed? Is it too skanky?" I say tugging my shorts lower as my lack of confidence rises.

"No baby you look sexy as fuck, any of these guys given you trouble or tried anything with you?" he says looking me over and biting his lip making me tremble beneath his lust filled stare. He knows what he's doing to me; this is probably how he gets the girls in his bed…not that he has to try hard.

"No Jace and I can handle it myself if I need to. Move… I need to get back to work." I say. As I shove past him he grabs me around my waist and brings me up against his chest as his arms wrap around my stomach.

He whispers in my ear, "If any of these guys give you shit, find me babe and I'll deal with them." He kisses my cheek and let's go. I don't say anything and turn to walk away but he grabs my wrist and pulls me against him again.

"Did you hear me Harley? Answer me…" he says through grated teeth.

"Yes Jace, I heard you. Can I go back to work now?" I don't care how hot this boy is… he is really starting to piss me off.

"Raven, let the girl go." Hunter says coming up to Jace and smacking his back chuckling at Raven's behavior towards me. I however, don't find it funny at all.

"What? She needs to know her place…" Jace says looking me over once again smirking suggestively.

This stops me in my tracks as I turn back to look at him. "Know her place? Who the fuck do you think *you* are?" I put my hand on my hip and glare at him with a raised brow; *he so shouldn't have said that*. Hunter drops his head back and lets out a deep chuckle that echoes over the loud music. Jace crosses his arms over his chest , tilts his head looking at me while tensing his jaw but doesn't say a word. I know I'm about to make him angrier but I don't really care.

"You know what Jace? You can go fuck yourself!" I say loud enough for him and Hunter to hear but not loud enough so that everyone else in the bar overhears. Hunter continues to chuckle at Jace's side but Jace has a cold expression on his face and he's still clenching his jaw. I know he's holding in whatever he wants to say to me now but I know later I *will* get it. I quickly walk away before he can catch me again.

I stand behind the bar and take a deep breath trying to control the anger surging inside of me. I am stunned by his condescending behavior towards me. I don't like the way he spoke to me in front of Hunter, as if he owned me and I was just a pet he was training to be obedient.

Chapter 11

"The MC boys already have their eyes on you; I'd watch out for that Jace Hun, he's a dangerous one, unstable too." Jesse says as he comes up to me and hands me a glass of water.

I take the glass and down it in one gulp thinking about the unstable part of his sentence.

"Yeah he thinks he owns me and its really starting to piss me off! I've never been in this situation before? I don't know how to deal with all this... possessiveness." I look back at Jesse, the way he portrays himself is so manly; you'd never think he was into guys.

"Sweetie, all these men are like that with their woman. However, I think he's more possessive over you because of the innocence that radiates off you. Don't get me wrong, you're hot as hell dressed up like that, but your innocence drives these wild men crazy. After all the dangerous and sinful things these men do? They all want a taste of something sweet and innocent. I tend to have possessive tendencies too, it's in all of us men who were brought up around this lifestyle." He motions his hands to the people that surround us.

"Some know how to control it and some don't. Jace may be fucking sex-on-legs but he just can't control himself, be careful with that one." He says giving me a hug.

I hug him back speaking against his chest, "Thanks Jesse."

"No problem babe, I'm here if you ever want to chat." He says smiling down at me.

"Anna! What did you do to my baby girl?" I hear Daddy yelling. I look behind and see my father's wide eyes looking at the clothes I'm wearing; I start laughing.

Jesse chuckles as he whispers in my ear, "I don't think daddy likes his baby dressing up." I smack his arm and walk up to my shocked father giving him a hug.

"Doesn't she look hot babe?" Anna says giving my father a kiss on the cheek.

"That's the problem..." Daddy mumbles making all three of us laugh.

"Don't worry Daddy, Jesse told me all about *the bat* and I know how to use it if anyone causes shit." And I hold up his baseball bat.

His frown disappears and he chuckles. "That's my girl."

We continue to serve the customers throughout the night. The place eventually starts to die down with only a few club members remaining and a few of the regular girls that hang around. It's past three in the morning, I'm exhausted and my feet hurt from standing all night. I'm not in the best of moods because of Jace's earlier behavior and the random drunk guys that wouldn't leave me alone. Anna reckons I'll get used to the strange men hitting on me but I'm not sure if that's even possible. To make things worse I've felt eyes on me the entire evening; I know who it is and I've been trying to avoid him at all costs because I know I'm bound to be "scolded" for my behavior once we're alone.

Walking out of the bathroom, I notice a man holding a girl up against the wall. She seems to be struggling against his grip; she tells him to stop then tries to shove him off but he continues to push his body against her, kissing on her neck.

"Dude get off her." I yell.

"Yes! Get off me!" the girl screeches. I've noticed this girl hanging around a couple different guys from the bar. She's one of the *hoes* as Anna would say; she's wearing a tight black dress with red stilettos.

The man who's wearing the MC's patch on his leather has his hand under her dress between her legs but she continues to push and shove him.

"Girl, stay out of it!" The big guy says not looking my way. He grabs hold of the girls face and roughly smashes his lips to hers while she continues to squirm underneath him.

"Fuck it!" I say as I make my way back to the bar to collect some help. Jesse looks at me and his eyes widen when he sees me grabbing the baseball bat. I make my way back to where the girl is struggling under the large man.

She looks over his shoulder and catches my eye as I point the bat at the man; she gives me a small smile and nods slightly. I swing the bat hard and hit his back. He screams out and the girl lets a huff of breath out as his body bounces off hers. He stumbles away from the girl then bends backwards clutching his back and I take this as an opportunity to raise the bat again and hit him between his legs.

"What the fuck!" the man yells in pain on the brink of tears.

"I told you to get off her!" I shout back. At the corner of my eye I notice my father and the rest of the people in the bar watching the scene I just caused. I turn fully to face them; my breathing is heavy from the anger racing through me. Anna has a smile on her face but my father and Jace seem to be seriously angry...

"She's a fucking whore! She's doing her job!" The man rumbles still clutching his hands between his legs as he sits on his knees. I hear the girl gasp at the man's words.

I lift the bat again ignoring Jace as he runs up to me but I've already hit the man in the chest with the bat, I watch him roll over on the ground and scream out, holding the bat in my shaking hands. Jace snatches it from me and glares.

"I don't give a fuck what she is! She didn't want you groping on her but you totally ignored her when she was telling you to stop." I yell.

"The slut wanted it, it's her job!" the man shouts making me angrier. I look over to the girl who seems shaken up.

"Stop calling her that! What the hell is wrong with you?" I reach for the bat that Jace has in his firm grasp but he yells, "Stop this shit Harley! Right now!" Then he throws the bat to Hunter who's leaning against the wall snickering at the standoff between Jace and me.

"What do you mean - stop? You allow *this* to happen?" I push Jace out my way and face my father who's now staring at me blankly as if I'm a stranger.

"You allow *your* boys to treat woman like this?" I ask furiously. I can tell he's getting angry because his face is now red and his body is tense.

I've never seen my father angry, especially not angry with me and it's a scary sight. I'm trying my hardest to hide how terrified I am on the inside.

"*She*...is *not* a woman...we don't disrespect *our woman* like that Harley." My father says in a deep angry tone. *Why the hell is he angry with me?*

"What is that even supposed to mean? Is this why you kept me away from your *brothers* and your *club*? You didn't want me to see how you all treated woman?" This situation has really made me livid. I'm absolutely fuming, my father is no better than the rest of them.

"Harley, she is *not* a woman! She's a fucking whore! She knew what she was getting into when she started coming around here. You need to mind your own God damn business when it comes to *my* club because this isn't going to change." He is yelling now making me wince.

"Whores are just that... whores! And they are treated as such. Tell her Rachelle." Jace's bark makes me jump.

She looks down at the ground as she stutters clearly afraid. "Yeah Harley, you should mind your own business."

"She's clearly scared of you Jace! The chick is petrified! She didn't want him on her and stop calling her that." I run my hands through my hair, taking deep breaths trying to get my heart rate down.

"She's not a whore? That's what you *really* think?" He glares at me, then turns to Rachelle.

"Come here." She almost runs to him as he opens his arms for her. He runs his hands down her arms and she leans into him. Jealousy hits me like a bag of bricks and I'm about to rip the girl I just saved out of his arms. He stares at me the entire time, he leans down moving her hair out of the way as he bends down to speak in her ear loud enough for me to hear every single word.

"If I let you wear my colours for the rest of the night will you suck me off? Right here, right now?" The girl wastes no time as she bends to the floor and starts unbuckling his belt, I don't waste any time getting the fuck out of there.

"I don't give a fuck what any of you say, if I see *anyone* treating *any* girl like he did?" I say pointing to the guy who's sitting on the floor now leaning against the wall.

"Whether they are *whores* or otherwise… I will do what I just did *again*, without a second thought. If you got a problem with it then I'll leave and you won't have to see me again." I look at my father when I say this and I immediately see when the shock registers.

I bend down to the guy on the floor and look directly into his eyes as I say, "If you go anywhere near her again, whether she likes it or not? When I'm done with you, you won't have a dick left to play with." I stand up, refusing to look at Jace, not wanting to know if Rachelle is going to be wearing his colours after all tonight. I walk out of the bar through the back entrance slamming the door behind me as I hear a few people whistling and shouting.

I continue to walk until I reach the park two streets down. I sit on the grass and pull off my shoes, my feet are killing me and I'm exhausted. I know it's dangerous to be out alone in the dark but I can't bear to see any of their faces right now and I have nowhere else to go.

I sit there for a few minutes, thinking about what Jace did and how jealous I was when he was touching that girl. I feel disgusted when I think about Rachelle and what she was willing to do just to wear Jace's club jacket for one night. I don't regret what I did at all, even if it was a wasted effort.

"You did good back there sweetie." Jesse says walking over to me and sitting closely.

"Thanks… didn't even hear you coming." I look up at him and smirk. "Did you follow me?" I stretch my legs out in front of me on the soft grass.

"Yeah, had to make sure you were safe, you know how we possessive men are." He chuckles.

I playfully nudge him and mumble, "Not funny."

"I'm proud of what you did back there, no one ever has the balls to question the brothers of the club and you went all out your first night working the bar." he says playing with a piece of my hair.

Something about Jesse's nurturing nature makes me feel comfortable and protected with him.

"Thank you Jesse but you get why I was upset right? I don't understand how they can be okay with what that guy was doing! Does that happen often?" I ask leaning my head on his broad shoulder yawning.

"Yeah, that's just how those men are. They were brought up like that, watching their daddies fuck the clubs groupies while the old ladies sat at home knowing full well what their husbands were up to." He wraps his arm around me pulling me into his side.

"That sucks. I won't be treated that way and I won't watch other girls be treated like that either." I say yawning again.

"I don't understand why my father was upset with me though? Why would he be angry with me?" I ask him confused.

He wraps his arms tighter around me and places his chin on my head as he says. "This is the only life your father knows, he grew up with his father being President. Like I said, no one has ever stood up to these MC men, especially not a woman. People sit back and watch... too afraid to say something and I guess your father didn't see your "boldness" coming when you did what you did. No one disrespects your father's brothers; I think the rage from that overwhelmed him before he noticed that it was you standing up for someone that wasn't part of the club. I think you surprised him Harley. Don't stress babe." I nod my head not knowing what to say and let out another yawn.

"Come on, let's get you home." He says starting to get up.

"No Jesse, I'm not going back yet. I can't deal with Jace or Daddy right now. I'll stay here till the sun comes up." I look up at him looming over me.

"I'm not leaving you out here; you can come home with me till you're ready to go back." He drops his hand to pull me up, picking up my shoes.

"Jesse I'm fine here. You can go, I'll be okay."

"No, you're coming with me. I've already texted Annalie telling her your safe and I'm going to make sure I keep to that." He says dragging me away from the park.

We arrive at his apartment and I'm completely floored. It's absolutely spotless and everything has its place.

"The bathrooms over there, you can borrow some of my clothes to sleep in." he says pointing down the hall.

I head to the bathroom; as I'm under the shower enjoying the warm water and cleansing my skin I hear the door open and footsteps. I wrap my arms around my body afraid he might be able to see me through the steamy shower doors.

"Don't worry Hun I'm not looking, just brought clothes for you." He says, and then leaves the bathroom.

I get out of the shower and dress, his clothes are rather large and it looks as if I'm drowning in them. I walk out into the lounge and spot him in the kitchen, he turns around and smiles at me in his clothes. I sit on the stool by the kitchen island and watch him take glasses out, followed by a bottle of vodka.

"I think you deserve a drink after standing up to those men tonight." Jesse says as he starts poring the clear liquid into a glass. I freeze, he isn't aware of the fact that I'm pregnant.

He places the glass in front of me. "Oh none for me Jesse, I ...uh...don't drink." I say as I push the glass back to him.

"C'mon, just one, I won't tell if you don't?" he winks at me and I laugh.

"No Jesse really… I can't. You have it."

"Why don't you want it? Is it because of your age? I told you I won't tell." He smiles and leans on the table in front of me.

"It's not that Jesse, I'm just not allowed to have alcohol." I smile at him as I try to brush it off but he won't drop it.

"Why?" he asks confused. "When I was your age all I wanted to do was drink and party?" He sips his drink and winces as he swallows the strong clear spirit.

"Well… when you were my age you weren't pregnant now were you?" I say sarcastically and watch as he almost chokes on his drink. I start laughing at his reaction.

"What! You're pregnant?" he takes my glass and downs it. "Please don't tell me it's Jace's…please God." He says closing his eyes and crossing his fingers praying.

I laugh at his exaggeration. "No Jesse it's not his." I say. Jesse looks at me then sits next to me on the bar stool, he holds me in a tight hug rubbing my back.

"Where's the father?" he asks softly.

"Not in the picture." I mumble.

"I'm so sorry Hun." He whispers into my neck.

"It's okay. I'm fine." I laugh and shrug him off.

"Well, since you can't have a drink with me, can I make you some hot chocolate?" he asks walking back to the cupboard for a mug.

"Now that sounds good, yes please."

He makes a mug of hot chocolate and calls me to sit with him in the lounge. We chat and I tell him my story about Caleb and Ashley as I rest my head on his shoulder.

"What a dick!" he says harshly. I've come to terms with the fact that the Caleb that I once loved wasn't at all the person I thought he was. I never pictured my life without him part of it, it was always Caleb and Harley…always. I would never have imagined him betraying me like he did. I must have fallen asleep on the couch but I'm half-awake as I feel my body being lifted and placed under the covers of a warm bed. I feel the bed dip and I cuddle into the pillows but instead of soft pillows I feel another hard warm body beside mine. I'm too tired to care, my body is exhausted…mentally and physically. Jesse places his arm around me and pulls me into his chest, then kisses my head as I fall into a deep sleep.

I wake up in a comfy bed and I'm not fully sure how I got here. The smell of bacon immediately wakes me up though and I jump out of the bed and run towards the toilet. After wiping my face clean, I use Jesse's toothpaste with my finger and "brush" my teeth.

I walk into the kitchen and watch as Jesse sits with two plates dished out in front of him. He gives me a toothy grin.

"Morning sickness must suck ass!" he teases.

"You have no idea." I sigh as I take a seat next to him. I feel safe with Jesse just like I do with Jace; but with Jesse I'm a lot more relaxed, it's probably due to the fact that I know he's gay, I know he won't try anything with me. When I'm around Jace his intensity messes with my emotions, he uses his sexiness to his advantage. I'm not sure what's going on between us but I know there's chemistry, that's for sure. Jace frightens me, he's volatile and can be cool one minute then raging the next. I'm scared of Jace even if I am too chicken to admit it to him…he scares me…a lot! I know he wouldn't hurt me but he's very controlling and it causes me to surrender to him even when I don't want to.

Jesse is sexy but in a more relaxed manner… I can let my guard down with Jesse knowing he won't use me and replace me like damaged goods.

"Don't you eat bacon?" He asks eyeing the bacon on my plate sitting untouched.

"No… I do but I can't right now. The smell alone makes me gag, I can't do it." I say disgusted.

He chuckles then picks the bacon off my plate and eats it. "We better get you home before Grimm comes knocking on my door… or better yet Jace." He says, taking our plates and placing them in the dishwasher.

I change back into last night's outfit but don't put the shoes or socks on, and we head down to Jesse's car. As he stops in front of the Club I'm hesitant to get out. He opens my door for me then leans in and bends down so we are at eye level.

"Everything is going to be fine Harley, if you need me for anything…even if you just want to talk, you can call me and I'll pick you up okay?" he writes down his number on the back of a receipt. "It's safe here Harley, everything is going to be fine… Come." He shows me his hand and I take it; holding onto it tightly as he leads me to the door.

"I'm okay from here, you don't have to come in." I tell him, I don't want my father or Jace to take out their frustration on Jesse for helping me. He nods and gives me a hug then leaves.

I open the door and make my way up the stairs. The house is quiet…too quiet. I make my way through the kitchen and lounge but I don't see anyone around; it's usually noisy and filled with guys from the club.

As I tiptoe towards Jace's room, a feeling of dread washes over me. I know he's going to want to discuss last night so I might as well get this over with, doesn't mean I want to though.

I notice Jace's door is open so I walk in, the bed is still neatly made and Jace isn't anywhere to be seen. I look out of his window which faces the back of the club to see if my father's car or bike is out there but there's only one bike parked outside and it's Jace's; Daddy's shop doors are closed and no one's there either, my thoughts are interrupted though as Jace enters the room.

"Where the fuck have you been Harley? I've been looking everywhere!" Jace yells, making me move away. I notice he's wearing the same clothes he wore last night, his hair is messy and his eyes are bloodshot. It doesn't look like he slept at all and I suddenly feel terrible.

"You don't have to yell!" I say back.

"Don't yell at you? Are you fucking kidding me! I'll do whatever the fuck I like!" He comes up to me and I back away as far as I can but my ass hits his desk; I can't move away from his dark eyes. I'm scared shitless but I won't allow him to see what he's doing to me so I stand my ground.

"I don't know what the fuck your problem is! I stayed with Jesse and Anna knew about it?" I say, moving away from him as he reaches out and grabs my arm tightly bringing me closer to him.

"Jace get your hands off me, now!" I say through gritted teeth staring at his chest in front of me.

"Jesse? You were with *him* this entire time? No one fucking told me! Why didn't you tell me? I don't want you with him. You don't sleep next to anyone besides me, do you understand?" he roars. When I don't answer he grabs my face and pulls it close to his.

"I *said*, Do. You. Understand. Me?" His voice is menacingly soft but still harsh; I can feel his breathe on my face.

"Yes! I understand you! Okay?" I shout and shove him off me.

He walks right past me and I stand there quietly as he leaves the room. The house is so quiet that I can even hear the shower as he turns it on. After ten minutes the shower goes off I start to panic, I don't want to have another screaming match with him. As I'm about to leave his room, he walks in zipping up his jeans, I avoid looking at his shiny muscular chest and turn to look out the window again.

"Where is everyone?" I ask.

"Your father had a meeting and Annalie went with him, the guys who didn't go are at home with their families." he says and I hear the bed squeak as he sits on it.

I don't say anything but that doesn't stop him from talking.

"That shit you pulled last night can't happen again, understand me?" he says again in that harsh tone.

"What shit?" I say flatly knowing full well what he's referring to.

"Playing superwoman, hitting one of my brothers with a bat? It's not on Harley, do that again and you *will* regret it. You may be Grimm's kid but no one fucks with our boys… not even you." he spits out. I feel smaller than I already am.

"What I said last night I meant, if I see *"one of your boys"* forcing themselves on someone that doesn't want it, I won't sit and watch. I don't care whether you agree with it or not." I walk closer to him and I know he's already fuming by the way he clutches the bedding in his hands. I need to say these words to him, I need him to know I don't agree with the way they treat women.

"Harley, I'm going to say this once and I'm not going to repeat myself. You will *not* do what you did last night again, do you hear me? You are a woman and you belong to this club but you need to know your place." he says pulling me onto his lap so that I'm straddling him.

I struggle to get off but he won't budge as he holds me tightly against him. We are at eye level as I speak with venom.

"What exactly is *my place* Jace?"

"At my side…with me, I can only do that if you listen to what I say. I have to keep you safe, your father agrees with me. You don't know how it is to be part of this life but I'm going to show you." His voice is softer and his hold on me loosens. He looks sad and exhausted. My heart hurts for him, melting away at the ice queen role I'm trying play. I want to wrap my arms around his much larger ones and comfort him.

"My father agrees with the way you treat me?" I ask raising an eyebrow confused.

"Yes, he trusts me with you and he knows I'm the best person to keep you safe. He knows what my intentions regarding you are." He says looking down at my chest now very openly; the sleeve of my shirt hangs off one of my shoulders and the top of my pink bra is sticking out along with a lot of cleavage. I watch as he looks at my body lustfully and he bites his lip.

"And what are your intentions Jace?"

"I want *you* baby…all of you and I'm not going to let anyone stop me, not even you." He looks up at me intensely.

"Really Jace? You want me? Last night it looked like you wanted Rachelle? So which is it? And while we're on the topic of her…" I bend down and put my lips near his ear. "Did she get to wear your colours last night Jace?"

I let my lips linger near his neck. I feel his shoulders bouncing, laughter starts coming from his mouth. The idiot's actually laughing at me.

"Jealous baby?" he says pulling my head back to look into my eyes.

"Oh shut up." I push him down onto the bed and attempt to move off him but his hands go firmly on the undersides of my knees making sure I can't move. I'm straddling his lap while he lies on the bed laughing at me. When I felt his arousal against me through his jeans I jump forward, stopping myself from falling into his chest by putting both hands on the bed next to his head. Now I'm leaning over him, his eyes on mine now more serious as he whispers, "Not jealous baby? Not at all?"

I shake my head unable to move my eyes from his.

"What if I told you that I let her wear my patch...all... night... long? That it was worth what she did to me while people watched... that she suck-" I interrupt him by shoving one of my hands over his mouth, squeezing my eyes shut.

"I don't want to hear about it... I can't." I shake my head breathing heavy, full of jealousy.

He manages to pull my hand away and I hear him say, "I knew it."

Suddenly his one hand grips my hair roughly and he tugs my head down to meet his. His lips are hard and forceful against mine; mine are equally determined as his. I'm lost in the nirvana he creates around me, forgetting all he's done.

I turn my face from his but he continues to press his lips against my neck and collarbone. Breathlessly I say, "Jace stop... I can't do this. Not after you and Rach-"

"No." he says and goes back to kissing me.

"No?" I'm confused.

"No." he repeats.

"What do you mean *no*?" I pull away from him again yet this time he rolls me over with him now looming above me. I push at his chest.

"What are you saying Jace? I don't understand? I'm telling you to stop; so stop!" I push him again and he chuckles shaking his head then dives in for another kiss. I bite his lip and he flinches back, checking his lip if it's bleeding; luckily it's not.

"No, as in I didn't do shit with that whore. No, I'm not going to allow you to overthink this and no, I'm not letting you throw away whatever is going on between us. It's going to happen and no, I'm not getting off you. Now wrap those pretty little legs around me." This time it's me who grabs his hair and forces his lips to mine.

He drops his body and I wrap my legs around his hips like he asks, he pushes against me one more time and I moan into his mouth feeling his body move against mine. His tongue enters my mouth finding mine, he's slow and gentle, caressing my tongue with each stroke. After a few more minutes he pulls away and leans his forehead on mine letting out a deep breath.

He moves away and pulls me with him so that I'm back to straddling his lap as he sits on the edge of the bed.

"I was so worried about you last night baby, don't ever do that to me again. I need you here Harley...I need you with me. Do you understand?" he whispers the last words and I know he wants me to answer. He looks miserable so I drop the wall I've been trying to keep up as I place my hands on either side of his face moving the damp hair from his eyes. I gaze into his eyes then kiss his cheek. I wrap my arms around his neck and hold him. His chin rests on my shoulder and mine on his; I turn to whisper in his ear, squeezing him tight as I do this.

"I understand Jace."

"I can't sleep without you, I need you next to me...I told you I can't sleep without you and you weren't here last night. I was alone and I couldn't sleep, I needed you... I missed you." He whispers in a husky voice against my ear making me shiver.

"I'm sorry Jace. I missed you too." I pull from his embrace, look into his beautiful sparkling eyes and turn my attention to his lips giving him a soft peck. When I release him and move off his body, I notice how dejected he looks; but I need some distance before I do something I may regret... like make use of that bed he's sitting on.

"Where did you go with Jesse last night?" he says as he clears his throat and gets comfortable on the bed, leaning his head against the pillows watching me.

"He found me at the park and took me to his place. I stayed with him." I say as I start looking inside my bag for clothes.

"What?" his voice rises.

"Jesse from the bar? I stayed with him at his apartment. I already told you this." I repeat myself.

I hear the bed squeak and hear his loud footsteps come up behind me, I ignore him and place my clothes on the desk in his room, then search for the medicine the doctor issued.

"What do you mean you stayed there?" he asks again as if in disbelief.

"Jace... seriously? I'm not repeating myself a third time." I say walking past him. He reaches towards me and grabs my arm roughly.

"You sleep in his bed?" he asks angrily glaring at me.

I swallow down remembering that I did and I clearly remember him climbing in bed beside me. He held me most of the night. He clears his throat and raises an eyebrow.

"Yeah. What's your problem Jace? He's gay." I say brushing him off, attempting to get passed him again.

"You sleep next to him?" he asks again flatly glaring at me. This part of Jace scares me, I can't even bare to look at him in the eyes.

"Jace...he's gay."

"Fuck it Harley. I know he's gay. Don't mean shit to me. You sleep beside another man in his bed and that man isn't me...we got a problem." He turns and heads for the door, opens it... then stops, looks back at me then crushes me with his parting words.

"You carry on acting this way and I'll treat you exactly how whores should be treated." Then he walks out. I stand there frozen as I hear his fading footsteps down the stairs, the door slamming followed by the rumble of his bike as he speeds away.

I stand there completely numb. My body is shaking but I'm not sure whether its fear from how angry and terrifying Jace was, or whether it's the hurt that's flowing through me from the callous words he spoke after he kissed me the way he did.

In a daze I make my way to the shower, clothes in hand. I wash my hair and body and sit under the hot water rubbing my tummy. I can't believe how he spoke to me. I don't deserve that. I can't wait to get the furniture for my room, we need space and I need distance from him, even if it is just the room opposite his.

After showering and dressing, I decide to do a load of washing; I only have a few clothes, not enough for a full load. I pick up clothes that are lying around the apartment, all of which are Jace's since he throws his clothes wherever he tends to be during the moment.

I do the washing and clean around the apartment trying to keep myself busy. I'm not used to this place being so empty and quiet. After folding the washing and placing all Jace's folded clothes on his bed I hear a honking downstairs; looking out of the window I spot the furniture delivery truck. I run down the stairs excitedly and show the guys which room to place all my things.

After the guys have delivered and assembled everything, they leave. I make my bed and place all my clothes in my new drawers and cupboard. I fill the adjoined bathroom with all my toiletries thankful to have my own space.

I lie back on my new comfortable bed and sink into a deep sleep.

Chapter 12:

I wake up to the sound of the loud bass coming from downstairs, I don't feel well at all, my head is pounding and I'm nauseous. I'm usually only ever sick in the mornings so I really hope I'm not coming down with something. The windows are rattling and the floor vibrating beneath doesn't help the headache. I look at my phone and see that it's already after seven in the evening, I slept the day away.

"Shit, I'm late for work."

I notice a text message from Anna and I open it:

ANNA AT 01:36PM: Hey Babes, we're still at the meeting, weather is bad this side and things are running late so we'll be staying here tonight. Don't worry about work, the Bar is closed tonight. Only a few of the boys will be there. Love you lots see tomorrow!

HARLEY AT 07:47PM: Have a safe trip. Love you guys.

I know I should type more but my head hurts so bad, I can't even concentrate.

I make my way to the bathroom and wash my face. I'm still wearing a pair of jeans and a Blink 182 band shirt. After washing my face, I make my way to the kitchen to see if I can find any headache tablets. Finding some in the cabinet, I take two and down them with cold water. I don't take notice of the various people around the apartment but they take notice of me and say their hello's; I nod my head not in the mood to start conversation.

I rest my head on my arms over the cold counter.

"Decided to join us?" Hunter says in his deep voice.

"Mmmhmm…" I mumble enjoying the coldness of the counter on my warm cheek.

"You okay Princess?" he asks, sounding more concerned.

"Yeah…just a little dizzy, haven't eating much today. I just need to take my medicine and I'll be good as new." I stand up and look at his concerned face.

"You want me to get you something to eat?" he asks seriously.

"No thanks Hunter, I can do it. Thanks though." I rub his arm as I walk pass him weakly.

Making my way back to my room to get my medicine, I lean against the wall in the hallway as spots blur my vision. The door to one of the spare rooms is a little open and it's a foot from where I'm standing, but I can see everything that's happening.

I see the body of a man sitting on the corner of the bed, his pants down to his ankles, I can't see his face yet but I hear his grunting and the girls fake moaning. I watch as the girl between his legs bobs her head up and down in a rhythm. I see her face clearly now as she moves away and uses her hands before placing her mouth back on him and it's the girl I defended last night, Rachelle. I stand there frozen as Jace's face comes into view. He pushes the girls head down harder onto his manhood. I can't stand there any longer and I run the rest of the way to the bathroom. It's as if the entire Caleb situation is on re-run, but this time I see it with my own eyes, I witness it. I was so stupid to think Jace was any better. I seriously don't have the energy for any of this.

I'm disgusted in Jace, I'm regretting ever standing up for that girl or letting Jace ever touch me. I know we don't have a relationship as such, but the way he explained to me that I was his; I thought that would be a mutual thing. I guess in his opinion I am his, but he isn't mine and never will be. The way he touched and kissed me this morning convinced me that he actually cared about me.

"I'm so stupid… So fucking stupid!" I say out loud.

I continue to throw up even as I hear the door open and close behind me. Tears that shouldn't be there are rolling down my cheeks and I want to tell whoever is behind me to go away but I can't speak.

"Here's some water babe, I'll go find Jace for you." Hunter says placing a glass of water next to me on the counter.

"No! Don't!" I stutter through coughs. "I don't want him near me." I hear him as he lets out a huff.

"He cares a lot for you Harley, I know it doesn't seem like it but that's just how we are. He cares about you, he just doesn't know how to show you; I know he's serious about you though." He says in a softer more soothing tone as he bends down next to me and leans against the door.

"Getting the girl that I defended last night to suck him off shows that he cares about me? Well Damn…if-" I start to say sarcastically.

"What?" Hunter interrupts me in disbelief. I throw up again and curse because this is so damn embarrassing. He continues to sit there calmly while my head is facing the toilet bowl. He doesn't seem fazed at the fact that I'm throwing up, he doesn't even seem disgusted.

I finally get a break to breath and I quickly get the words out before I'm hunched over the toilet again. "Yeah…tell him next time he should shut the fucking door."

"I'm going to fucking kill him!" Hunter roars and steps up, ready to leave. I panic and quickly grab his pants above his knee. I can't see anything as I'm facing the toilet but I watch out of the corner of my eye, where my hand is holding onto his jeans.

"No….don't go…Please." I say through coughs, there's nothing left in me to come out.

He tenses but I don't let go, his body relaxes and he leans into me. I flush the toilet and move my body from the toilet now panting, fully exhausted. He picks out a clean cloth from the cabinet and wets it then pulls me into his body as I'm sitting between his legs on the floor with my head and back against his chest. Slowly but soothingly he wipes my face clean.

"I'm sorry Princess." He says quietly.

I let out a deep breath my whole body is weak and exhausted from getting sick but I find the words I need to say.

"Don't be sorry Hunter; you're sitting here helping me. I guess I can't even be mad at Jace for whatever's he's doing now." I say sadly, thinking that they're probably hooking up by now.

"We aren't dating or anything, Jace only feels protective over me because of the accident and that. It's cool, I'm good. I think it's best if I just keep my distance from him for a while." I say, trying to convince myself more than I am him.

I move my body from his and wash my face and brush my teeth. I'm still a bit shaky but I need to get out of here.

"Thanks for everything Hunter, I know you don't think I belong here and I promise you if I had somewhere else to go I would… I just don't right now." I say avoiding his eyes.

"Princess, I said that because you are too good to be around people like us." He chuckles. "But after the show you put on last night, I think you belong here just fine." He laughs again remembering the events of last night.

"You did good last night. Proud of you, you have balls hitting a dude as big as Tom Cat." he chuckles again. "Don't let anyone change that Princess, not even Jace."

He pulls me in for a quick hug and gives me a quick squeeze before releasing me. I smile at him as we make our way out of the bathroom.

I walk to my room and slip on a pair of socks quickly.

"Where are you going?" Hunter says leaning on my door frame.

"Nowhere, my…err…feet are cold. I think I'm going to sleep, I'm too tired and don't feel well." I say sitting on the bed.

"Yeah how are you feeling? You were pretty sick back there, if you don't feel better in the morning you should go to the doctor. I can take you if you like?" he asks genuinely concerned.

"Thanks Hunter, I'll let you know." I say, putting on my bedside light and opening my bed, trying to get him to leave.

"Night Princess… and… sorry about Jace." He switches the overhead light off and leaves my room.

I almost flinch at the mention of Jace's name but recover when I remember what he is most likely doing with Rachelle. I quickly put my shoes on and grab my hand bag and cell phone.

I hear loud noises outside the room and then suddenly the music stops and everything can be heard perfectly.

"So nice of you to join us *Raven.*" Hunter almost growls.

"Fuck off Hunt…" Jace yells back.

"Next time your busy with a whore, make sure you close the fucking door." Hunter says louder.

"What's it to you brother if people see who's sucking me? Huh?" Jace says back with his smug attitude.

"Well when it comes to Harley, I guess *now* it becomes my problem. Girl was so sick she couldn't even walk straight; saw you with that bitches face in your lap working you, got her even sicker *brother*, I've spent the last twenty minutes watching her face over the toilet. So now I say, shut the fucking door next time Raven." Hunter roars.

"Fuck." I hear bustling and movement. "Where is she? Is she okay? Let me get to her."

I don't wait to hear the rest because I'm already making my way out the window looking to see if the fire escape still reaches the ground safely and if the ladder works. Thank goodness it works perfectly, I make my way down quickly ignoring the loud smashing and banging noises coming from upstairs. The ladder stops a few feet above the ground but I land on my feet just fine.

I'm in the alley behind the bar leading to Daddy's mechanic shop. I quickly run past and place the hoody over my head so the bikers that are standing on the street don't notice me. I know there's a Diner on the next street and I need something to eat, I'm starving.

As soon as I'm in front of the Diner I pull back the hood of my jacket and walk in. I order food and sit in the corner away from any windows. The phone Anna bought me starts vibrating; Jace's name pops up on the screen. It rings a couple more times. It rings again and I watch as Daddy's name lights up my screen. I sigh knowing I have to answer him; I don't want him worrying about me.

"Hello?"

"Harley! Thank God! Where are you? Are you okay?" he asks worriedly.

"Daddy I'm fine, just getting something to eat, the apartment is full and I…just needed to get out." I stutter. I hate lying to my father but I suppose the story is partly true.

There's silence on the other side of the line and I can hear his deep breathing. When he speaks it's in a softer tone. "I'm sorry about last night baby girl, I didn't mean to get angry with you and I never want you to feel that you can't come home. I know the club is not…err….perfect for you but me and Ann need you with us. We've been without you for too long and we want you safe…with us."

I feel a tear slip down my cheek and watch as it hits the table; I wipe it away with the sleeve of my jacket. "It's okay Daddy we'll talk about it when you guys are home, I have to go, foods here. Please drive safely tomorrow. Love you guys."

"Okay baby girl. Send me a message when you are home safe okay? Love you Harley." He says as he ends the call.

An older lady brings over my food and I quickly wipe away any remaining tears, my face is probably all puffy and red but I'm too exhausted to worry about that .She lingers by the table looking sadly at me as she places my plate in front of me, then she gives me a small smile and pats my back. I give her a reassuring smile and that seems to make her happy as she strolls away.

I relax and eat the cheeseburger I ordered, I'm starving and I know it won't stay down for long but I need to eat something. I try to keep thoughts of Jace out of my head; trying to think of anything other than him is hard. I think about Momma back at home and wonder how she's doing. Even though she was hardly around when I was there, now that I'm not with her I really do miss her.

Chapter 13

I hear the bell of the door go off and a bunch of rowdy guys come in laughing and joking. I try to scoff down as much food as I can quickly so I can get out of here. I don't look up to see who they are and it's unlikely I know any of them but I'd rather be alone than in this noisy diner.

I keep my eyes on my food and ignore the noise as it comes closer toward where I'm sitting in the back corner.

"Harley? Is that you?" I hear a familiar voice say. I freeze hoping if I ignore them they will get the picture and leave.

I hear their footsteps as they walk closer to me then I see their shoes in my line of vision. I slowly raise my eyes and look at them.

I don't get a chance to respond as I'm being lifted into large warm arms; squealing as I'm pulled from my chair making it scrape against the floor.

"Oh my God, I was so worried about you." He lets out a deep breathe. "I tried calling a couple of times but you didn't answer?" Brent says finally putting me down as he looks at me, almost inspecting me.

"Brent...my phone broke in the crash. Daddy transferred my number though to my new phone but I hardly answer anyone's calls these days. What are you doing here already? Doesn't your semester start in a couple weeks?" I sit back down and he sits opposite me taking a fry off my plate and eating it, I shake my head and smile. Typical Brent...

"I came up early to stay with my cousins, wanted to check things out and all. The best parties are before college starts." He winks at me, his expression then changing as what I just said suddenly dawns on him. "Wait, what do you mean *your semester*?" he raises his eyebrow.

"I pulled out of full time, decided to study through correspondence. No big deal." I say taking a sip of my Coke.

"Yeah Harley it *is* a big deal, you won't get to enjoy everything the College has to offer , you're going to miss out on so much." He says sadly.

"Brent things have changed, I have more responsibilities now. I have to do things on my own, before, when I was with...him...things were easier but now that I'm not, this...this is the way it has to be. This is what's best for me." I try my best to give him a smile but it doesn't quite reach my lips. I can't eat anymore, apart from being full, I've lost my appetite. I push my plate away.

He looks at me genuinely, and then places his large rough hand on top of mine, I tense and look up at him.

"Have you been crying?" he says softly.

"No." I say pulling my hand away trying to avoid his gaze.

"You are a terrible liar babe, how have you been?" he asks in a caring tone.

"I've been better…but I'm getting there slowly. It's funny how when you feel things are finally looking up for you and you're ready to lose those crutches that've been keeping you up, something gets in the way, trips you and you fall a few more steps back; but yeah…I'm getting there." I say out loud thinking more to myself than him.

He's quiet still looking at me with sad eyes. "You are so strong Harley; you didn't deserve what he did. He doesn't deserve you babe, you can do so much better. I can't believe he did that to you. You were so good for him and he fucked it all up." He runs his hand through his thick messy blond hair and whispers the last bit as if not wanting me to hear.

"If it makes you feel better he hasn't been himself since you left that night. After your accident, he blamed himself, he wanted to see you and speak to you, try explain to you why-"

I interrupt him. "Brent…no…I don't want to hear it and I seriously don't want to speak about him or hear how he's doing. I want to forget him and that night. Please." I beg him.

"Sup Brent, who's the hottie?" Some jock comes over to us and puts his hand on Brent's shoulder, looking down at me winking. I just shake my head and look to Brent who's now eating my half eaten burger and drinking the rest of my soda. I smile; many people have changed through the years but Brent has stayed the same no matter what. Of course he's flirty and always joking around with me but he will always be like a big brother to me. I shouldn't have shut him out like I did, guess he's really one of the only true friends I had.

"Trevor, meet Harley. Harley this is my cousin, Trevor. Harley's off limits got it?" Brent says with his mouth full of food glaring at his cousin.

Trevor greets me but I hear the door bells go off again and once again I tremble praying Jace hasn't found me. Instead in walks a group of the girls that hang around the club, Rachelle included.

What the hell? Is this the local hang out or what?

"Why do you look so jumpy every time the bell rings?" Brent asked confused.

Trevor looks at the door and spots the group of barely clothed girls. His lip curls in disgust, "Argh…look what the cats dragged in." He winks at me then walks back to his table with the other guys.

I look down at my hands, shake my head and let out a deep breath, "Tell me about it."

"You know those chicks? Please don't tell me you hang out with them." Brent says looking concerned whilst pushing my now empty plate to the side.

I almost want to stand up to the girls and ask him what he means but I know exactly what he means; he thinks we are better than them, that I shouldn't be associated with girls like that. I don't bother standing up for them. *Look where it got me last time? Those girls did this to themselves...*

"Nah...don't know them but know of them." I look back to where Rachelle was minutes before, looking up just in time to see her walking towards me.

"Harley, I'm so sorry about earlier. I heard you saw us." She looks down at her long red fake fingernails ashamed.

"No Rachelle, don't bother apologizing to me. I stood up for you last night. That dude was double my size and I fucking hit him with a bat for you. I risked mine and my child's safety for you, only for you to act like the slut that they were accusing you of being. Then I find you sucking him off? No-" I shake my head, "-don't bother, I'm done with apologies, they don't mean shit." I get up and throw money on the table, enough for the meal and a big enough tip.

"Y...your child?" Brent stutters, in my angry state I forgot he was even around.

"Oh. My. God, you're pregnant. I...I'm so sorry Harley, I don't know what I was thinking-" Rachel trembles but I ignore her and Brent and run out of the diner.

I lean on the side of the wall trying to get my breathing to return to normal; I can't have a panic attack out here.

Breathe...just breathe Harley...In...out...in...

"Harley! Wait! Shit, you need to stop running away like that!" Brent comes running up to me out of breath leaning his hand on his knees hunching over.

"I'm sorry..." I mumble finally catching my breath looking up at him as he stands up, waiting to see the judgment in his eyes.

"You're pregnant?" he simply says.

"It's not his Brent, don't ask me questions...just know, it's not his..." *It's mine,* I don't say that out loud though.

He looks at me with a shocked expression on his face and then surprises me by pulling me in for a hug. "You need anything babe, you call me."

"Thanks." I say squeezing him tight.

"Come with us to the park? I'll take you home after. Please?" he begs me.

"Okay..." I smile and he pulls me along to his truck where all the guys are already sitting on the back making a ruckus.

We're sitting at the park in the middle of the night. I'm sitting next to Brent as I watch the other few guys hanging around down by the pond all chatting and laughing with drinks in their hands.

The park is my favorite place around here; it's so beautiful and peaceful especially at night.

"So who was that chick and why did you hit some guy with a bat?"

Brent says, interrupting my thoughts.

I sigh knowing he isn't about to let me get away with it.

"Well last night, she was struggling to get away from this guy that was forcing himself onto her. When he didn't listen to me telling him to stop - I got a baseball bat, hit him a couple times and yelled at all these guys when they called her a slut. When they told me that she was doing her job I defended her but then…" I mumble not really wanting to bring up the memory of seeing them together.

"Then what babe?" Brent's looking intensely at me obviously engrossed in my story.

"Then I kinda found her…with Jace a few hours ago…she was um…giving him head." I say sadly. Brent looks at me and I can tell he's confused.

"Who's Jace?" he asks.

"He's the guy that I crashed into and well it's complicated. I don't know what we are or what we were. It's weird but I thought we were together because he kind of acted like we were but I guess I was wrong. I suppose I can't even be upset with him or what he did. It reminded me of the whole Caleb and Ashley thing." I say sadly wiping away a stray tear and looking away from him, not wanting him to see my watery eyes.

Brent pulls me closer to him so I'm snuggled into his side, putting his arm over mine. "I'm sorry you have bad taste babe." This makes me laugh underneath him and his chuckle joins mine.

"Do you want me to beat him up for you?" He winks.

"Who do we have to beat up?" Trevor says lying next to me leaning on his elbows.

"Sweetie, no offence…Jace will destroy you. Both of you. Same time." I tease them and they chuckle; little do they know that all of what I'm saying is true.

We hear the roar of motorcycles come up and I know my time is up. I roll my eyes and snuggle closer to Brent, he smiles at me then looks up to the parking lot to see a couple bikes as they park.

"Wonder what these guys want." Trevor says twisting his head to see a couple of guys jumping off their bikes. I turn my head back to the pond, wishing that I had a little more time to enjoy the peace.

"They're here for me." I simply say and both boys' heads whip around to look at me.

"What? Whoa! Check out that big dude. Please don't tell me that's Jace…" Brent says quickly, taking his arm off my shoulder. *Good idea…*

I take a glance back and turn my head back to the pond.

"Nah that's Hunter…Jace is scarier." Brent chokes on his beer and I chuckle.

"Bad taste huh?" I say winking.

"Princess, up…let's go." Hunter simply says. I let out a deep breath and Brent helps me up. Hunter gets in between us but I manage to slide past him and grab Brent in for a hug. He feels so familiar and harmless. I whisper in his ear. "I'll call you and we can catch up okay?" I try pull away but he pulls me back tighter against him.

He whispers, "Are you safe with him Harley?"

"Yeah…he's good." *I'm safe with Hunter…not so sure about Jace though.* I kiss his cheek and he smiles. I swear I hear Hunter grumble from behind me but I don't care.

Brent reluctantly lets go and Hunter takes my small hand in his. He pulls me along with him up the hill back to where their bikes are parked.

"Raven isn't going to like that." he says as he puts a helmet on my head and makes sure everything is buckled tight.

"What?" I ask confused.

"You cuddling up to the Jock, he won't like it… I don't like it." he shakes his head.

"He's the only friend I have left here; I don't care what anyone says. I've lost too much already, I'm not losing him as well." I say looking away from Hunter's concerned face.

"I'm your friend Harley, aren't I?" Hunter says. I look at him and notice how hurt he looks.

I smile at him and squeeze his large muscular tattoo covered arm. "Yeah…you are. Thank you Hunter." He smiles at me and seems to relax a little.

"Okay good, where's my kiss then? Huh?" He gives me a cheeky grin. I'm not fooled by his good looks, I know a player when I see one but I oblige and give him a kiss on his cheek as he bends down.

"Thank you for looking after me in the bathroom tonight and…everything else." He smiles.

"You're welcome Princess. Let's get you home before Rave rips the entire club house to shit." Hunter climbs onto the bike motioning for me to climb on behind him.

Arriving at the house, I don't know what to expect. As I get off the motorbike, Hunter helps me take off the helmet. I looked up at the dark apartment above the bar and shiver. I'm scared. I text Anna telling her I'm home safe and delete all the missed calls from Jace and a few unknown numbers.

Hunter places his heavy arm over my shoulders and guides me in.

"Don't stress cupcake; he won't do anything you don't want him to. I'll be right there." He takes my hand and guides me in.

The noise gets louder as we head up the stairs. I hear banging and a few guys shouting. I hear glass cracking and I shiver. Hunter squeezes my hand.

We open the door and Hunter stands in front of me. I sneak a peek from behind him as I watch three guys holding Jace down on the floor as he continues to scream and shout at them.

"Where the fuck is she? You need to find her!" He screams out loud, pulling his hair roughly and rocking back and forth. "Why do I have to fuck up everything?" he mumbles and the guys continuously tell him to calm down.

I move around Hunter, I don't like the way they're holding Jace down and even though I should hate him, I want to make sure they don't hurt him.

I step closer and I feel Hunter step up behind me. A few guys notice and then Jace looks over their shoulders; his raging eyes spotting me.

This isn't my Jace...Jace is gone....Raven is here and I'm afraid of Raven.

His black hair is all messy; his face is red, eyes bloodshot.

"Harley, it was a mistake... please come to me. I miss you. Come here." Jace says sadly standing now with open arms looking from me to Hunter continuously as if trying to piece something together.

I stand still and don't say a word, the guys eventually let go of Jace but I can see they're cautious.

"Baby?" he says coming closer. I want to run away and lock myself in my room but I'm not sure if that can keep Jace away from me.

"Come here..." he repeats seriously.

"Now Harley!" he roars and I flinch. He walks closer to me and I back into Hunter. Hunter puts his hands on my shoulders protectively.

Jace looks at Hunter's hands then glares at Hunter full of hatred.

"Better get those hands off my girl." Jace says in a more quiet tone; I can see the anger and it's about to resurface any moment.

"Raven brother, you need to quit, you're scaring her." Hunter says from behind me.

"Don't fucking tell me what to do! You don't know shit about her! You think you can just come here and take her away from me? You're not my fucking brother! She's mine!" Jace jumps for Hunter behind me ignoring the fact that I'm standing in the middle. He grabs Hunter's shoulder tackling him, in the process elbowing me in the nose and tackling me too. I land on the ground with a heavy oomph, the air is smacked out of me by the force of the fall on the tiled floor. I managed to crawl away from the two men who are now punching and fighting each other. I feel a few hands help me up but I push them away, I can't stand to have any man's hands on me right now. I look at the floor and see blood.

Oh God no...please not again.

I look to see if the blood is coming from between my legs and notice it's on my shirt. I touch my nose and wince. My nose is bleeding. Thanking

God my baby wasn't hurt I ignore the pain in my face from being elbowed and cover my nose with the sleeve of my jacket.

"Get a fucking sedative! Hurry!" someone shouts and I turn my attention back to the two boys that are rolling on the floor.

"You don't get her Hunter, not her! You can have everything but her! She's mine!" Jace says as he pushes Hunter into the table causing beer bottles and glass to fly everywhere.

I watch as a few guys attempt to stop them but Hunter tells them to stay out of it.

Hunter doesn't say anything, he doesn't punch Jace back just keeps trying to block the punches coming from Jace's fist.

"I got him, hold the boy down!" I watch as someone brings a syringe near Jace.

"No! Don't hurt him!" I cry out but it's too late the guy has already injected Jace. I watch as Jace's body becomes clumsy and Hunter places him on the ground. I crawl up to Jace and place his head on my lap. His eyes are droopy and I can see he is fighting for control. He looks like a little boy in my arms.

"I'm so sorry I left, I just needed some space away from here…I'm so sorry Jace. I don't want to cause you pain." My hand strokes his cheek and he gives me a small smile.

"Need you baby. Don't leave me alone. It's dark inside." He says breathlessly, putting his hand over his heart. I bend down and kiss his forehead. As I lift my head to look down at him, he's already fast asleep.

"Harley, let the boys put him to bed and let's clean you up." Hunter says as the guys pull Jace away from me. Hunter picks me up and leads me to the bathroom.

He sits me on the counter and wets a cloth, he brings it to my nose and I wince. "Sorry Princess…" he mumbles.

He cleans all the blood away from my face and wipes my hands down. I look at his face noticing a small cut and swelling around his jaw.

"That boy's my brother but he's not good for you babe. He's got too much shit going on in his head and it's going to kill him one day or worse…hurt you."

He looks sad, I saw how hurt he looked when Jace told him that he wasn't his brother. I don't say anything instead get another cloth and start wiping away the blood off his face. He gives me a sad smile and stands there as I clean him up.

He helps me off the counter and I head to my room to change into pajamas. I place a large shirt of Jace's on and my normal sleep shorts.

The apartment is a mess and it's very quiet. Everyone has either gone to sleep or has left. I peek inside Jace's room to find him sleeping on his bed. I close his door and quietly walk down the passage towards the kitchen, after getting an ice bag for my nose I spot another door open, one I haven't been in before. I find Hunter sitting on the bed, he hasn't got a shirt on and I see his back covered in tribal designs, his head is resting in his hands; he looks so torn and sad. I just want to give him a hug and tell him everything is going to be okay.

I walk quietly into the room but he doesn't notice me coming in. I sit next to him on the bed and rest my cheek on his shoulder. His body relaxes and he sits up straight looking down at me; I notice his watery eyes. I pick up the ice bag that was intended for my nose and place it gently on his jaw. He covers my hand with his.

"Thanks Princess." He says continuing to use my pet name. I don't mind though, if that's what makes him feel better.

I place my arms around his waist and place my cheek on his chest. I know he doesn't expect it because he tenses for a few seconds before relaxing against me. He places the ice bag on the bed next to him and wraps both arms around me.

"I'm sorry Hunter, all of this is my fault, I shouldn't have left like that. It's what I do...I run. I'm sorry. Jace didn't mean what he said to you, he was just upset. He is your brother and will always be. He loves you very much, if he didn't you'd probably be dead by now." I squeeze my arms.

"Christ, you really are a life size Teddy Bear. Ya' know sometimes we big guys need hugs too." Hunter says into my hair.

I giggle, "He told you about that huh?"

"Yeah Rave tells me everything. He didn't tell me about the baby though." Hunter says and I freeze at his announcement.

"Don't worry babe, God knows I can't judge." Hunter says, looking intently at me as I pull away. He places the ice bag back on my nose.

"How'd you find out? And how did you know where I was?" I ask him taking hold of the ice bag now.

"Fucking Rachelle called Jace and I had his phone so I answered it. She told me she was worried about you running around this time of the night with those college boys, and that you were upset. So I asked what she meant and she told me; I understood why you were so sick earlier now. Called Jesse to see if you were with him, he said you weren't but told me you might be at the park. Didn't expect to see you with that Jock though" He grunts at the mention of "*That* Jock".

"You don't have to scowl like that every time you mention him. He's actually a great guy. We've probably been friends for as long as Caleb and I were, never best friends though. We only really became close these last few years." I lie down on his bed looking at the ceiling holding the ice against my nose. I sound as if I have a blocked nose but the ice is easing the pain.

"I may be able to control my anger but Jace can't, don't ever let him see you like I did with that boy tonight, you hear me?" Hunter says in a firmer tone he's never used on me before.

"Okay…" I say quietly.

"Who's Caleb." he asks.

"An ex." I simply say hoping he doesn't ask any more questions.

He nods his head. I raise the ice pack and he takes it from me and places it back on his jaw.

"This is the only family I have. I have no one else. This club… is all I have." He says quietly almost as if talking to himself. I lie on my side, resting my head on my folded arm.

"Daddy and Anna are all I have. Momma back home doesn't really want me… I think I was a reminder of everything she couldn't have, all the things she missed out on because she gave birth to me. She only kept me so she wouldn't be alone and to spite Daddy. She left me alone a lot though. You'd think I would learn from her mistakes right?" I let out a chuckle, "Funny, I'm sitting in her situation now too. At least I had Daddy… my baby isn't going to have one."

"You have us Harley don't you worry, your baby will have plenty of father's to fill that role. You'll never be like your mother, don't ever compare yourself to a woman like that. Come here." He says pulling me into his arms. We lay there together in silence. After a few minutes I decide I better get to bed.

"Goodnight Hunter, thank you for everything." I said kissing his cheek and stepping away from him.

"Night Princess, sleep well. I'll make sure Prince Charming doesn't choke on his own vomit in his sleep. Damn idiot was wasted." Hunter says shaking his head.

I fell asleep quickly knowing Hunter would make sure Jace was okay. I prayed the drug was strong enough to keep Jace from having his nightmares.

Chapter 14

I wake up to the sound of a door closing and then I feel movement behind me in the bed. I keep still and act as if I'm asleep. I feel a large hard body snuggle against mine and I smell minty breath as they kiss my shoulder. As soon as he places his hand under my shirt and onto my belly I know who it is.

Jace must have just got out the shower; his skin is soft and his scent fresh. He's shaved too, I can feel his soft chin against my collarbone as he lifts the hair away from my neck and places it higher on the pillow giving me a soft kiss on my neck letting his lips linger there for a few seconds. I can't stop the shivers he causes from running through my body.

The room's still dark with curtains closed, even though it's about midday only a slit of light comes through. My body is a little stiff and my nose hurts like a bitch.

"It was a mistake…it meant nothing." He whispers against my neck. I flinch…*Please tell me he didn't feel that. Please…*

I lay there hoping an apology will finally make its way out of his mouth but nothing comes. He's not sorry about what he did…only sorry he got caught. It feels like a repeat episode…memories of what happened the night I caught Caleb come rushing in.

"I know you're awake baby please talk to me."

"It doesn't matter Jace. I don't care what you two did." I say in a ruff soft voice.

"You don't care?" he says as he tenses behind me.

"Jace…you can do whatever you want, we are not attached or anything, you're not my boyfriend. I don't care what you do and who you do it with." As I say the words out loud I know I'm lying, they are so far from the truth. I don't know why but I want Jace; I want all of him and I don't want to share him but I'm done being weak in front of these men. I've been weak and look where it got me? I need to keep my distance from these men, I need space.

"Really?" he says letting out a deep breath as if my statement just gave him freedom. *Guess it did.*

I turn to look at him. "Yeah Jace, all good."

His eyes widen. "Shit baby what happened?" he gently touches my nose and I wince and pull away from him.

I climb out of bed and leave a dumbstruck Jace staring at me as I make my way to the joined bathroom, I don't want him to see me breakdown. I close the door and lean against it and whisper, "You happened Jace…"

I wipe away the tears and look into the mirror, the bridge of my nose is just a little purple but I'm sure some make up will cover it up fine.

I make my way back to my room expecting Jace to be exactly where I left him but he's gone. I pick out clothes and head for a shower.

I'm busy putting makeup on in front of my floor length mirror when Anna walks in with a plate of pancakes, the smell makes my stomach rumble.

"Afternoon babes, how you feeling? Oh my God! Who did this?" She says cupping my chin and placing the food on the counter so she can inspect me.

"It's okay, I'm okay it was just a wrong place - wrong time thing. Someone bumped into me. It's cool I swear." I smile at her and continue to put foundation on my face to cover my nose up.

"And the baby? Are you sure you're fine? Maybe we should go to the doctor sweetie." Anna says worriedly as she starts making my bed for me then sits on it.

"I'm fine Mom thank you. What time is Daddy opening the bar today?" I say grabbing the plate and sitting on the bed next to her. She smiles at me and grabs a pancake off my plate.

"In about an hour babe, it's already after lunch sweetie. Your father's not in a good mood honey, especially after coming back to find our home wrecked. He was furious with the boys but they don't want to say who's to blame; do you know what happened?" she asks me curiously.

"No actually I was out last night. I met up with a friend of mine." I smile thinking about Brent.

"That's great Harley, I'm so happy for you." She says giving me half a hug.

"Oh Honey before I forget I made an appointment for you for Friday with the doctor."

"Thank you for everything, you don't know how much I appreciate everything you and Daddy have done for me. I'm sorry for how I behaved the other night, I just-" I pull away from the hug and she interrupts me putting her hands up.

"No no no, don't apologize for what you did. You did great, you are such a brave strong girl don't let anyone change you. You stood up for what was right. You were right Harley. Well in your mind that's what you thought was right. You've only been here for a little while honey but you'll see how those girls behave around our men. You may stand up for them but don't ever expect them to do the same. They'll walk over any woman just to get into this club. I'm so proud of you Harley, just be careful though" She says before giving me another tight hug before leaving.

After eating the pancakes and making my way out of my room, I notice Jace's door is closed. I continue my way down the hall to the stairs. The house is clean and there's no evidence of what happened last night. Apart from a missing table and a few ornaments the place looks the same as it did two days ago.

There's a few guys laying on the sofas in the lounge and they greet me as I pass. I make my way down the stairs to the bar as Jesse walks through the kitchen with a few clean glasses from the kitchen.

"Harley! How you doing babe?" he says setting the glasses on the bar and turning to give me a hug. I squeal when my feet lift off the floor and he spins me around.

"Jesse stop!" I giggle, wiggling out of his grip before he finally lets me down.

"Baby girl, you've finally decided to get out of bed." Daddy teases as he gives me a hug.

"Yeah sorry… wasn't well last night and I guess my body was exhausted." I make my way over to the glasses and start placing them on the shelves.

"What's wrong? Was it the baby? Are you two okay? Maybe you shouldn't work this evening." He says concerned, Jesse seated next to him looks just as worried as they wait for my response.

I laugh at them. "No I want to work, besides tomorrow I have to collect my books so I can get a head start with my studies so I may only work a few hours. I'm working tonight, okay? Stop stressing."

"I always stress about you sweetheart." My father rumbles in his deep voice.

I walk over to my father as he's placing money in the register. "Daddy I want to talk to you about the other night. I want to apologize for-"

He interrupts me, "No Harley don't, let's just forget that happened and move on. You don't need any more stress than you already have from this club."

I kiss him on the cheek, I really wanted to talk to him about it but I don't think now is the time or place to argue with him about it.

"Can't believe those fuckers wrecked my house." He mutters to himself continuing to put money in the register; looking over at Jesse I smile.

The bar filled up soon enough and I managed to keep a distance from Jace and Hunter's table. There were a couple of guys sitting with them and also the usual girls hanging around too. Although I avoided his eyes I could feel them on me the entire evening.

It was a little after midnight; only the club boys were left sitting around. Jesse and I started cleaning the tables whilst Anna was sorting out the tips and petty cash. I wasn't as exhausted as my first night but my feet sure did hurt. I was standing behind the bar wiping it down when Daddy got a call. I watch him across the bar as he drank with his boys, his tone sounding angry and his face frowning. I watch as he throws the phone down and speaks to a couple of the guys. They rush out of the bar as Daddy whispers into Jace's ear. Jace then nods over to Hunter.

Something has obviously gone down for them all to rushing out of here. Before he leaves, Jace looks at me with a sad expression then strides out. I notice the gun tucked into the back of his pants.

I overhear Daddy telling Anna that another club has come onto their turf and blown up a gas station just out of town, before he also follows his boys out of the bar.

"What the hell just happened?" Jesse says planting his ass on the stool in front of the bar.

"Fucking Club North decided to make an appearance. Blew up a gas station; Grimm and the boys went to see if the cops had any clue to where the guys are hiding." Hunter says pouring herself a drink and sitting next to Jesse.

"Why aren't you with them?" I ask him curiously.

"Someone has to look after our woman; couple of the boys are on watch outside as well." He says taking a sip. I notice his bruises aren't as bad as they were last night and the cuts aren't as red. He looks better.

I make my way to the bathroom. As I'm washing my hands I hear the door open and close behind me. I look in the mirror and see Rachelle leaning against the counter.

I ignore her and continue to wash my hands.

"Harley I know you probably regret everything you said that night when you defended me but I…" she falters and I take this as my opportunity to interrupt.

"No Rachelle I wish I did regret it but I don't. You shouldn't let these guys walk all over you and degrade you like that." I say feeling sorry for her.

"I know but you don't understand, you were born into this lifestyle, they respect you. My mother is a cokehead who gets naked for money; this is the only life I know! As much as you are a part of this club, so are we…we have a purpose too." She says as if trying to make sense of her own words.

I raise my eyebrow. "I was born into this lifestyle? No Rachelle actually I wasn't, I stayed with my mother who funny enough is also a stripper. I was born into *that* lifestyle but I didn't let it become who I am. I didn't choose to be part of this club! I don't want my child growing up thinking its okay to treat woman the way these men treat you. Do you like it when they treat you like a whore? Is that what you want? I don't understand why it means so much that you become part of the club?" I shake my head wiping my hands on a paper towel. "You know what Rachelle? Our mothers at least got paid to take their clothes off, is what you do really any better? Do the guys that you "*serve your purpose with*" at least pay you? You really need to take a good hard look at what you're doing. You are a beautiful young woman, don't let them walk all over you." I make my way to the door.

"Your mom's a stripper too?" She smiles as tears fall down her face smudging her makeup.

I can't believe after the whole speech I just gave, that was all she got from it but I smile, "Yeah she is."

As I leave the door I hear her shout out. "You are going to be a great mom!" smiling to myself I make my way to the bar.

Only Jesse and Hunter are left sitting at the bar.

"I think I'm going to head upstairs. I've got a long day tomorrow. Goodnight boys." I say attempting to walk away but Hunter catches my hand. He turns his body on the stool and pulls me so I'm between his legs.

"Give me a hug." He pulls me into his chest and wraps his arms around me protectively and immediately I feel safe right there. "That's a good Teddy." He whispers against my neck. I giggle and push him away.

"Nah-uh. I'm your friend too remember." He taps his cheek and I lean in to kiss it.

"Goodnight Princess." He smiles.

"Night Hunter."

Walking back towards the doors that lead up to the apartment another arm grabs me and I shriek with surprise.

Jesse chuckles and I punch his arm as I catch my breath. "Not funny."

"I'm sorry sweetie… Damn you're cute." He says pulling me into a hug.

I pull away from him but he doesn't release me, he cups my jaw and inspects my face his eyes clouding over as he tenses his jaw.

"Did he do this?" Jesse says in a rough voice I've never heard him use before.

"He didn't mean to, I got in the way. It was a mistake."

"Come." He says pulling me up the stairs into the apartment.

"Which one's yours babe?" he asks and I lead him to my room.

He shuts the door and I watch him as he slips his shoes off then goes to sit on my bed leaning against the headboard.

"What are you doing?" I ask him confused.

"Just go get changed then come here."

Returning into the room Jesse is still in the same position. He motions for me to sit by him and he places a pillow on his lap. I rest my head down and he pulls out my braid that was in my hair. He brushes my hair with his fingers so softly that I'm close to falling asleep. It reminds me of a time when Momma would have her moments, actually wanting me around. She would climb in bed with me and do the same until I'd fall asleep.

Those days are long gone though.

"Tell me what happened." He says quietly.

I huff, "I don't even know where to start."

"Start from what happened after I dropped you off yesterday morning." He says as he gently brushes his soft fingers on my hurt nose, up and down the bridge.

"Okay, well Jace and I were arguing and then things got out of hand because he found out I slept in your bed next to you. He didn't like that and he said some ugly things to me. Then-" Jesse's hand pauses in my hair and he says flatly, "What did he say?"

"Something about if I carried on acting that way, he was going to treat me how whores should be treated." I hear Jesse's deep intake of breath obviously trying to control his anger.

I continued to tell him about how I fell asleep after my furniture was delivered and only woke up later. "I woke up sometime yesterday afternoon to the bass from the music. This place was packed and I wasn't feeling well. I went to the kitchen and I found Hunter there, I took a couple headache tablets and headed back to my room. On the way there I caught Jace…um…he…err…was…"

"Spit it out Harley." Jesse says impatiently.

"Rachelle was sucking his…" he interrupts again putting up his hand.

"Okay I get it, did they sleep together?" he asks.

"Probably, I didn't stay to watch the end of the show, I was so disgusted I rushed to the bathroom to throw up. Hunter found me there and helped me. It was the worse morning sickness or well… evening sickness, I've ever had. Hunter was kind though. After I went to my room I kinda climbed out of the window before Jace could confront me. I went to a diner where I met an old friend of mine; we went to the park and caught up there. That's probably when Hunter called you; anyway Hunter brought me home and when we got back here, Jace saw me with Hunter and lost it. Jace elbowed me by mistake and then they gave him some drug to calm him down. I was so scared Jesse. I didn't want them to hurt him. I was so worried about him." I say wiping away tears trying to hold myself together.

"Yeah I can imagine. It must have been very scary but Jace is a big boy babe, he wouldn't let them hurt him. I can't believe he did that though, I can't fucking believe him. If he doesn't treat you better I'm going to say something. This is pathetic." Jesse says shaking his head still running his hand up and down my nose.

"No Jesse, stay away from him! I don't want any more people getting hurt because of me." I beg sitting up to face him.

"What happened this morning when you saw him?"

"He climbed in bed with me and said that it was a mistake. I told him that it didn't matter and that he could do whatever he wanted. He's not my boyfriend and we aren't together." I say desolately looking everywhere but him.

"That's bullshit and you know it. He acts as if you are his old lady and that you are off limits, the same should have applied to him. Now you basically gave him the go ahead to screw every one of those whores and still come back to cuddle you at night. Is that what you want Harley?" he says sounding angry.

I place my head back on the pillow. "No but I need to keep my distance from him Jesse. He doesn't want me like that, he's just possessive and protective because I nearly lost my baby because of the accident he caused. Stay away from him Jesse; I don't want you to get hurt. Please." I beg him as I rub his upper thigh. He tenses and I feel him move underneath me as if uncomfortable.

"Um... babe... I don't think you should...uh...do that." he says placing his hand between his legs.

"Shit...I didn't realize I was moving around so much." I say worriedly looking down at his hands as I notice the rise is his jeans. I cover my mouth to hide my laugh.

"I think I better...ah...go." He says getting up uncomfortably putting his shoes on. "Uh yeah..." I say quickly trying to keep a straight face.

He reaches the door and opens it as he stands behind it obviously trying to hide his erection. "Next time he does something like that, don't go running away. Give me a call and I'll fetch you. Okay?" I nod. "Goodnight Hun." And he slips away shutting the door behind him.

I lie back on my bed with my hands covering my face as I burst out in giggles. "So embarrassing..." I mumble.

I've never had a gay friend before so I'm not sure how to act. He's too manly for me to treat him like I would one of my girlfriends. I'm comfortable around him knowing I can be myself when he's near. I can open up to him about everything and he always has good advice. I guess I can only learn going forward and resting my head on his lap is a definite no-no from here on out. Maybe he is bi after all....

I open my window and sit on the window sill looking at the various buildings and enjoying the cool breeze. Looking at my phone I notice I have a message.

BRENT at 08:32pm: Jus texting to make sure you're safe and sound. Want to meet up tomorrow?

HARLEY at 12:16am: Sorry I'm replying so late. Hope I don't wake you. I have to fetch my books today & then I'm going to the library. What about tomorrow afternoon? Let me know.

I place my phone on the bedside table then rest my head on my pillow on top of the covers.

Chapter 15

I wake up as I'm being lifted up then placed under the covers.

"Shhh baby, go back to sleep...I'm here." I hear Jace's rough voice.

I pull the blanket up to my chin and cuddle it as I fall back asleep. I feel him climb under the covers and cuddle up to me close.

I get out of bed the next morning before Jace wakes up. I know I've been avoiding him but it's the only way I know how to deal with the situation. After showering and dressing I pick up the laundry noticing Jace's clothes lying on my floor. He obviously used my bathroom last night. *So much for having my own space...*

I pick up his clothes and notice dark red smudges on the white floor tiles. I bend down to get a better look and realize its blood. *Where the hell did that come from?*

I look through Jace's clothes in my arms and realize there's dry blood on his dark green shirt. I look at his club cut that he left hanging behind the door, inspecting it closer I notice blood spatters on the leather.

I looked at Jace this morning before getting out of bed I didn't see any marks or cuts on him, he looked beautifully untouched. This isn't his blood.

I walk into my room and notice him sitting up in bed with no shirt on watching me. I stomp up to him and throw his clothes at him.

"What is this?" I watch as it dawns on him what I just threw at him. He's quiet for a few moments then speaks.

"You need to forget you saw this. Keep your nose outta my business and keep your mouth shut. You hear me." he says raising his voice in that tone I hate so much.

"Then don't use my bathroom? Don't put your shit with my stuff then. And please...wash the fucking blood off you before you climb in bed with me." I say noticing dry blood on his neck where he missed a spot cleaning last night.

I watch as Raven makes his appearance and back away. "Who do you think you're talking to? I can do whatever the fuck I want. Don't make the mistake of thinking you can tell me what to do. Do I make myself clear?" he says in a menacing voice making me shudder.

"I asked you a question!" he shouts and my door flies open. Hunter comes through looking worried. He stands in front of Jace moving him toward my bathroom and shutting the door. I hear talking but can't make out what they're saying because my heart is beating so hard in my chest that I'm trying to focus on breathing. It looked like he was about to hit me, what if Hunter hadn't come in when he did? What would Jace have done?

I take the opportunity to put sandals on, not even caring if they match my denim shorts and shirt. I don't have time to brush my hair or put makeup on. I grab my handbag and cellphone and rush out. It's already half past ten. I avoid all of the people hanging around the apartment and make my way down the stairs to the street.

The College is only a few blocks away so I start my walk. My heart is beating fast and all I'm focused on is the concrete beneath my feet. I reach the college, the lady that issues my books to me has a constant frown as she looks my face over. I just need to get my books and get to the library where I can hide in a corner and hopefully no one will bother me.

Walking up the steps to the library I hear my phone going off indicating someone's calling. I quickly put it on vibrate and ignore Jace's call. I don't plan on bumping into anyone I know near the library, I know for a fact that neither Ashley nor Caleb would ever be near a library. The lady at the counter tells me to sign the relevant registration forms and she makes a copy of my student card. The old lady won't stop eyeing me, making me feel self-conscious. I won't be able to sit and study with her eyes on me the whole time. As I'm walking down the stairs leaving the library, thinking about going to the park to study I notice a couple of people sitting around on the grass just outside. I find a quiet spot and sit leaning against one of the trees; it's a hot day today but luckily it's cool under the shade. I take out my books looking them over.

My phone starts vibrating again and I see Hunter's name appear. I click the end call button and send him a text.

HARLEY at 11:26am: Hunter I'm fine. At the small park near the library, please don't come. I need some space from everything. Please keep Jace from coming to get me. I'll call you if I have to. Thanks.

HUNTER at 11:27am: Okay Princess, I'll keep the beast at bay but when u get home we're going to have a chat about you running away every time the shit hits the fan.

HARLEY at 11:28am: Thanks Hunt, sorry. Xo

I'm busy organizing a timetable in my diary when I feel a tap on my shoulder. I jump at the contact and whip my head around to see who it is. I let out a deep breath when I spot Brent. His laughing stops as he stares at me oddly.

Shit! That's probably why people have been looking at me funny. In my rush to get out the house this morning, I haven't brushed my hair and I've forgotten to put on makeup to cover my nose.

"Who did this?" he says gripping my shoulders getting a closer look. I push him softly.

"Stop that, I'm fine." I say looking back at the books on my lap.

"That's not fine, looks like someone punched you." He says lying on his side on the grass in front of me clutching one of my text books and paging through it casually.

"Elbowed actually." I say smoothly as I pack away my books. He stops paging through the book and looks up at me clenching his fist.

"What? Who hurt you like that? Was it that guy that picked you up at the park?"

"No it wasn't Hunter who did it, it was Jace and it was a mistake." I snatch the book from him and place it on top of the other books.

"Who did what to you Harlz?" I hear a familiar deep voice on my left.

I look at Brent wide eyed. "You didn't!"

"I'm sorry Harley but you guys need to talk." Brent says trying to stop me from packing my things. I need to get the hell away from here.

"Please babe, just stop a sec and listen to me... please." Caleb says, but I can't bear to look at him even though I can hear the pain in his voice.

"I thought I could trust you Brent?" I say getting up, I can already feel my eyes tearing up.

"You can Harley, I'm sorry, Trevor told him we met up with you last night and-." Brent says reaching for me but I push him away.

"I needed to see you. I miss you baby please just let me explain myself. Please...I'm so sorry...I need you back." Caleb says coming up to me, pushing Brent away.

He stops in front of me, pulls away the books from my hands and gives them to Brent; placing his big familiar hands on my jaw making sure I have nowhere else to look but his beautiful eyes. I look straightforward directly at his chest. I forgot how tall Caleb is and how it felt when I was with him, with his hands on me.

"Jesus Harley! Who hurt you like that?" Caleb says cupping my cheeks, I can't help but look at his beautiful green eyes. He is so gorgeous; I hope our baby has his genes because he really is such a beautiful boy. I shake my thoughts away.

"It doesn't matter Caleb, this-" I say pointing to my nose, "Is nothing compared to what you did to me. Stay away from me." I pull away from Caleb's arms and snatch my books from Brent. "Both of you." I rush away before they can catch up. I hear Brent telling Caleb to give me time and luckily neither of them follow me.

I make my way to the jam-packed club house. I greet the guys I pass and make my way to my room, putting the heavy books on my desk.

After making something in the kitchen to eat I head back to my room. I hear a banging sound coming from the room next door then I hear moaning, when I hear a girl screaming out for "Raven" to slow down. I put the sandwich down, my appetite lost. I plug earphones in my ears and climb out the window to sit on the metal floor of the fire escape. I play the music loud so that I'm void of all noise. The metal flooring beneath me is uncomfortable but I need to get away and I need fresh air. I sit on the top of the staircase, cover my face with my hands and cry. I cry so hard that I battle to find my breath and my whole body shakes. I don't know how much heart I have left to break. All the stress and sadness within me surely can't be good for the baby. *I have to sort my shit out…*

I feel someone's presence behind me and then I feel them reach over to touch my stomach. I know its Jace but I can't stand to have his hands on me after he was screwing someone a few minutes before. I pull out my earphones.

"No! Get away from me! Don't touch me!" I scream at him and push him away.

"Please Harley let me hold you. It didn't mean anything…It never does, not like when I'm with you, none of them do Harley. I thought this was okay? You said you didn't care?" He says backing away from me.

"No I said that because I needed space from you, I knew you would do this! Make me have feelings for you them throw me away like trash, just like he have! I only said that to stop you from hurting me more than you have already." I wipe away the tears as he stands there in shock. "I don't want you to touch me anymore. You don't have a heart, do you *Raven*?" I say his name with such distaste, I now see Hunter making his way to my window.

"I didn't think you would actually go and fuck someone in the room next to me. Really Raven? Do you only think of yourself? You act as if you own me! You act as if you care for me? You told me I didn't deserve the way *he* treated me and what *he* did? Is this what I deserve? You're doing the same thing he did to me on fucking repeat! Every day is a new way to hurt me? Right Raven? I don't have any heart left for you to break." I push at his chest but he doesn't budge or make a move to stop me and the sad look on his face only makes me angrier. I shove him again. "You speak to me like I'm a piece of shit and you terrify me. You don't realize how fucking scared I am of you! Then you expect me to be fine with you fucking other people and climbing into my bed so I can be your fucking *Teddy*?" I scream the last word not caring who sees me and how terrible I look all snotty nosed and tear faced. I sniffle then say in a softer voice. "You know what happened today *Raven*?" I notice he flinches every time I call him by his road name but I continue. "I ran into Caleb and all I could think about was how safe I was with him and how much I missed the feeling when he held me. How fucked up is that?" I laugh bitterly wiping away all the tears.

"Oh my God…" Jace whispers, running his hands through his hair. Finally realization hits…

My fight or flight instinct kicks in.

I pick flight…

I climb through the window and run but Hunter grabs me as I make my way across my room just before reaching the door. "Nuh uh, you're not running away again Princess. No more running." I notice Anna and my father have entered my room, both looking horrified by the scene.

"Boy, I told you to look after her, not fuck with her feelings." My dad shouts pointing at Jace.

"I know Grimm...I fucked up." I hear Jace from behind me as I kick and push to get out of Hunter's gentle but tight grasp.

"Please... Let.Me.Go! Please." I cry as I use all the energy I can find to push and shove Hunter but it does nothing to weaken his hold, instead he pulls me so than he's holding me close against his chest. His big hand rests on the back of my head holding me tight as I sob into his shirt. My body is exhausted as my legs give way; he helps me to the floor not releasing his hold once.

"Shhh... calm down babe before you hurt yourself. Shhh..." he whispers into my hair trying to calm me.

"Please...please just let me go Hunt...please." I cry exhaustedly. He only holds me tighter.

"Let her go Hunter. The rest of you out. Now!" Anna yells.

I hear footsteps and I feel Hunter loosen his grip. "I'm sorry he did this Princess." He whispers before letting me go. I cry into my hands pulling my knees to my chest.

"You too Raven...out." Anna yells again making me flinch.

"Son, we need to have a chat." I hear Jace's dad call.

"It meant nothing baby...I promise. What we have means everything." Jace mumbles. I hear his footsteps stop near me then continue out of my room closing the door behind him.

Anna comes to my side and pulls me to her chest. I weep for my broken heart, what Jace has done to it and for seeing Caleb today looking better than ever while I'm breaking from the inside out.

I feel hands underneath my arms and I try to get away from them. "It's only me baby girl...let's get you off this cold floor." My father says softly as he picks me up and places me on the bed. I rest my head on Anna's lap as she strokes my hair just like Jesse did the night before. My father sits in front of me at the edge of the bed with his hands on his knees shaking his head.

"I shouldn't have brought you here. You shouldn't be around this environment. You are too good for this. I'm so sorry Harley, I only ever wanted what's best for you and I thought keeping you close was that but I see how this place is changing you." He says sadly. I sit up and lean my head on his shoulder and he puts his big arm around me.

"Don't apologize Daddy, none of this is your fault. I thought I could do this and be here but...I just don't think I can. This is not the type of lifestyle I want my child to grow up in. I don't know if I can stay here Daddy..."

"I know sweetie... I kinda knew these boys would be too overwhelming for you. We've sheltered you from this and I thought that maybe if Raven kept an eye on you, you'd be okay. I didn't think he would be the one hurting you. I kinda knew that eventually the club house would be too much for your pure heart to handle and that's why we bought an apartment in the building next door for you...just in case." He says smiling down at me.

"What? You guys bought me an apartment?" I say bewildered looking back and forth between the two of them.

"Yeah babes we did." Anna says smiling. I notice she too has been crying. I jump onto her as she laughs and hug her tight.

"You guys are the best...I love you so much. Thank you." I say hugging her tight.

Then I reach over to my dad and hug him the same way. I feel his body shake as he lets out a deep chuckle.

"We have to make sure you and that grandbaby of ours are safe." he chuckles.

I lean back and rest my head on Anna's lap and she continues to stroke my hair. I close my eyes.

"At least I won't be far from you guys." I yawn.

"No we will be close by...always" I hear my dad mumbling as I drift off to sleep.

Chapter 16

"I swear to God Jace, you do one more thing to hurt her and I will make sure you can't use that thing between your legs!" I hear Anna shout at Jace in a soft tone but still very much full of anger. I remain still as I eavesdrop on their conversation.

"I promise I'm done, I don't ever want to hurt her or see the look she gave me today. I promise Anna. Please let me stay with her, I'll look after her…. please." I hear Jace's sad voice as he whispers to Anna.

I feel Anna move away, placing a pillow under my head. I hear her footsteps disappear then the door close. Jace climbs onto the bed and lies in front of me. I feel his eyes looking over me and I flinch when his fingers touch my lips.

"I won't hurt you baby. Not anymore." He whispers.

I open my eyes and look into his sad ones but don't say anything.

"I can't believe I did this to you …I'm such a fuck up." Jace says softly as he cups my cheek running his thumb gently over my jaw, staring at my bruised nose.

I find my voice. "You need to stop talking about yourself that way. You are not a fuck up but the choices you make have a tendency to mess things up."

I look him over noticing his wet hair and the fresh smell coming off him. Thankfully he showered before he came to me. I don't think I could lie next to him while he smells like the girl he was banging earlier today.

"It's true though…I could never have something as untainted as you. I'm surprised I didn't fuck it up sooner. You are too good for me baby." He says clearing his throat. I don't know if it is his intention to make me feel sorry for him but it's working.

"People need to stop saying that. I'm not the perfect little girl everyone thinks I am. If I was, I wouldn't be sitting in this situation now would I? I don't know what to do with you Jace, I don't know what you want and what you expect from me? I'm scared I say the wrong thing and you get upset with me. I get so nervous when you get angry." I say grimacing at the memory.

"I just want *you* Harley; I want you safe…with me. Please baby…don't be scared of me…I'm done hurting you…I promise." he says sadly as he lifts my shirt and places his hand on my lower belly and rubs it softly. Once again I'm stuck in a nirvana like state and I forget everything he's put me through.

"I had a sister once, well I never met her but I had one. Mom was an addict and we thought she would stop with the drugs when she fell pregnant. She was eight months pregnant when she overdosed. She killed the baby…. I lost my little sister." He says out of the blue, the sadness coming from his voice causes tears in my eyes. *No wonder he is so protective over me and my baby.*

"I'm sorry Jace. I'm so…so sorry. That is horrible." I let out a shaky breath as the tears fall and soak into my pillow. I cover his warm rough hand that's resting on my belly with my much smaller cold one.

"Yeah…me too." He whispers.

I pick up his hand, kiss it then place it back on my tummy.

"Did you really feel that way when you saw him? Did you feel safe with him? Even after everything he did?" Jace says flatly.

"The truth?" I ask him and he hesitantly nods.

"Yeah I did, I'm scared of you Jace. You can do really hurtful things. One minute you say you want me and you care about me then the next you're… you're… the next I hear is some girl screaming your name or see some girl's head in your lap. I'm only good enough to be your sleeping buddy because you sleep easy when you're next to me? How do you think that makes me feel? It hurts so much Jace. I feel used by you Jace. That hurts more than what Caleb did to me… with you it's as if that night I caught him with Ashley is on repeat, except it's a different girl and you're trying to rub it in my face continuously to hurt me." He tries to talk but I place my hand on his mouth to stop him.

"I know this is ridiculous because it's not as if I'm your girl. I don't know why it hurts so much seeing what I did or hearing it but it does. It's okay though…now you can do whatever you like to whatever girl you want. I just won't be here when you do it…" I trail off.

"I…I'm so sorry Harley. Please don't leave, just stay here please. I promise I'll be good. You are good enough baby…you are too good for me and I get so frustrated. The only way to ease the tension is to fuck someone or fuck them up. You know which I chose…"He whispers ashamed.

"I'm sorry you saw what happened with Rachelle, I didn't mean for it to happen but she was around and…Yeah…I was just upset about you staying with Jesse and I had to get back at you somehow. Childish, I know. I'm sorry about earlier too…it doesn't mean anything with any of them you must know that…it's just sex baby. I didn't know it would hurt you, I swear it feels like you hate me sometimes and I felt like I was pushing my feelings onto you. I've never felt what I feel for you with any other woman and that is nerve-racking. I thought pushing you away would do the trick but I can't get you out my head. I didn't know you feel the same way as me. Baby you *are* my girl…you always were. I was too stupid to see that. I only want you Harley, well both of you…please don't leave me. No more of these sluts…I promise baby. Just us." He leans on his elbows looking down at me. His damp hair tickling my collar bone he's so close. Looking from his pink lips, I look down at his neck at the tribal tattoos that runs from just behind his right ear following it as it travels over his one pec, not touching his pierced nipple, and then over his arm. I look back to his lips as I notice a small little mark there on the right, just below his bottom lip line. I lift my index finger and gently touch the mark.

I've seen the same mark before. Ashley and I went to a tattoo parlor to get our tongues pierced, instead she wanted her piercing to be seen so she got her lip pierced but once her parents saw it they forced her to remove it; leaving her with a small little mark where the hole once was. The night of the crash I took my tongue ring out, I forgot it and haven't put one back in since.

"My lips pierced babe, haven't worn the ring for a while, being punched in the face with that metal in hurts bad." Jace says and I watch his lips move. I don't look up at him, instead I keep my gaze on his perfect lips.

"I'm moving out." I whisper in my daze.

"What?" This makes me look up into his eyes.

I shake my head trying to clear my head. "I'm not going far, just next door. Daddy got me an apartment. I can't stay here Jace, not only because of you but also because of this place. It's not healthy for a baby."

"I know Harlz…I know. This environment isn't good for either of you." He says as his hand starts to rub my stomach again. The way he says Harlz reminds me of Caleb and the way he used to say it.

"It's going to be scary staying by myself though. I know when I stayed with Momma I was alone most of the time, but this is different… I know you guys will be next door but still… I'm worried." I mumble as my eyes drift down to his lips again.

"You won't be alone baby. You'll never be alone again." I watch his lips move.

"You'll be with me? You'll stay with me?" I whisper afraid of his rejection.

I watch his short intake of breath then I watch as his lips form into a perfect smile making me grin in response. "You still want me with you? You still want me to sleep next to you?"

"Yeah I still want you…" I know I'm making a terrible mistake but I can't help the words from spilling out my mouth. I don't correct myself because what I've said is true. I want Jace; I want him all to myself. He said he would stop with the girls and I've finally got an apology from him. I know I've given him too many chances and I don't know if I'm only letting him stay with me because I'm afraid of being alone but all I know is I want him with me. He may scare me and when he's upset says horrible things but I want him… despite all of that… I still want him.

I watch the dimples in his left cheek, I place my finger over it, I'm close enough to feel his breath on my skin and his eyes on mine watching my every move.

I trace my fingers on his jaw line. His hand moves from my stomach to my hip then gently makes its way to my lower back as he pulls my body into his closing the distance between us.

The room is quiet, not sure if it's because I'm so focused on Jace or if it's because there isn't music playing from downstairs. I lean my face into his and run my nose up and down his. I lean my lips closer to his as I feel and taste our breaths intertwine. I run my lips over his feeling the softness of his warm ones. His lips part and he lets out a moan before his hands wrap around my waist; he doesn't deepen the barely there kiss, he's letting me take control.

The butterflies in my stomach are wild but I force my nerves to remain calm and gently slip my tongue out as I watch his eyes close and his hands squeeze me into him. I run my tongue over his bottom lip and then the top as I taste his minty breath on my tongue. I feel his lips spread wider. I latch my lips around his bottom lip, biting it and letting it go. I kiss it gently and he lets out a deep moan causing goose-bumps to break out down my entire body.

He's obviously given me all the control he can muster because his lips attack mine with such hunger and want. He rolls me over and climbs over me with his large body pushing me deeper into the mattress. He lifts both my legs so they wrap around his waist, then leans down and rests on his one elbow as his other hand moves from my upper thigh up the length of my body and rests on my jaw. He is so gentle with me and I recognize this kindness as the Jace I met the night of the accident. His thumb brushes against my jaw line gently and I open my lips a little and suck on his lower lip. He gently slides his tongue into my mouth and soon our tongues are colliding. I feel his chest rumble as he moans out, pushing his lower body into mine.

I've only ever kissed one guy, I've only ever touched one person the way I'm touching Jace but that person wasn't a man. Jace may only be twenty five but he acts as if he carries the world on his shoulders. He's mature and even though he portrays that hard scary edge, I know this sweet loving man was hiding inside somewhere; right now is evidence of that. He doesn't need to speak, I can feel the emotion rolling off as he touches and caresses me.

Our lips part and he starts down my neck as he speaks for the first time since I kissed him.

"I've been waiting for you to do that from that first night I held you in my arms." He says looking down at me smiling.

"Why? You've kissed me before and I've kissed you?" I ask as I try to catch my breath.

"I'm usually the one to initiate it so I wanted you to kiss *me*. I can be controlling and I suppose it can be overwhelming for someone like you. I didn't want you to feel like you had to be with me because I was forcing my lips on you. I wanted you to choose it…to choose me…and you did." He smiles again pecking my lips.

"I did…" I smile back at him.

"I'm sorry for hurting you baby. I never want to see that hate in your eyes like I did today." He says looking off. "Don't think I can live without you." He whispers but I catch it.

"What does this mean Jace?" I whisper.

"It means you're my girl now baby, it means no other guy gets to put their hands on you. Not even Hunter; I saw how he held you on that floor today and didn't like it. It means you sleep with me and only me. It means you are the girl I come home to after a long day's work, you are mine and only mine." He says planting kisses down my neck. I remember the night I told him about having a girlfriend, having someone to come home to that was waiting for you and only you. In his own way he's telling me I'm his girlfriend. I don't care for labels but as long as he knows we belong to each other I don't care what he wants to call us.

He bends down as he kneels between my legs, he lifts my shirt just enough to see my bump. Then he plants soft kisses on my tummy. This melts my heart. *Why can't he be this compassionate person all the time?*

"Are you mine too Jace?" my voice is shaky and even though I'm scared to ask, afraid what the answer might be, I need to hear him say the words.

He stops kissing my stomach and looks up at me. Then smiles. "If you want me, I'll be yours forever Harley."

"I want you Jace." I whisper loud enough for him to hear and then smile.

"Then I'm all yours." He smiles at me.

"This doesn't mean I'm over all the shit you put me through. We have a lot to deal with and sort out. I don't trust you Jace but I'd like to sometime in the future." I look down at him as his lips linger on my belly.

"I know Harlz…we will work through everything. I'll do anything to make this right." He whispers looking down at my stomach beneath him. He continues to kiss my belly and I let him, enjoying the moment.

"Come with me tomorrow… I mean you don't have to… I just wanted to ask if you'd like to."

I stammer then shake my head at the stupid idea. "Never mind… don't worry about it… stupid idea, you're probably busy in any case." I ramble on shaking my head. *What guy would want to go to a doctor's appointment that has to do with a baby that isn't even theirs?*

He chuckles against my stomach as he lets his lips linger there.

"Where do you want me tomorrow baby?" he asks.

"I have an appointment with the doc-" he interrupts me.

"Okay." He says and continues to kiss me.

"Okay?" I ask.

"Yeah, if you want me to come then I will."

"Thanks Jace, hopefully I get to find out whether it's a boy or girl." I say smiling and he abruptly stops and looks up at me.

"Appointment? To see the baby?" he says all serious now. He obviously didn't realize it was for the baby specifically.

"Yeah... it's okay if you want to back out. I didn't think you would want to go with me anyway. Anna's going to be there so I'll be fine. Don't worry about it, forget I asked." I say smiling down at him and brushing my hands through his long hair, reassuring him its fine if he doesn't go.

"No, I'll go with you. I want to be there." He looks down at my stomach, smiles then looks up at me. "You really want me to go with you when you find out the sex of the baby?" He smiles so happily.

"Yeah, I want you there. Aside from all the shit you've put me through these past days, you've been here for me from the moment we met. I want you there, Anna too because she never got to experience all of this when they were trying to get pregnant. I think it will make her happy." I continue to run my hand through his hair as he rests his head on my stomach.

"So sweet. She'd love that. Thank you for this, you don't know how much this means to me." he smiles then looks down at my stomach and whispers, "Your mommy is one amazing person."

Chapter 17

"Ready babes?" I hear Anna shout as she knocks on the bathroom door. I've had bad morning sickness; I've been awake since five but finally after a shower I'm feeling better. Jace stayed with me the entire time until I had to force him to go get ready so we weren't late for the appointment.

I open the door to a smiling Anna. They're both really excited about the appointment today.

Jace comes running in as I'm braiding my hair, picks me up and swings me around. I start giggling. He plants my feet back on the ground then squishes my cheeks between his hands and gives me a big kiss. "I'm so excited to see the little one." I laugh at him and continue to braid my hair.

"Sooo... are... you two?" I forgot Anna was in the room; I open my mouth to speak but Jace beats me to it.

"She's my girl and I'm her man. Right babe?" he smiles at me.

"That's right." I wrap my arms around his waist and hug him before he walks out of my room. I look back to where Anna is sitting on my window sill and notice the big smile on her face.

"It's the big scary ones that are the kindest when no one's watching. Those boys can be a pain in the ass but when they're sweet like that, they're hard to resist. Jace doesn't know how to treat woman. His mother wasn't a great role model and even though he has a temper from hell, I've never seen him this happy before. That boy may be dangerous but he will be good to you and look after you well. After the scare you gave him yesterday and the talk your father and his gave him, I pray for his sake he treats you right. We all just want you happy and seeing you with him just now like that... you looked so happy my girl." Anna says with a grin on her face.

"It's crazy though right? I haven't known him all that long but it feels like we connect, like all the shit he puts me through is okay as long as I get that little bit of Jace that carried me from my wrecked car. I think I'm obsessed? That has to be it. He's just too damn hot for his own good." I giggle. "I don't know why I can't resist him, I tried, I really did. But when it's the two of us and the real Jace comes out...I fall...hard. He is really sweet and gentle and I want him close all the time. I feel safe with Jace...its Raven I'm afraid of." I mutter adjusting my summer dress.

"Babes, Jace may be the gentle one but it's Raven you should feel safe with. Raven will protect you no matter what. You couldn't picture one without the other though, can you? The naughty wicked side of Jace attracted you to him, am I right? And the sweet gentle side pulls you in. So either way, you want both sides of him, you may not think it but you do." She winks at me and I smile. I'm lost for words because she's right.

I feel Jace's eyes on me the entire time I've been staring at the question on the doctor's form these past five minutes. It's an optional question but my hand is still frozen unable to move on to the next question.

Name of Childs biological Father. Should I fill it in? I should just leave it blank. Caleb doesn't deserve to have his name on that dotted line.

Jace pulls the forms from me and I watch as he writes *Jace Alexander* on the dotted line.

"Jace…" I whisper and pull his hands away.

"Baby I'm doing this." He says in that don't-argue-with-me tone. He's glaring at me and I sink into my chair afraid he may cause a scene in front of the people sitting in the waiting room. My hand shakes as I take the form from him and complete the remaining questions. Before I have a chance to scratch out his name he snatches the clipboard from me and walks up to the receptionist to hand the forms in.

I look at Anna to see her smiling brightly at us, looking back at Jace I whisper, "Isn't it illegal to lie on those forms or something?"

He lets out a deep chuckle and my eyes meet his sparkling ones. "Better give me a big kiss before the cops take me away babe." He pulls me into his chest and gives me a kiss. I try pulling away from him, I'm not one for PDA and luckily enough my name being called gets Jace to release me from the kiss.

Jace and I stand up to follow the lady, I look behind me expecting to see Anna but she's nowhere. "Wait a second…" I mutter quickly walking back to the waiting room. I notice Anna sitting where I left her looking at her hands.

"Mom? Aren't you coming?" I smile at her. She looks shocked by my question.

"What? You want me in there? With you guys?" She says as her eyes fill with tears.

"Of course!"

She jumps up and hugs me then rushes to where Jace and the nurse are waiting for me.

I get dressed into a gown and I'm thankful Jace isn't standing there staring at me. The doctor comes in and introduces herself. Anna knows her from when she was trying to get pregnant many years ago.

"So Harley, we're going to find out the sex today? Is Mom and Dad excited?" Doctor Smith asks Jace and I presuming he is the father of my child.

I'm about to correct her but Jace speaks too soon.

"We're very excited." Jace smiles, kissing my forehead. The doctor covers my legs with a piece of material then lifts my gown to reveal my growing belly.

"Let me guess, Dad wants a little boy?" The doctor gives Jace a friendly smile and he chuckles.

"I just want a healthy baby. I don't mind either way…as long as the baby is healthy."

I swallow down the lump in my throat as I remember the story he told me the night before about his little sister and mother.

"What do you say Granny? What do you want?" The doctor asks Anna.

"I agree with Jace, we just want a healthy baby, right babes?" Anna smiles at me from the corner of the room.

"Yeah, I don't mind as long as he or she is healthy. That's all that matters to me right now." I say looking at Jace as he watches the doctor's every move. She pushes soft gel onto my stomach and soon the room is being filled with the sound of my babies beating heart. I smile and look at Jace and Anna. I've heard it before and I probably had the same love filled expression on my face as these two do.

"That's one strong heartbeat right there." The doctor says as she moves the screen so we can look into it.

"That… that's her baby?" Jace stutters from next to me looking into the screen.

"That's *your* baby." The doctor corrects him. He smiles down at me with teary eyes. I look in the corner to see Anna with tears flowing down her cheeks as well. I squeeze Jace's hand and he pecks my lips so tender and soft.

"Let's see here…ah….I was right." She says pointing to the outline of my baby on the screen. "Looks to me like you're having a little girl sweetheart." I look at Jace as he wipes his tears away with the back of his ring clad hands; I don't think his smile could get any bigger but it does. I see Anna in the corner and smile at her, she comes up and gives me a hug.

"Congratulations Mommy and Daddy. This is your daughter." The Doctor says, giving Jace and I the ultra sound photos of the baby.

"Daughter…" I hear Jace whisper beside me as he stares at the picture in his hands.

"Daughter…" I repeat grinning at him. He pulls me in for a hug and plants small kisses all over my face. I feel his tears fall onto my cheeks. I know this is wrong and I know he's not my child's father but I need him here, I don't know why but I do. Maybe I'm latching onto him because of the lack of Caleb in my life? Maybe it's because I'm not used to being alone without someone at my side? I know it sounds weak and pathetic but I've always had someone with me. Even before Caleb and I started dating, he was my best friend; we were always together, how am I supposed to fill the void he's left? Maybe Jace can help complete me again? This is most probably why I've been keeping him close, even though at the back of my mind I know he has the ability to break my heart; the same one he's unknowingly been repairing.

As we arrive back at the apartment, I spot my dad sitting in the lounge with a couple of the guys watching TV. I come up behind him and place the picture on his lap. "That's your granddaughter Daddy." I smile down at him.

He picks up the picture and I watch as a grin spreads across his face. "It's a girl?"

"Yeah…" I sit on the arm of his chair and watch as he stares at the little black and white picture.

"Congrats sweetheart…"

He pulls me in for a hug and kisses my cheek. The guys in the room give their congratulations and each has a turn hugging me.

"That's going to be one cute little kid." I hear Hunter say as he comes up placing his arm over my shoulder, pulling me into his side and taking a look at the picture

"Yeah she is…" I say thinking about Caleb's features more than my own.

"Congratulations Princess." He kisses my cheek.

"Hands off Hunt." I hear Jace grunt as he steps closer to us.

Hunter chuckles then reluctantly removes his hand.

I walk back to my room and place the picture next to my bed on my bedside table. Thinking about the events of today and how great it was. Even though we seemed like a perfect little family I know I need to speak to Jace about the whole "Father" situation. I need him to understand that this isn't a joke, if he wants to be part of our life I need to know if he's serious because I don't want this to affect my child negatively.

Jace comes in and closes the door. He flops himself on my bed and rests his head on my lap taking the picture off the bedside table.

"I need to talk to you Jace." I tell him and watch as he tenses underneath my touch as I run my hands through his silky hair.

"Is this about me signing those forms?" he says looking up at me as I stroke his hair out of his face.

"Yeah." I say. He sits up and moves to the corner of the bed next to me.

"I'm not trying to take the place of her father. I know I'm not the father Harley. You just seemed so torn staring at that fucking question and I needed to ease at least some of that pain." He lets out a deep breath. "I guess I got so caught up in that beautiful moment that part of me wished that it was my baby inside you… but I know this isn't a game and I'm serious about all of this. I want to be here for you and her. I don't care if the kid calls me uncle instead of dad, I'll make sure she knows that she can come to me if she needs anything Harley but please…let me be here for you both. That's all I want babe. Even when it comes down to the point where you want her to meet her real father, I want to be there for you and her. Please." He says with such compassion that I hear the truth in his words.

"Why do you want this Jace? You're still young... and gorgeous, why would you want to be stuck with someone that's in this situation? If you really want to help me with this then I need to make sure you're serious because I don't want someone that's going to be constantly in and out of her life. She needs a stable upbringing Jace and I just want to do what's best for her." I lean my head on his shoulder as he interlaces our fingers together holding my hand tight in his.

"We all want what's best for her and I won't be stuck with you baby. I want to be with you and I want to be part of your life. I promise you baby...I'm not going anywhere." He kisses me softly letting his lips linger.

Chapter 18

The past few months with Jace have been amazing. He's been perfect and although I don't get to see him as much as I would like due to school and work, he's made sure to sleep next to me almost every single night since the day I moved into my new three bedroom apartment. The apartment is great and apart from the furnishings in my old room at Daddy's place, I refused to let them buy me anything for my new little home. They've already spent too much money on me as it is, I couldn't let them furnish it for me as well; even if my father insisted. I was making good money at the bar and when I looked too pregnant to be seen working at the bar Anna asked me to help her at her tattoo studio's front desk with her books and answering of calls. Eventually after many hours at thrift shops, I finally managed to furnish the apartment. Of course none of it is designer and most of the furnishings are second hand but it's home to me.

My father still gets Jace to do whatever it is he does for the Club, therefore some nights he doesn't make it to my apartment until morning and even then Jace makes me lie in bed next to him while he sleeps.

I'm already thirty five weeks into my pregnancy and apart from the last few days, Jace couldn't seem to keep his hands off my big belly. The heated make out sessions are a regular occurrence but we haven't gone any further; I'm at the point in my pregnancy where I've grown to accept how my body is changing but I don't feel pretty and comfortable in the way it's changing. I've become self-conscious even though the boys keep complimenting me about how good I look, I just don't feel all that great.

I'm not sure how Jace has been able to go without sex these past months. I have moments when he's not around and my mind goes into overdrive thinking that maybe he's getting it from someone else because he doesn't want to touch me while I look this way, but then when he's cuddling up to me or telling my belly stories at night I forget about all my insecurities and think of how great he truly has been throughout my pregnancy.

Anna organized a surprise baby shower a few weeks ago and because I don't have many female friends we had a barbeque with all the boys and their old ladies. It was amazing and I got thoroughly spoilt. Jace surprised me that same evening when I got back to my apartment. He'd painted the baby room and decorated it beautifully with help from Hunter and Jesse. He even purchased a beautiful crib with the matching dark wood furnishings every baby room needs. I cried so hard when I saw what they did to the room; its lilac and white. It's so perfect and I wasn't expecting the boys to do something so sweet for me.

College has been going great and I haven't run into anyone that attended the same High School I did. Caleb called continuously and left messages those first few weeks after seeing him at the library, so did Brent. I deleted each and every one without reading them. After a few weeks all the calls and messages gradually stopped.

We' had a weekly Sunday lunch where the boys from the club bring their families. I've gotten to know the guys really well and they all seem to love the whole idea of the club Sunday lunch.

Today I'm supposed to go to another checkup since I've been cramping a little, it's making me uneasy but I can't get hold of Jace and haven't seen him since yesterday because he had "work" to do.

Walking into my father's club house, I see there was a party the previous night. I heard the music last night but presumed it was from the bar downstairs. There are beer bottles and half naked people all over the place. My father and Anna went away for the week to stay at their cottage by the lake; they wanted me to go with but I thought they needed some time alone. Clearly these guys were celebrating not having the President around.

Letting out a deep breath I make my way to Jace's room. Although he stays with me most nights, we decided he should keep his room. I reluctantly open his door afraid to see what's in there, but apart from the messy bed the room is empty.

I'm running late to my appointment so I quickly make my way to my car, which my father bought me when the insurance from my previous car paid out. It's the same Fiesta I had before but this one is blue.

Trying to find my keys in my handbag, I hear the rumble of a motorbike coming to a stop behind me. I look to see Hunter climbing off his Harley.

"Hey Princess where you off to in such a rush?"

"I have an appointment, Jace was supposed to take me but I can't get hold of him; now I'm running late and I can't find my keys!" I yell getting frustrated.

"Whoa, calm down babe. Come… we can take my car." He says putting his arm over my shoulders dragging me away towards his jeep.

Getting into his car, I let out a frustrated sigh as I battle to put the seat belt on over my protruding belly. I rest my head back on the head rest and let out three deep breaths as I count to ten just like I used to do when I got panic attacks.

"You okay?" Hunter says softly as he leans over me and gently puts the seat belt over me.

"No Hunter, I'm not. My feet are killing me, I'm grumpy, I don't feel comfortable, my fucking stomach gets in the way of ev-ery-thing and Jace was supposed to take me to this damn appointment and I can't find him; so… *no* I'm not fucking okay." I say folding my arms like an immature child. Hunter just nods and starts driving. I let out a deep breath feeling guilty for shouting at him when he's only trying to help.

"I'm sorry Hunt. I don't mean to take it out on you, it just hasn't been a good day and I hate going to these things alone." I say softly rubbing my stomach.

"It's okay babe, I told you to call if you ever needed anything besides… I'm glad I'll be there to see this." he says smiling down at my larger than life baby bump.

Hunter comes into the room with me and I introduce Hunter to the Doctor.

"I'm Harrison, her best friend and the baby's godfather." He announces before I even get a chance to open my mouth. He winks at me; I chuckle and shake my head.

So Harrison is his real name…

The doctor leaves the room and Hunter helps me onto the bed, I place the blanket over my waist and pull my shirt up and wait for the doctor. I rub my tummy and can't help the giggles erupting.

"What's wrong?" Hunter says looking confused.

"She's kicking again, she's been so active these past few weeks. Here…Feel." I say grabbing his hand and placing it over the spot she usually kicks.

A smile forms on his face and I let go of his large hand and he moves it over my stomach smiling.

"That's amazing…she's kicking so well." he mumbles.

"Tell me about it." I laugh.

The Doctor comes in and does her usual checkup telling me how healthy the baby is and that I should be prepared for the coming week since she could come at any time. This makes me nervous so I'm glad Hunter is with me and I'm not alone.

"Thanks for coming with me today." I say to Hunter as we stop outside the apartment.

"Between me and you? I'm glad you couldn't get hold of Jace, I'm so happy I got to be there and see that; It's pretty amazing Harley." Hunter says with a look of awe covering his face.

"If you ever have a problem reaching Jace, just give me a call babe and I'll be there." He says as he helps me out the Jeep.

"Thanks Hunt…thanks for everything." I hug his waist tight and feel him wrap his arms around me too.

He walks with me into the bar to see how Jesse and the two other guys my father hired to work in the bar are doing. I spot Jesse instantly; he smiles as he pours me a glass of orange juice and sits next to me at the bar. I show him the new ultrasound photo and he gives me a big hug.

"If you were at the appointment then why wasn't Rave with you? He's been sitting with that crowd all afternoon drinking it up and making a big noise." Jesse says nodding his head to the back corner of the Club. I spot Jace sitting there with a few guys and the usual girls, Rachelle included. He has his arm over the back of her chair, she looks me in the eye and gives me a sad look.

I knew it was too good to be true. I never wanted to change Jace, I wanted him to change for me...well I wanted him to at least try to change for me but maybe someone like him is unable to think of anyone else but themselves. His boys are his main priority, who was I kidding thinking that we could be that perfect little family. Fact is, this isn't his child and we are not his responsibility.

"Shit...he forgot, didn't he? Fucking tool! I'm sorry sweetie." Jesse says rubbing my back resting his head on my shoulder.

"It's okay Jesse, it's not like this is his baby in any case. I should have stuck to my gut from the beginning." I take one last sip of my orange juice and try to give Jesse a reassuring smile but I just can't do it.

"I stuck with him even though I knew it would eventually boil down to him doing this, I hate the thought of being alone but maybe I just need to get my shit together and stop thinking I can rely on him. I don't need him... I want him sure..." I turn and take another look at Jace who hasn't even noticed me yet, even though the bar is basically empty. "...but maybe this is something I need to do without him, I'm not really alone, I have all of you guys supporting me and I don't ever want my daughter to think when she grows up that her mother was weak and had to rely on others all the time. This is my responsibility and I guess it's time I grow up and face that fact." I give him a sad smile and I know he senses that it's fake but he doesn't say anything and I quickly leave before he can.

After eating, taking a shower and going over some class notes I sit in the lounge in front of the TV and listen to the loud music coming from the apartment next door. I know Jace must know that I'm back by now because Hunter would have told him, but it's been two hours and he still hasn't arrived. Maybe the novelty of the pregnancy has worn off for him.

Looking down at my phone I scroll through my contacts stopping at one in particular. It's only five o'clock and hopefully she doesn't have the night shift. I press dial and listen to the dial tone until I hear her soft voice on the other end.

"Hi Momma." I say.

"My baby! I've been so worried about you! Are you okay?" she says sounding worried. I hear the television is the background.

"I'm fine, haven't spoken to you for a while." I mumble.

"I know sweetie, I've missed you so much." She sounds as if she's crying and it breaks my heart to hear her this way.

"Why didn't you call me?" I say softly.

"I wanted to Harley... your... your daddy threatened me, told me to stay away from you or he would make sure I regretted it. I almost drove up there just to see how you're doing but your daddy scares me baby."

I can hear her sobbing into the speaker.

That's something my father would do and I guess I can't blame her but if the situation was reversed I wouldn't let anyone in the way of my daughter and I... but then again I will never treat my daughter the way I was treated as a child.

"I miss you too Momma." I whisper wiping away a stray tear. "I have to tell you something..."

"What's wrong baby?" she asks sniffing.

"I'm pregnant Momma." I say softly and listen for her response but she doesn't say anything for a few seconds and I hear her turn the volume of the television in the background down.

"Oh Harley...You're going to be a great mother. I know I was a pretty crappy example, I was a terrible mother to you but I know you baby, you are going to be an amazing mother. I wish I could see you all big and pregnant sweetie." She says surprising me. I was at least expecting her to yell and tell me I would turn out like her but instead she's *kind of* apologized for not being the mother I needed and told me I would be nothing like her.

"Thanks ...that means so much to me. I know I never told you this enough but I love you Momma." I tell her and I hear her cry on the other end of the call.

"I love you too and even though I've been a shitty mother, I swear I'll be the best fucking grandma you've ever seen." She chuckles.

"I want to see you. I miss you so much." I blurt out as the tears fall.

"You can come whenever you want to Harley, this will always be your home and I'll always be here for you sweetie."

"Can I come now?" I say and I'm met by silence again.

"You want to come see me? Now? I want to see you too baby but is it safe for you to drive here? It's a few hours away and it's going to get dark soon." She asks concerned.

"It's okay mom, if I leave here now I'll get there by nine and I'll stay the night then leave in the morning. Can I come?" I say already making my way to my room to pack an overnight bag, eager to get away from the music next door and as far as possible for a little bit.

"Of course baby, I'll wait up for you. I can't wait to see you!" she says excitedly.

I know I'm running away again but I just need to see my mother and get some space from the noise coming from the club. Maybe driving a few hours away is a bit extreme but as far as I'm concerned the further away from this place the better the chances of my mind not thinking about what Jace is probably doing at this point and with whom.

I find my car keys in the fruit bowl on the kitchen counter and quickly make my way out of the apartment towards my car.

I finally make it to my mother's and my entire body is aching and sore but I'm so happy I've finally arrived. I haven't received any calls so Jace probably hasn't made his way to my apartment yet. That's if he's even going to go back there tonight at all.

I hear the door open and see my mother come out. She still looks as beautiful as ever as she runs up to me. I've never seen her so happy to see me before and it brings a smile to my face.

"Oh Harley look at you! You're so beautiful. It's true what they say about pregnant woman, you're glowing baby!" she says wiping away tears. After she takes my bag, putting it into my old room, she pulls me to the couch and then all the questions start. She asks about Caleb and how he's doing; I have to tell her all about that night and what happened, then I tell her about Jace and everything that has led up to me arriving here tonight.

"I'm so sorry my baby. Your daddy was one of the good ones honey. Not many men are willing to take the responsibility of looking after a baby while they're so young." She says as she pulls me to her chest and runs her hands through my hair.

"Yeah I know Momma." I say sadly.

"You have so many people that are there for you. You don't need someone to take the place of the father. You are such a strong smart woman, you can do this sweetie." She says softly as she continues to stroke my hair.

We spent most of the night chatting and catching up. She apologizes for the way she treated me and tells me how much she regrets not spending more time with me when I was younger. Telling me that when she found out I was in the hospital she went crazy and wanted to come immediately but my father threatened her. She cried hard when she told me about how much she missed me around the house and how alone she felt.

When I wake up the next day, I find a note from her telling me she had to be at work and didn't want to wake me. *Wonder how many guys would be at a strip club at eleven o'clock in the morning?*

Looking at my phone I notice I don't have any missed calls or messages and my heart drops a little at the thought of Jace not even making it home last night.

I write Momma a note thanking her for the talk and tell her I will see her soon.

As I drive away from my old home and closer to my new one, the nerves within me build up. I take a slow drive home and stop for food along the way. I only reach the Club House after 3 in the afternoon. Dropping my clothes on the bed I notice the bed is still neatly made; he didn't stay here last night.

I make my way next door to finally find him and it's like déjà vu all over again. Everyone lying all over the place and the entire apartment is trashed. *Daddy is going to freak out when he sees this…*

I make my way toward Jace's room just as Rachelle is stepping out zipping up the side of her dress. She freezes when she spots me and her eyes start to water but I don't pity her this time.

"I'm so sorry Harley." She says walking up to me.

"Bullshit, how long has it been going on?" I say moving past her to see a bare chested Jace lying on his bed on his stomach, out cold.

"It never stopped." She says softly.

I feel the pain in my chest and I back away until my back hits the wall. I rest my head against it as I feel the tears fall. She tries to console me but I shove her off and she bursts out crying.

"Don't cry. You can have him. I give up. You win." I whisper trying to stop myself from sobbing keeping my eyes closed.

"What's going on?" I hear Hunter next to me. I open my eyes to see him looking back and forth between Rachelle and me.

"Fuck sakes Rachelle, you were supposed to be gone already." He yells at her confirming what I thought all this time.

My mouth drops open and I'm out of breathe. "You knew? You knew this whole time?" I ask in disbelief. I see the regret written all over his face.

I watch as Jace's door opens. "What's all the shouting for?" he says wiping his face, the lines from his pillow still imprinted on his face. He sees me and looks at Rachelle.

"Fuck!" He whispers.

I step around Rachelle and walk away but he grabs my arm. "Wait baby please…" he begs but I turn around and push him away from me as the tears pour down my face.

"What Jace? What? Wait; let me guess, it didn't mean anything? You telling me I'm your girl while you're fucking a tramp on the side these past few months, means nothing right? Fuck you Jace! It means… I'm not your girl…not anymore. What happened to not letting any girl in your bed? I was the only one right?" I look at Rachelle then back at him. "Right… You look like you slept just fine…you don't need me anymore." My voice dies down to a husky whisper as the tears fall. He attempts to touch me but I feel disgusted and want to get as far away from him as possible so I step away.

"I'm so sorry Harley. I do need you, I took a sedative before we… and I've been stressed out and…" he stutters.

"And what? The only way to deal with the stress was to fuck someone else? Fucking hell…" I shake my head. "I'm such an idiot! To think you would actually care about someone other than yourself?" I shake my head and run my hands through my hair.

"I do care about you and that baby-" he says coming closer but Hunter stops him. We have an audience now.

"Really? Really Jace? You missed the appointment yesterday and Hunter had to stand in for you, you didn't even fucking realize I wasn't home last night? You care about me? Really Jace?" I rhetorically ask wiping away the tears. He looks at Hunter then back at me.

"Where were you? Why the fuck were you with her?" he asks Hunter and I ,ignoring the rest of what I just said.

"Where were *you* when I needed you Jace?" I ask him. He looks at Rachelle but says nothing. The guilty look he's giving me says it all.

"Yeah while you were fucking her I was hours away trying to get the thought of you out my head." I say backing away. Jace shouts out for me and starts shoving Hunter as he tries to get to me.

"Stay away from me! All of you… just stay away from me." I say as I back away from them.

"Wait Harley, don't fucking walk away from me. Please let me explain…please." Jace begs as he comes running, kneeling on the floor and holding his head against my stomach. I try removing his arms but he's too strong.

"No Jace, I'm done. You can be with Rachelle freely now, you don't have to get everyone to lie to me for you." I look up at Hunter purposefully as I say this, he gives me a pained look and steps closer but I shake my head making him freeze and look down at Jace.

"You knew what Caleb did and how it broke my heart and that was once! You've done it how many times now? You're worse than him! I can't be around you right now Jace, I feel like such an idiot for believing everything you said; all those promises you made. I can't…I can't even look at you right now." He reluctantly lets go as I say this and I watch his eyes gloss and watch his jaw work as he swallows the tears.

"Please don't leave me baby…. I was thinking about you when I was with her." He says softly.

"No Jace, don't even say that. I can't do this anymore. You don't get it, you don't see how much I cared for you, how much I love you…." I hear his quick intake of breath as he hears that and I cover my mouth. *I just told him I loved him.* We have told each other how much we care for each other but never used that four letter word… ever.

He smiles at me and stands up, "Baby I lo-"

"No Jace…don't you dare say that to me! Not after all this shit." I say backing away from him as I feel the tears falling again.

"It's true though… I want you to hear it. I lo-" He yells coming closer to me but Hunter grabs him again. Hunter turns Jace to face him with his hands on both of Jace's shoulders looking him in the eyes.

"You need to calm down bro. Have you taken your pills today?" Jace ignores him and Hunter's words have left me completely confused.

What pills? Are these the same ones I saw Jace take that first morning? I hear something fall and the glass shattering breaks my thoughts. I look to see Hunter and Jace struggling, Jace has him up against the wall with his hands around Hunter's neck.

"Jace stop! Stop!" I shout and he quickly drops Hunter and looks at me full of panic.

"Is this a fucking game to you? Do you enjoy breaking my heart? Well, you win Jace…it's broken and there's nothing left for you to destroy. Are you happy? Does that make you happy?" He looks down at his hands then back up at me but doesn't say a word.

"I think it's best if I stay away for a little while." I say and turn toward the door; I mumble a goodbye as I shut the door behind me. I run as fast as I can down the stairs and out the door towards my apartment. I hear Jace's shouts from the street. Making my way into my apartment out of breath, I'm leaning against the door trying to control my breathing when I feel warm liquid running down my legs.

"God no…" I cry out as I see the liquid pooling at my bare feet.

It's not blood though…thank God.

I run trying to find my phone. I don't know who to call; my father and Anna are hours away, so is my mother. I can't call Jace or Hunter. I lean against the counter, clutching my stomach. I try Jesse's number but his phones switched off. I burst into tears feeling really truly alone for the first time.

I look down at my phone as I find his number.

"Hello? Harley?" I hear his deep voice on the other end.

"Brent? I need your help." I say sniffing trying to control my breathing.

"What's happening babe? Are you crying?" he asks sounding worried.

"Brent…I think my water just broke and I have no one here to help me. I would drive myself but I don't think it would be a good idea in my….." I say softly unable to finish my sentence as the sobs take hold again.

"No, I'll be there soon Harley. Just give me your address and stay calm. Everything will be okay babe." He says as I hear keys jingling in the background.

I tell him my address and he says he's just around the corner from me. I call Dr. Smith and she says she will be waiting at the hospital for me.

I hear my door open and Brent comes running up toward me. He helps me up and looks me over.

"You okay? Where's your boyfriend? Do you need to take anything with you?" he asks looking worried.

"Yeah I've got a bag; this shouldn't be happening… it's a week too soon Brent." I say, ignoring his question about my boyfriend.

"Where is he Harley? Why isn't he here for you?" Brent repeats.

"It's only me and my daughter Brent, can you just get me to the hospital and then I'll be out of your hair." I say getting frustrated with him.

"I'm sorry babe. You're *not in my hair*. I'm glad you called me Harley. I thought you would never speak to me again." He says sadly.

"Brent…as much as I'd like to sit here and reconcile, I'd much rather get to the hospital and have this baby. Okay?" I sigh pushing him out the door.

"Right. Sorry babe let's get this baby out." He smiles and I shake my head.

We arrive at the hospital, I'd called my parents on the way telling them about the baby; Daddy said he was leaving right away and ordered me to keep that baby inside me until he got there. He didn't even ask about Jace, guess he just presumed he was with me.

My father paid for me to get a private room that allowed for Anna and him to be in there when I gave birth. I wasn't too fond of the idea of an audience while I was giving birth, but at the rate my baby is going I think she will be out of there before they arrive.

As the doctor gets me comfortable in bed she asks, "Where's Jace? He better hurry and get here, looks like your baby wants out of there." She eyes Brent cautiously.

"He's not coming." I say flatly.

"Doesn't he want to see his daughter born?" she asks confused.

"She's not his daughter and no he doesn't. If my parents don't make it in time then it'll be just me." I say looking away from her judging eyes.

"And me." My head whips to Brent as he announces this. He takes my hand and kisses it.

"You don't have to sit with me through this. I'm scared and I don't want to be alone but I can't ask you to do this." I say looking up at him.

"You don't have to ask me Harley. I want to be here and besides, I owe you at least this much for that whole going behind your back and trying to set you and Caleb up. I'm sorry for that by the way. I will never betray you again Harley."

I smile and nod then turn my attention back to the Doctor who stands watching Brent and I the entire time. *She probably thinks I'm the biggest whore around with the number of different men she's seen me with.*

"The baby isn't due for over week, why is this happening now?" I ask her worriedly.

"Stress does that to you. Just by standing here I can see how stressed you are sweetheart." She pats my hand. "Sometimes these things happen but your baby is healthy and I just need you to calm down so that everything runs smoothly. You can never plan things perfectly when it comes to the birth of your baby. Just stay calm and all you need to focus on now is the fact that you'll be seeing your little girl soon." She smiles and pats my baby bump.

I hear my phone ring and Brent picks it up. "Jesse?" he asks and I take the phone from him.

"Harley, you alright?" he says sounding concerned.

"No Jesse I'm…um…in the hospital." I hear him gasp.

"I'm alright now, a friend picked me up. My water broke and I panicked because I didn't know who to call." I say.

"I'm on my way babe. Why didn't you call Jace? Or Hunter?" he says as I hear doors being opened and closed on his side of the phone.

"Uh…Jace and I aren't… I mean, I caught him with Rachelle…again. I ended things. Hunter knew about it the whole time. I didn't have anyone to call. Brent's with me now but I don't know if Mom and Daddy are going to make it in time." I say looking at Brent as he brings me tissues.

"Fuck babe…I'm so sorry. We will talk about this later, you just focus on that baby of yours. I'm on my way, I'll see you soon Hun."

I hand the phone back to Brent and notice him frowning at me.

"I know… okay? I have bad taste…I get that now. I'm done with guys… my heart can only break so many times." I say avoiding his eyes as he sits on the bed next to my hand and puts it on his lap.

"You deserve so much better." He says looking down at me with a sad smile.

Chapter 19

A few hours later, after all the pushing and squeezing of Jesse and Brent's hands I hear the first cry from my baby girl. They place her in my arms as Brent and Jesse bend over to have a look at her. She is the spitting image of her father and I wouldn't have it any other way; even if it means I'm reminded of him every second of the day. She has a mop of black straight hair and although her eyes are dark blue which is usual for new born babies, I have a feeling her eyes will eventually be as green as her daddy's. The similarities between Jace and Caleb are scary; I guess people would think that this was indeed Jace's child if they'd never met Caleb, but I know she can only be Caleb's.

"She's beautiful Harley." Brent says softly placing his finger on hers; she clutches it immediately.

"She looks a lot like you sweetie." Jesse says kissing my forehead.

"No…she's the spitting image of her daddy. She's perfect." I smile down and kiss her soft cheek. She immediately stops crying and looks up at me as if she trying to get her eyes to focus.

I reluctantly let the nurse take her away to get cleaned up and the boys give me a few minutes so that the doctor can clean me up too. I can't wait to have her in my arms again; I could sit and look at her for hours on end.

After another hour, I'm sitting comfortably in my bed anxiously waiting for my baby. The boys sit on either side of me chatting to each other about how cute she was and how scary the experience was. I'm exhausted but I just want my girl in my arms.

The nurse brings her in and the sound of her cries cause a pain in my heart. As soon as I hold her close to my chest over my heartbeat she stops crying and I smile.

"Dear thing knows who her mother is." The nurse smiles, then asks the boys to sit on the other side of the curtain so she can show me how to breastfeed.

After my little girl has been fed the nurse allows the boys back in as I continue to stare at the bundle sleeping in my arms. I brush my finger up and down her soft little nose then watch as her little hands move around in her sleep. I put my finger near her left one and she immediately clutches it.

"You have a name for her yet?" Brent whispers, being careful not to wake her.

"Willow." I say smiling down at her.

When I was about seven, Caleb won me a teddy bear at the fair. He told me that I would never have to be alone again. I don't know what caused us to name it Willow but we did and I think the name suits my daughter perfectly. I'll always have her, she'll always be mine and I'll be hers…I'll never be alone again…

Watching her little body sleeping in my arms, I don't care about how exhausted I am, how my body hurts or that there is a loud commotion going on outside my room.

The door opens but I can't keep my eyes off Willow.

"Aw my baby girl…we're too late. I'm so sorry we didn't make it in time." I hear my father's voice as he closes the door.

"You're not late…you're just in time…" I say, smiling at my baby.

He comes closer and I look up just in time to see his big smile as he looks down at his granddaughter. Anna follows behind and just stands there staring at us with tears in her eyes. They're both speechless.

"Willow, meet your granny & grandpa…" I say to the baby in my arms as she starts to stir. Her eyes open and Daddy steps closer ignoring both Brent and Jesse who are sitting on the other side of the room. I reluctantly hand her over to my father. He's quiet but I don't think I've ever seen him smile this hard before.

"A beautiful name for a beautiful girl." He says through a thick voice and I look up to see tears rolling down his cheeks. He's crying.

"Don't cry Daddy." I smile as he holds my daughter so gently in his big leather clad arms.

"Tears of joy baby girl, tears of joy… I'm so damn proud of you. You made this beautiful girl… she's perfect Harley."

Eventually he passes Willow off to Anna who is sobbing like a baby herself. Willow doesn't cry; she just moves her eyes around taking in the people surrounding her.

Anna sits on the comfy chair next to my bed and holds Willow to her chest staring down at her.

"I'm so sorry we were late baby." He says kissing my forehead.

"It's okay Daddy. I wasn't alone." I tell him looking to the two quiet boys in the corner.

This gets his attention, my father looks at Jesse and smiles then looks at Brent and frowns.

"Who're you?" he grunts.

"I'm Brent sir. Harley and I went to High School together, I've basically known her since pre-school." Brent says smiling at me. I can see how exhausted the two boys are, but neither of them wants to leave my side.

Then my father does the last thing I expect him to. He walks up to Brent and I watch as Brent takes a step back not knowing what my father is about to do. My intimidating father pulls his hand out to shake Brent's then pulls him in for a man-hug. Brent smiles at me over Daddy's shoulder then winks.

"Thanks for looking after my girl's son. You ever need anything… you call me, okay?" My father says firmly.

"Yes sir…thanks." Brent says nervously.

"No… no sir here. The name's Grimm." Daddy then turns his attention over to Jesse and does the same routine.

He comes back up to me just as Anna places a sleeping Willow into the little baby bed trolley the nurse brought in earlier. I wrap the blanket over her and run my fingers over her little beanie the nurse put on her.

After an hour my father forces Jesse and Brent to go home to shower and eat since they've been here since I arrived at the hospital; we are all exhausted. The nurse takes Willow away and even though I tell my father and Anna they can go home, they won't leave me alone and secretly I am grateful.

Waking up the next day, my body is exhausted but I'm feeling a lot better. Touching my flatter stomach makes me kind of miss the feeling of having my baby inside me; where I could protect her from the big bad world. The nurse woke me up a couple times to feed Willow but I fell back asleep straight after they took her away again.

Daddy just walked in the door as the nurse handed me Willow again. The Doctor came and checked on me and told me that I was looking good and so was the baby. She asked if I wanted to stay another night but I told her I'd much rather go home as soon as I can. She said I would be able to leave this evening as long as I had someone there to look after Willow and I. Of course Anna said she would be with me.

"What's all that noise outside? Idiots are going to wake the baby up." Dad grumbles walking towards the door. Anna has already gone home to get my apartment ready for me and the baby.

I look down at Willow, whose eyes are wide open. "You're already awake aren't you baby girl." I say softly to her as she lets out a flow of incoherent mumbles making me laugh.

I continue to talk to her while I hear my father chuckling at something someone outside my room has said. I watch as I see the arms of another big guy give Daddy a hug then pat his back.

I am dumbstruck when Jace confidently strides into the room clutching a large bouquet of flowers.

I turn my attention back to the baby. if I was thinking sensibly right now I would ask him to leave, but I'm so high off the feeling of having my baby in my arms I probably wouldn't even care if Ashley walked in right now.

Jace comes up to me and places the flowers on the table next to me. He gives me a one arm hug over the bed then kisses my head. I don't return the hug but continue to stare at Willow praying Daddy won't leave us alone, but then I hear the door click and I know he's done just that.

"I wanted to be in there with you but Hunter kinda knocked me out after he told me you were in hospital. I'm so sorry Harley…I'm sorry for everything." He says with a deep rough voice.

"Jace... let's not do this now... I just want to enjoy this moment... please."

I look up to him and notice his sad beautiful eyes have tears flowing from them. He wipes them away then finally acknowledges Willow. He bursts out crying and then starts chuckling. I look at him not sure what to make of it, but he has a huge grin on his face as he wipes the fallen tears with the back of his hand.

"She's beautiful baby...she's so perfect." He says placing his index finger that has the silver club emblem ring on it over her little hand. Willow's quick to latch onto it as she starts making her usual baby sounds. Jace and I both start laughing.

"Jace meet Willow."

I look up to his happy face forgetting all that he put me through the day before; only focusing on this moment with him and my baby girl, knowing that whatever Jace and I had before last night will never be the same again. My main priority lies in my arms right now and I won't let him hurt her like he has me.

"Willow..." he repeats in a whisper. "I like that."

"You want to hold her?" I ask him, watching as his face whips up to look at me as if in shock.

"You'd let me hold her?" he sounds surprised.

"If you want to?" I smile at him.

"I'd love to, just show me how."

I slide my body slowly and he helps me so that my feet are hanging off the side of the bed then move over to the double seater comfy couch next to the bed.

"Sit here. I'll hand her to you." I say motioning for him to sit on the couch.

I gently hand her over, telling him where to put his hands. I sit next to them and watch as big scary Jace holds my baby so gently and carefully in his arms.

"You're such a beautiful girl Willow, just like your momma. Your mom did an amazing job baby girl, I'm so proud of her... just wish I wasn't such a f... uh... naughty boy, then I would've been here for mommy when she brought you into the world...." He says in the gentlest tone I've ever heard from him. As I hear the door being opened I quickly wipe away a tear before he can see. I watch as my father comes in with a smiling Hunter.

"Harley, you have another visitor." Dad smiles obviously out of the loop about what happened the previous day with the three of us.

I look up at Hunter and he gives me a sad smile as he kneels in front of me. Jace is so fixated on Willow he doesn't bother to look away from her.

I look back at Hunter in front of me and he whispers. "I'm so sorry

Princess, for everything. You should have called me. I would have been here for you."

"I know Hunt but at that moment, after what happened I didn't know who to call. I felt so betrayed. I still do." I say looking down at the little package he's carrying.

He pulls me in for a hug but is careful to be gentle with me; even though I don't hurt that much due to the various meds I've been given. He whispers in my ear. "I will never lie to you again...from now on you come first...club second. Family is more important."

"Thank you." I say pulling away from him. I know how important the club is to him and how he sees it as his family because he never had one. I know how hard that must be for him to tell me something like that and mean it.

"Jace and I bought the kid something." Hunter says handing me the pink gift bag.

I open it and feel cotton; pulling out the material I see a little pink beanie along with other baby clothes. I open the beanie to see the words *My Mommy is the Best!* I laugh and shake my head as I look at the next article of clothing. It's a little jacket, the material is so soft but it's a replica of Jace's club jacket. It even has a mini club patch on the back with a black matching beanie with the words *Devils Grimm Property* written on it.

"I love it guys, thanks so much." I hug Hunter then give Jace a half a hug due to our position.

"Let's see how this looks..." I say pulling off Willow's current yellow beanie.

"Whoa...check out all that hair! Little Mohawk too." Jace says looking down at Willow as she makes funny sounds.

"Brother... are you sure you two didn't hook up before the crash? Swear that kid looks like you." Hunter says and I smack his arm.

Jace chuckles but doesn't say anything.

Opening my apartment door with Willow cuddled tight to my chest, I'm surprised to see Brent and Jesse sitting by the kitchen table laughing and chatting with Anna. I hear Hunter grunt as he notices Brent; Jace just looks at him confused.

"Brent don't you want to come help me quick." He quickly rushes and takes Willow from my arms and we walk to her room.

Once we enter the room I shut the door. "Is that other dude, the mean looking one, Jace?" he whispers as he gently places her in her crib.

"Yeah that's why I wanted to talk to you. I know you Brent and I know you probably want to have a chat with him about what he did but I'm asking you not to." I say looking up to him.

"Harley, how can you even let him into your home after what he did to you? Someone needs to confront him about the way he's been treating you." Brent says in an angry whisper.

"Brent please, you don't know how dangerous he is. I will talk to him about everything, just not now. I'm not getting back with him, I don't think I ever will but I just don't want arguing right now. He can hurt you Brent and I don't want that." I say giving him a hug.

He chuckles. "What? Don't you think I can handle a guy like him?"

I raise my eyebrows. "Hun... Jace will skin you alive."

I put the monitor on next to my little sleeping Willow then Brent and I make our way back to the others in the lounge.

Anna's made pasta for dinner so I dish out some for myself and Brent handing it to him knowing if I don't give him his own bowl, he'll just eat out of mine.

I watch from over the kitchen counter as Jace and Hunter sit chatting with my father in the lounge area. Every now and then I feel Jace's eyes on me and Brent as we chat. Jesse is chatting away with Anna about changes that she wants to make in her tattoo parlor.

I excuse myself so I can get dressed into comfortable sleep clothes. As I'm looking through my drawers I hear my bedroom door close behind me. I turn just in time to see Jace making his way to my bed. He sits on the side and rests his head in his hand, his long dark hair falling over his hands. I dress in the en-suite bathroom spotting Jace in the same position when I return to my room. I sit on the bed next to him but lay down and look at the ceiling.

"Who is he?" he says softly.

I know who the *he* is that he's referring to. "His name's Brent, we've been friends a long time."

"Just friends?" Jace asks now looking down at me.

"Yeah Jace. If I ever had a brother, I would pray he was just like Brent." I say looking up at the ceiling.

He leans on his one arm looking down at me then he gently lifts his hand and runs it on my stomach.

"Going to miss that... so proud of you Harley."

"I'm going to miss it too, but I'm so happy she's out... I get to hold her and love her. She gets to be my little teddy bear." I say smiling thinking about my beautiful little girl sleeping down the hall.

The room goes quiet and then Jace finds his words. "I never slept with her Harley. We did... uh... other stuff... but I never slept with her. I was so stressed out about you and the baby. It wasn't because I didn't want to be part of your lives... I did... I do. It was just the fact that I knew I was going to fuck something up. A girl like you doesn't belong with a guy like me. You're perfect and you deserve the whole white picket fence fairytale but I'm... I'm not that guy Harley, you won't get any picket fences with me." he says looking down at his hands.

"Jace… the fact that you guys didn't have sex doesn't mean shit to me. You promised me; no other girls and you… you lied Jace." I let out a deep breath as I calm my nerves. I don't want to yell and shout at him, I don't have the energy. "I don't care about the whole fairytale ending crap. I didn't want that… I never wanted that… all I wanted was you Jace. I hoped that this could work out between us, that I could be enough for you; but I was so… so fucking wrong. A girl like me will never be enough for guys like you and Caleb. I can't go through this again Jace… I can't." I sigh.

"Don't say that babe, don't. I know my word doesn't mean shit right now, but you are too good for me Harley. I will get better, I will be the man you deserve… I promise you baby. I want to be here for you and Willow. Let me please…" He begs me looking so sad.

"Jace… you can be here as much as you want, but your lifestyle… the club one… I don't want her around that ugly stuff. You can visit her whenever you want but we can't be together Jace. We tried… it didn't work. I just want to focus on Willow now. I don't know what the future holds but right now? This is what I want." I say sitting up and looking up at his sad eyes.

"I fucked us up for good, didn't I?" he says running his hands through his hair letting out a deep breath.

I don't say anything so he continues, "You really go visit your mom?"

"Yeah, I needed to get away. I saw you at the bar with Rachelle and I… I knew something was up the last couple of days if I'm being honest. After seeing you two together I put two and two together and figured you were over me. Of course, you're a guy and you weren't getting any from me in my… ah… condition. I knew you probably thought I looked repulsive especially with the swollen feet and that. I mean, I thought I looked terrible and I guess that's why you hardly touched me, so yeah…when I saw you and Rachelle… you guys looked good together." I say looking away from his confused gaze.

"What?" he says shocked. "You thought you looked horrible? Baby you were the hottest looking pregnant woman I've ever seen. I haven't touched you the last few days because I knew if we started something, I wouldn't be able to stop and I…I was worried that I would hurt you or the baby if I took it further." He looks down at his hands then rests his elbows on his knees with his head in his hands. "Fuck… I'm so sorry Harley… for everything. I should have been with you for that last appointment." He says softly shaking his head.

"Jace, it's too late for all of that… let's just… move on and focus on the future yeah." I say as I sit up and close the curtains.

He agrees and after saying goodnight to me, holding me closely against him, he kisses my cheek and leaves.

Walking into the lounge, I notice everyone has left apart from Hunter and Anna. Anna excuses herself to check on Willow and to take a nap until I have to get up and feed the baby again. She made up a bed in the spare room so that she can make sure I wake up to feed the baby through the night. I'm left sitting in the lounge next to Hunter feeling rather awkward.

"She's perfect Princess." He says turning to look at me as I curl into a little ball on the corner of the couch resting my head on the armrest.

"She is…" I smile thinking of her.

"I meant what I said at the hospital babe. You and that baby will come first from now on. I've had a long talk with Jace and he regrets the decisions he's made these last few weeks. He's going to be better Harley. I promise you." Hunter says pulling my feet onto his lap.

"No Hunt don't promise anything, especially not on his behalf. I'm done with people promising me things." I say looking at him directly in the eye.

"I gave you my word Harley and I mean it. Princess… the only reason I didn't tell you about Jace when I found out what he was doing was because I know how out of control he gets when he's angry. He's got a problem babe but it's not my place to give his secrets away. I was afraid if you confronted him he would lose his shit again and possibly hurt you. I swear I would have made him tell you everything once the baby was born, you just found out too soon. From what I know he never slept with her; I know that doesn't change shit though. Betrayal is betrayal…" Hunter says rubbing my feet gently.

"Hunter, I'm done with this, all of this… the reasons don't matter to me anymore. What's done is done but you're right about one thing. Betrayal is betrayal. Let's move on and focus on what's ahead of us. I'm too exhausted for this conversation right now." I yawn.

Later that night I find myself in my bed. I don't know how I got there but I'm pretty sure Hunter had something to do with it.

<u>Chapter 20</u>

Four years later...

As I'm placing the dishes from breakfast into the dishwasher, I hear my daughter giggling in the lounge. Smiling to myself I think of how much she has grown over the last four years. I remember the first time she called me *Momma*.

It was during one of our family Sunday lunches with the guys from the club; I was watching her play with a few of the other kids on the grass. Jace and Hunter had just come back from a job out of town and the first thing Jace did before greeting anyone was pick up a squealing Willow and hug her tight. We were so use to her gibberish and we spoke to her a lot even though we didn't know what she was saying most of the time.

As Jace held Willow close he asked her, "Where's your Momma?" Willow replied by turning her head pointing directly at me and squealed *Momma*, before bursting into a fit of giggles.

I broke down in happy tears, I felt so loved and proud of her in that moment.

Willow was the perfect baby. She always seemed happy and I made sure she never had to go without. I struggled at first but I refused my father's money. I saved a lot and when I had to go back to work Anna, Brent or Jesse was always there to help. As I expected, Willow turned out to be the feminine version of her father. Her hair is pitch black and she has beautiful green eyes, just like her father. She has his bubbly happy personality too and even though she reminds me of him every minute of the day, I wouldn't have it any other way.

Sometimes I wonder about Caleb as I watch Willow. I think about what he's doing and how life turned out for him. I often think about whether he ever considers his daughter and whether he even cares that she exists. I watched as Willow grew older and started to notice that other kids have two parents and not just a mommy; I know one day the question will come and I don't quite know what I will say, but she hasn't asked me yet. Maybe it's because she has so many male figures in her life; she hasn't realized yet that she doesn't have a father around.

I know Brent knows who Willow's father is, but he has never confronted me and we have never discussed it. After my father found out about Hunter and Jace's behavior the night I gave birth to Willow, he made sure to give them all the out of town jobs. They didn't argue with him, they felt they deserved it and who was I to argue when I knew it was true too. Whenever they come down though they stay with me and spend time with Willow; she loves her two favorite uncles.

A couple of times Jace was in town I would find him sneaking into my bed. He never tried to get closer than cuddle and being selfish I let him sleep next to me enjoying the comfort I got from him whilst I was in his arms. I found out that Jace was now on medication to help him deal with his insomnia and it was working; that made me feel better when Jace was out of town and not by my side. Brent is more like Willow's big brother; He play's Barbie with her and will sit and chat with her all day. She's really brought out his inner child and he looks after her like she's his own. Although he still has his immature jock ways, he has grown up so much these past few years and I'm so thankful for everything he's done for me.

My mother comes and stays with me one weekend every month so she gets to spend time with us and tomorrow I'm taking Willow to visit her. I haven't told my father about it yet because I know he will have something negative to say. My father and Anna are skeptical about my mother's presence in my life these days. I assured Anna that she was still my mother and I still love her as if she was my biological one. This seems to have reassured her, helping my case with my father. He worries and needs the assurance that my mother has indeed changed.

Today I'm going to the park with Brent, apparently there's a band playing on the college grounds. I usually avoid going to campus during the day, but Brent begged me and told me Willow would enjoy it so he eventually won me over. Brent fell behind on a couple of his credits so he was still finishing his last year at the college. Brent was never one of the smart kids and always enjoyed a good party. Since having Willow, I've completed my degree and now manage the bar as well as doing work at Anna's Tattoo parlor when she needs me.

I watch as Willow rolls around on the floor giggling at whatever she's watching on T.V. I hear a knock at the door and knowing its Brent I call out for him to come in. I watch from the kitchen as he strolls in and Willow heads running into his open arms.

"Bent Bent." She calls him and I laugh; when she was younger she couldn't pronounce the "r" in his name so she called him Bent. The name just stuck and even though her pronunciation is damn near perfect with other words she refuses to call him Brent.

"Pillow Pillow." Brent mimics teasing her. She giggles.

"Mommy, tell him I'm not a pillow." Willow says, now standing with her hand on her hip looking from me to Brent with a serious expression on her face.

"What?" I feign shock with a hand on my cheek. "You're not a pillow? But you're so soft and cuddly." I say tickling her; she squeals in my arms then runs away.

I give Brent a hug and he helps get Willow ready as I pack a quick bag with various toys in case she doesn't find the park all that interesting.

We decide to take a walk since it's not that far and Willow insists she wants to walk like a big girl. She's wearing a cute little floral strappy top ,little three quarter denims and I've left her long hair down. I couldn't bear cutting her hair as it grew longer, her shiny straight black hair reaches just above her belly button now and she loves it. I did a side braid in her hair this morning just to keep her long fringe from falling in her eyes when she plays.

After only a few meters, little Willow already has her arms up for Brent; wanting him to carry her the rest of the way to the park. He smiles at me knowing that we had anticipated this happening, but he happily picks her up as we continue to make our way to the park.

After giving birth to Willow, I lost my baby weight after a few months of working out and running. Apart from the various stretch marks in places there weren't before, my body has gone back to the shape I had before I fell pregnant. The fact that I'm wearing a pair of denim shorts I've owned over four years is proof of how hard I worked to get back to the healthy size I'm at now. I know I will never be model skinny, nor do I want that. I've worked hard enough, and I'm to a point where I don't wince every time I looked in the mirror. I feel better within myself and I am actually happy being me these days.

Brent finds us a spot on the grass and Willow immediately sits on my lap as she watches the many people and large built up stage down the hill from us with wide eyes.

There aren't many kids around and that's probably due to the fact that it's a college campus. I put some sun tan lotion on my little girl and offer Brent some. He's already in full conversation with Willow about what she was doing yesterday. I look inside the little bag I packed Willow to get her something to drink but realize I left it at home.

"Brent, can you watch her a minute? I'm going to get us something to drink. What do you guys want?" I say getting up and dusting my shorts off.

"I'll have a coke babe." He smiles at me.

She frowns at him and the next words that come out of her mouth make me hunch over and laugh till my stomach hurts.

"No Bent! Don't call mommy babe. She's not a piggy!" Brent and I finally compose ourselves but Willow is still standing in the same position she was earlier. Her hand on her hip, her face isn't angry anymore it's more confused as she looks back and forth between us.

"Yeah Bent don't call me that!" I wink at him. He chuckles, then pulls Willow into his arms and tickles her. I walk away to the sound of my beautiful daughter's laughter.

Standing in the queue for cold drinks, someone bumps into me.

"Oh sorry." I hear a familiar deep voice and I immediately feel butterflies in my stomach as I look into his beautiful green eyes.

"Harlz?" Caleb says looking shocked.

"Hi Caleb." I say turning my eyes away from him as he shamelessly continues to look my body over. He seems so much taller and his body has filled out well since the last time I saw him four years ago. He's not a boy anymore, he's all man.

"It's been what? Four years since the last time we... ah... saw each other. You're looking *really* good." He says running his hands through his black messy hair. I turn to look at him and can't help but run my eyes over his body, he doesn't look like the guy I left here at the same park all those years ago. Caleb has turned into a beautiful man. I notice one arm has a complete sleeve and I notice another tattoo peeking out under his black shirt near his collar bone.

I look up to see him smirking, dimples and all. I look away. "Yeah thanks, ah... you too."

"Honey, how long does it take for you to fetch me something to drink? I was beginning to – uh... oh... Harley?" I hear a whiny voice behind him and watch from the corner of my eye as Ashley wraps her arms around Caleb's.

Of course they're still together. I inwardly roll my eyes.

I turn to look at her. "Hi Ashley. How are you?" I can't help but feel the hurt that creeps in when I see them together. You'd think I'd be over him and what he does to me whenever I see him, but no not this heart, it flutters every time he's in my presence.

"I... I'm fine... and ah... you?" she stutters looking back and forth between me and Caleb.

I give her the biggest smile I can muster. "I'm great!"

"Mommy, Mommy look what Bent got me?"

Willow comes running up to my legs with a teddy in her arms. I bent down so I'm at her eye level. I don't miss the gasp from Ashley and I sure as hell didn't miss the shocked look on Caleb's face as he watches his daughter jump into my arms. I pick Willow and the teddy bear up and then look over at Brent's shocked face as he mouths sorry.

"Cutest teddy ever baby girl." I smile and kiss her cheek then look over to Brent again who seems rather pale as he gazes between Ashley, Caleb and I.

"Brent, you spoil her way to much." I smile at him and watch as his shoulders relax and colour comes back to his face.

Caleb and Ashley are speechless for a little while but of course Ashley is the first to speak up.

"Wow…" she lets out a deep breath looking from Caleb to Willow; it's so obvious since Willow is the spitting image of her beautiful father. "Is this… her?" She asks quietly. I watch Caleb's head snap in her direction as Ashley smiles at Willow.

I put my daughter back on the ground and my polite little girl introduces herself. She walks up to Ashley.

"Hello lady."

Ashley bends over not fazed by the fact that people behind her can probably see her underwear under the short mini she's wearing. I only hope Willow can't see any of that from where she's standing down there.

Ashley smiles at her and says. "Hello cutie pie. My name's Ashley." Willow giggles and moves her attention onto Caleb as she speaks to Ashley.

"No silly! My name's not cutie pie." Willow laughs and Ashley laughs while looking down at my daughter with a loving expression.

Caleb bends down so that he is eye level with Willow. We've moved out of the line by this point and Brent has already gotten our cold drinks. Willow smiles at Caleb and Caleb puts his large hand out to shake her tiny one. "What is your name baby girl?"

She puts her hand on her hip again and says with as much attitude that she can muster. "I don't know why everyone calls me that, even Jacey and Hunt Hunt, I'm not a baby. My name's Willow." Then she lifts her hand and shakes his big one with determination.

I watch as Caleb looks at her then up at me as he repeats. "Willow…" it's as if realization hits him, his eyes get all watery and I notice him swallow then he says with a ruff voice.

"Well Willow, I'm Caleb and it's very nice to meet you."

"Here Pillow, I bought you an ice-cream. I know how much your momma loves cleaning you up after you get chocolate everywhere." Brent chuckles and picks her up and throws her upside down and she giggles in his arms as they walk away. I pick up the teddy that she dropped just as

Ashley opens her mouth.

"She's so beautiful Harley, you did such a good job." Ashley comes in for a hug but I push her away.

"This whole little... ah... reunion was... nice, but I'd really like to spend the rest of my day with my daughter." I move past them but Caleb's strong arm stops me around my waist then pulls me against his hard chest.

"Whose is she? How old is she Harley?" he whispers in a serious tone.

I look back and forth between the two of them. Ashley has an ashamed look on her face and her eyes can't meet neither Caleb's nor mine. I push away from Caleb.

I laugh and shake my head. "You know exactly *whose* she is. Don't play stupid with me Caleb. How old do you think she is? That night I caught you two together? I was just over three months, so yeah...you do the math. Besides, you should know all of this? Why are you acting like this is all news? Your girlfriend here..." I give Ashley a pointed look. "...told me you didn't want Willow. I can understand the fact that you wouldn't want me in your life, but your own daughter? Really Caleb? I never expected that from you... then again, I didn't expect the cheating either. Even though you two were together, I still would have liked her to have a father around and I would have dealt with the fact that my ex was with my best friend or ex best friend... whatever. Why are you looking at me like that?" I ask Caleb. He looks like he may pass out and I'm confused as to why he looks so shocked.

"What did you tell her?" he roars at Ashley. She looks back and forth between us both. I notice various people watching us now; I've never seen Caleb this mad before. His knuckles are clasped and I see his jaw pulsing.

"I... I... I don't know why I said that baby. I promise if we just leave now I'll make it up to you later and explain everything." Ashley says in a flirty tone. I don't want to hear how and what *making up to him later* entails. My heart clenches at the fact that they're hooking up because even though I shouldn't, I still think of Caleb as mine. It's gotten a lot more crowded now and while they're now talking to each other I slip away to find Brent.

Walking up to Brent, I notice Willow's face is covered in chocolate and that she's fast asleep on his lap.

"I'm sorry about earlier Harley, I shouldn't of come looking for you but she was so excited about her teddy." Brent says looking upset.

"No it's cool, don't apologize. I'm tired of hiding away and we were bound to run into them sooner or later." I say getting the baby wipes out the bag and gently wiping Willow's little face careful not to wake her.

"Harley... I know I said I wouldn't ask questions but I can't keep this in any longer. Why did you keep her from him? You know how much he wanted to be with you and you know he would have been there for her regardless of whether you wanted him there or not." Brent says in a more serious tone than I'm used to.

"Are you kidding me Brent? He knew about her! He knew I was pregnant but he still chose Ashley over us. I... I think it's time I take her home, it's been a long day... for all of us." I say putting Willow's new teddy in her bag.

"What? He didn't know...or at least I don't think he did. He hates her Harley... they aren't even-" I interrupt him.

"Brent I'm done with this conversation, please can we just leave it?" I ask impatiently. He sighs as he picks up Willow and we leave the park.

Chapter 21

After Willow was bathed and dressed I started on dinner. I placed my phone on silent because I can't bear to deal with anyone else after the day I've had. After letting the dough stand for the homemade pizzas I was making, I decided to grate some cheese and get the toppings ready. Willow was sitting on the carpet in front of the TV watching the cartoons.

I don't hear a knock at the door; instead I hear the keys in the lock before Jace walks in and immediately picks up Willow. After greeting her and putting her back down on the ground she instantly goes back to watching her movie.

"Hey babe." He says pulling me in for a hug.

I haven't seen Jace the past few weeks, he's been on some job a few hours away.

"Hey, how have you been? Haven't seen you in a while." I say finally moving out of his arms and heading over to the fridge to pour him something to drink.

"I know. I've missed you guys. You miss me baby girl?" He calls out to Willow.

"Don't call me that. I told C…Caleb I'm not a baby anymore." She says, trying to remember his name.

I watch as she turns her attention back to the TV and Jace snaps his head back to me as he speaks slowly.

"What did she just say?" he asks seriously.

"We bumped into Caleb today. It was awkward, he was with Ashley and when he asked about Willow it sounded like he never knew about her." I say placing dishes into the dish washer.

"We'll have a word about this later." He says looking back at Willow as she lies on the floor on her tummy, head resting on her hands looking up to the TV.

After Willow has eaten her supper she went and sat on Jace's lap in the lounge. Jace handles her so gently; I know one day he will make a great father. The relationship between Jace and I has been strained since the night I gave birth to her but we don't let that affect his relationship with her.

She rests her head on his chest and Jace cradles her in his arms, it makes my heart melt at how caring he is. He looks up to me and smiles and I return it. After cleaning all the dishes and showering, I come back to an empty lounge. I walk to Willow's room just in time to see him tuck a sleeping Willow into bed.

I watch as he sits on the corner of her little bed and moves the hair out of her face. He sits for a few extra seconds then kisses her forehead. I leave before he catches me staring and start putting away all the clean dishes; some are still wet from my faulty cheap dishwasher so I place them on the table and rack to dry.

As I just about close the dishwasher door with my foot, I squeal as I'm being lifted in the air and placed on the kitchen counter. I squirm as the top of my bare thighs touch the cold counter; I'm only wearing pajama shorts and a strappy top. As I try to lift my ass to get off the counter, Jace positions himself between my legs and places his rough hands on top of my upper thighs.

Even after all that Jace has put me through I know my body still reacts to his touch due to the fact that I'm unquestionably attracted to him.

"Let's talk." He says looking down at me.

"What do you want to talk about Jace and why do I have to sit here?" I say raising an eyebrow.

"You know what about and because I can keep you here without the risk of you doing your usual running act when you don't feel comfortable." He says grinning at me.

"What do you want to know Jace? I saw Caleb, he asked about her and I told him. Just like I told Brent today, I'm done hiding away from them. I want Willow to see all the beautiful things out there. You should have seen her today at the park, she was so inquisitive and her eyes couldn't stop moving over everything. Apart from the club crowd and the quiet park by the pond, I never take her anywhere around here because I was too afraid of walking into either of them." I say looking down at his chest.

"Brent? You went with him today? What was it? Like a date?" he says raising his eyebrow and losing the grin he had before I mentioned Brent's name.

"Yes I went with him and no it wasn't a date. Why are you looking at me like that? Are you mad?" I ask him, watching as he tightens his hands on my upper thighs to the point where it hurts.

He shakes his head and looks down at my hands on my lap; he lifts one to his lips and kisses it, keeping his eyes on me the entire time. This makes me blush and look away from him.

"Baby when it comes to my girls and other guys, I never like it; even though I know you and Willow are no longer mine. My heart and my head tell me otherwise, I want to be the only man in your life. Even after four years you're still all I think about, It kills me to know I fucked that up babe. All I care about now is that you're happy and safe. But as far as that Caleb fucker is concerned, if he comes anywhere near you or her…I'll kill him." he says menacingly, making me shiver.

I gasp. "Jace, don't say shit like that! You said you would be cool when I decided it was time to introduce her to her father." I whisper yell at him.

"I mean it Harley… or do you *want* him around? I only said that when I thought you were both mine. If he comes into the picture now, it will fuck me up." He says raising an eyebrow taunting me.

"Jace if he didn't know about Willow and Ashley *did* lie then I want him to have a relationship with her. He is her father! I seriously don't ever want to hear you talk about killing someone else again. I don't care who it is. Okay?" I say backing away from him on the counter.

He places his hands under the bend of my knee and pulls me against him with such force that I gasp, he places his one hand on my lower back and the other behind my neck as he brings my face a few inches from his.

"Remember when I told you that I didn't like to be told what to do Harley; I meant it. I'm not going to let him take you two away from me. You are mine... you should know that by now." I feel his breath on my lips.

The look he's giving me is enough to make me shiver, not from want but fear. Jace has kept Raven hidden from me since that night four years ago; I guess tonight he's making a reappearance.

"Jace... you... you need to stop saying that. I'm not yours. Please stop this. Let me go before you wake Willow up." I move to get distance away from him but he looks at the hallway; when he notices that Willow is in fact still in bed he turns his attention back to me.

"But you are mine Harley, you and that little girl. Do you honestly think after all the time and effort I've put into you, I'd allow you to let that piece of shit back into your lives? In place of where I *should* have been?" he threatens. His hand on the back of my neck starts pushing my face toward his until our lips meet.

I push at his chest to get him off me but he continues to stick his tongue in my mouth. I feel like I'm suffocating and I need him to get away from me. When his hand reaches and harshly grabs my breast, I bite his lip and the next moment I'm thrown off the counter landing on the floor, smashing the clean dishes off the drying rack. I touch my lip and it stings, I look down to see blood on my index and middle finger. Looking up to Jace I realize what just happened....he backhanded me.

I see the shock in Jace's face as he looks back and forth between me and his hand that struck me. I'm frozen with disbelief; I never thought he would be the hitting type. Of course he looks like the hitting type but I never thought he'd *actually* do it. I look down at the floor and notice a couple of cuts on my legs, many of which have shards of glass still stuck in.

He tries to move towards me but I back away. His mouth opens and closes but no words come out, I guess I'm the same. He runs his hands through his hair and then in one quick motion he's gone; all I hear is the slamming door as he leaves.

"Mommy!" I hear Willow scream and I watch as she comes running to where I'm sitting surrounded by glass.

"Willow wait! Stay right there baby. There's glass on the floor, I don't want you cutting your feet up okay?" I gently try to get up off the floor but I have glass in my feet as well as in some of the cuts on my legs. Willow stands immobile by the hallway doorway, tears flowing down her face.

"I need you to do mommy a favor okay sweetie?" I ask her calmly and she nods through sobs.

"Mommy's phone is next to her bed, can you go and fetch it for me quickly?" she immediately turns and runs down the hall; a few seconds later she's clutching the phone to her chest waiting for my next instruction.

"Throw it here baby." I say and she tosses it my direction. I eventually get up off the floor and pick up Willow. I ignore the discomfort in my feet as I walk over the glass and place her in the lounge chair telling her not to come back into the kitchen. Her sobs are softer now.

I look at my phone, ignoring all the missed calls from Brent. I need to keep my phone close just in case Jace returns. I kneel down on the floor to pick up all the tiny pieces of glass that are shattered. I ignore the sting of the cuts in my legs and feet as I try to pick up as much of the glass as possible. I hear hard knocking on the door and internally curse myself for not locking it after Jace left. I hear Willow's cries increase, obviously she's afraid. I don't know if she saw the whole Jace ordeal, I pray she didn't.

I hear the door being opened and attempt to stand up quickly but as I lift my head over the counter the last person I expect to see cradling my weeping Willow to his chest is Caleb.

"What's wrong baby girl? Where's your Momma?" he says holding her tiny body to his chest.

"Mommy fell, she's bleeding, hurry." I hear her muffled sniveling.

"It's okay sweetie, I'm fine… just some scratches." I say to her as I try once again to lean up on the counter to avoid standing on the glass in one of my feet.

Caleb looks in my direction in shock, quickly placing Willow on the lounge chair and rushing to my side; catching me before I fall. "Jesus Harlz, what happened here?" he says looking around at the glass on the floor.

"I just tripped and fell that's all. What are you doing here? How'd you find me?" I ask him, trying to avoid looking at his face as I limp my way over to Willow.

"I've been calling you all day but you didn't answer. I had to talk to you about today, I couldn't just leave things like that Harley. I forced Brent to tell me where you live, so here I am." He bends down and scoops up the bigger pieces of glass and looks around for a bin. I point in him in the right direction.

I hold my daughter close to my chest as I pick her up. Even though the various cuts hurt like hell, all I care about right now is making sure my daughter is okay.

She wraps her arms around my neck and holds me tight as her cries die down. "Come on sweetie let's get you back to bed."

I limp my way towards her room but Caleb steps in front of me with open arms; his eyes still avoid mine.

"Let me help you with her Harley, your foot is bleeding." He says looking down at my foot.

I pass him, keeping Willow in my arms; not because I don't want him to hold her but because I need to hold her more right now. My whole body is in shock, firstly with the whole Jace hitting me ordeal and now with the fact that Caleb has found me and knows where I live. My heart is beating so fast right now that I'm battling to catch my breath.

I place Willow into her bed and sit on the side of it wiping her long hair out of her face.

"Mommy... where's Jacey? Why was he yelling Mommy?" she asks me innocently, making my heart beat faster.

"Did you see Jace leave baby?" I need to find out how much she saw.

"No Mommy. I heard him shouting, then the loud bangs and glass then I heard the door slam. I stayed in my room until I found you Mommy... I was scared." She says with a shaking chin as if she's about to burst into tears again.

"Don't worry, everything's fine. Mommy just dropped a couple dishes that all. Go to sleep my baby...everything's going to be alright." I whisper softly stroking the bridge of her nose. I sit and watch as her eyelids flutter closed. I move my hand away from her face and stand up to tuck her in. I leave her little bed side lamp on and shuffle out the room. I don't see Caleb anywhere in the hallway as I gently shut the door after looking at my baby girl sleeping so peacefully. I wipe away a few stray tears that I didn't even know I'd shed and then bump into Caleb.

His hands go around my waist to steady me and a shudder goes through my body at the feeling. I remember the many times his hands have held me tight and kept me safe. Caleb would never hit me - ever.

I move away from him and head back into the kitchen to see all the glass is gone.

"Harley, please answer me, what happened here?"

"I... uh... just fell. I slipped and fell. That's all. I know you want to talk but I don't have the energy to right now. Can we do this another time?" I say softly out of breath as I find my way to my bedroom en-suite to fetch the first aid kit. I can't bear to look at his eyes. I'm humiliated and ashamed of how things have gone down.

I don't want Caleb in my home. Caleb comes from a very wealthy family and my tiny apartment is probably the size of his room. I feel uncomfortable with him being here, it may feel like home to me but I know the furniture looks cheap. When I caught him looking around my apartment I could see the pity in his eyes.

I'm aware of Caleb following me but I don't have the energy to stop him. My legs are wobbly as I bend down to the bottom shelf of the bathroom towel cabinet and get the first aid kit.

Caleb stops me and picks it up. "Here, let me help you." He says heading out of the bathroom. He motions for me to sit on my bed; I do. He bends down in front of me then starts looking through the first aid kit. He takes my foot gently in his big warms hands then gently removes the glass and washes away the blood. He then takes the little shards of glass out of my legs; we both sit there quietly as he focuses on not hurting me. It's been so long since I've had his hands on me, but it still feels so familiar; It's as if my body has never forgotten the feeling of his touch.

I look down as he gently pats the cuts above my knees with the antiseptic. He's changed so much yet he's still the same gentle Caleb he was five years ago. His black hair now sits just above his shoulders, always falling into his face perfectly. He still has those dark eye brows and thick eye lashes with those lips; the bottom lip curling slightly. He used to always be clean shaven but I now spot light stubble on his jawline. I notice a couple scars on his face that weren't there before, the most prominent one being through his one eye brow. I look at his hands as he wipes the rest of the blood off my right knee and I notice scars on his knuckles that weren't there a few years ago either; his shoulders also seem broader and bigger. The outline of his chest and the muscles of his back can be seen through his shirt as he moves his body around my room putting away the first aid kit. He seems much taller and manlier than he was when we were together. He seems a lot more serious and a lot less playful than the Caleb I used to know too. I guess a lot has changed in both our lives.

I sit quietly watching him as he shamelessly looks my room over, checking the windows and making sure they're locked. He then disappears and I hear the front door being locked. He comes back into my room and I watch as his attention lands on the various frames on my wall. The photos consist of me during my pregnancy and a lot of Willow when she was a baby. A couple of her ultrasound pictures and then there are pictures of her with my parents, Hunter, Jace, Jesse and a lot with Brent.

Caleb strolls towards where I'm sitting on the bed and sits back down next to me with his eyes still glued to the collage of photos on my wall. I hear him let out a deep sigh.

"I like that photo of you with her; the one where she's cuddled up to your side on the sofa. I like the one where you were pregnant too. You look so beautiful Harley." He says sadly, still avoiding my eyes. I don't think he's looked me in the eyes since he got here. I lean over and take the photo out of the frame next to my bed.

"Here, you can have this one if you want. It's the day she was born." I hand over the photo of me cradling my tiny little baby in my arms. My face is all sweaty and tears fall down my cheeks but I have the biggest smile on my face as I look down at Willow. Her little finger reaches up and touches my chin and she's staring up at me. I wipe away a tear, thinking about that beautiful moment.

I look up at his face, he is staring down at the picture with a big smile. I watch his finger trace over Willow then he traces over my face in the photo.

"My girls are so beautiful..." he whispers to himself, but I hear.

He looks at me finally and his face immediately tenses as he looks down at my lip. I quickly touch it and I wince. My lip is split... *shit, how am I gonna explain my way outta this one.*

He puts the photo on the bed and reaches over to touch my face; I cover my lip and move away from him.

"It's nothing Caleb; I must've knocked my face on the table when I fell." I mumble avoiding his eyes, but it doesn't deter him. He leans right up to my side on the bed, pulls my hands away from my face then cradles my face between his hands as he looks at my lip.

"Who's Jace? Is he the one that you had that accident with?" he says, looking me in the eyes. I tense under his hands at the mention of Jace.

"He... yeah... he's the one I crashed into." I mumble, attempting to pull my face away from his hands; but he grabs my jaw gently in one of his large hands then moves my hair out my face and gently places it behind my ear like he always used to do.

"What else is he to you?" he says in his husky voice as he stares at my split lip making me feel uncomfortable.

"He... we ah... were together a few years back, it didn't work out but we stayed close friends." As soon as I see his shoulders sag I instantly feel guilty for loving someone other than Caleb.

"Together? What does that mean?" he says clearing his throat.

I look away from his sad eyes and his hands drop from my face. He leans his elbows on his knees and runs his hands through his hair, leaving it even messier than before.

"That day in the park where your face was bruised up, he do that too? How many times has he hit you Harley? How is he with *our* daughter?" he says sounding harsher.

"Caleb, Jace is very good with Willow, he has never laid a hand on her like that. If your trying to go somewhere with this then you better stop right now. No one's taking her from me, she's all I have Caleb. I need her." I say quietly.

"I'm not going to let my daughter live here while her mother lets some fucker beat on her." I gasp in shock as he spits this out.

"She's *my* daughter Caleb, you didn't want her remember? You didn't want me either. And don't *ever* threaten to take her from me. She's all I have

Caleb! I would never let anyone hurt her, ever! Don't do this Caleb, you took everything from me, you can keep Ashley and everyone else… just don't take Willow. Please don't take her from me." I'm now a sniveling mess and I cover my face with my hands not caring how pathetic I sound as I beg him. If it weren't for Willow I don't think I would have survived everything I did.

I feel warm hands covering me as I'm being lifted onto his lap. He holds me to his chest and cradles me tight. I feel his head in my neck line and hear him take a deep breath against my skin as if he's taking in my scent. I don't stop him, even though I should after everything he's done. I feel safe with him; it's as if I've never left his arms, that I belong here. It feels like home. I place my forehead on his shoulder and take his sweet smelling cologne in.

"I've always wanted you Harley, always. I'm so sorry, I know you would keep her safe. But when I saw your split lip and heard what Willow said about that guy being here, I lost it. I didn't mean for it to be harsh, I would never take her from you baby. I can tell you're a great mother, you've done a great job and I'm so proud of you. I just wish I knew why you felt you couldn't tell me? I've missed four years of her life Harley." He sounds so sad. The feeling of his warm breath against my skin as he talks makes me melt.

"You did know Caleb. You told Ashley that you didn't want us, you didn't want to be part of our lives." I whisper back, thinking about the phone call that crushed the little bit of hope I had left in Caleb.

"What?" he says pulling back from me. I move back a little, needing some distance from him but he won't let me off his lap; his arms are now wrapping around my waist holding me in place.

"I called you Caleb, a few days after the accident. I wanted to tell you but Ashley answered. She said you were busy, and then proceeded to tell me that she told me you already knew about the baby and didn't want *it*." I say looking down at his chest. I see a few lines of his tattoo sticking out the V of his shirt but I can't make out what it is.

"She knew you were pregnant from the start?" he asks in a stern voice.

"Yeah she was the first person I told, I was going to tell you that night…the night you two…" I can't even say the words. "After I moved to my father's, I tried to call you. When I did, she answered and yeah you know the rest…" I say sadly avoiding his eyes once again, but I feel his beautiful green orbs staring at me.

"I don't know why she had my phone Harlz, but I swear to you I didn't know about the baby. If I had I would have been there for you. I wouldn't of let you do this alone." I look up and I know he's telling me the truth. I can see that he's angry, obviously because of Ashley, but he also looks sad.

"I've never been alone Caleb. My parents are here for me, the boys from the club are and so is Brent." I say thinking back to the night my water broke and I'd had to call Brent.

"How did Brent even know about Willow?" he asks genuinely.

"I told him when I was a few months. I told him not to ask questions about it though and he never did. I was under a lot of stress and went into labor a week early. My parents were a few hours away and I had no one to call. I called Brent and he came, he was there when she was born and he's been so great with her." I smile.

I watch as a frown appears on his face. "I should have been there; I wish I was there... fuck!" He look up to me then asks. "And you and Brent, are you two?" he coughs, clears his throat and continues. "I mean... have you two... ah... hooked up?"

"Hook up with Brent? Me? No! I love Brent; of course I do, especially after the past few years." I watch as he winces and flexes his jaw as I say this. "...but I love him as family. Oh God no! I could never "hook up" with him." I say shaking my head looking up just in time to see his shoulders relax and a grin form on his lips.

"Not gonna lie...that's good to hear." He lets out a chuckle and this only pisses me off. I try to move off him but he holds his grip tight.

"Yeah it would fucking suck if I was sleeping with your best friend..." I say sarcastically continuing to push and shove him to let me go.

"Ah... fuck... I didn't think... Harley you need to know that was the biggest mistake of my life. Next to not trying harder to find you and make you take me back. I fucking hate Ashley, but I know I'm also to blame; I'm so sorry I cheated on you and hurt you like I did. I love you so much, I never want to hurt you the way I did back then." He says after he flips me over so he's on top of me and I can no longer struggle against him.

I don't miss the way he said he loved me, as in present tense.

"Caleb...why did you do it?" I whisper as I feel the tears spilling down the sides of my face. "Was I not good enough? Did you get bored?" I whisper even softer. He wipes away the tears with his thumbs; he's so close to me that I can feel his breath of my cheek.

"Oh baby... no... I fucked up Harley, it was all on me. You were perfect, you are perfect baby... I'm the fuck up. I had things going on and I needed to do something to get the thoughts out my head. I fucked up baby. I wasn't bored... ever. You're my soul mate. I was stupid back then, I made a bad decision that I have had to live with ever since. I'm so sorry... so sorry." He whispers as he leans his forehead against mine. He then lifts his head and stares down at the cut on my lip again.

He places his fingers near it and I watch the frown appear on his face. "He ever touches you again... I'll kill him." he says in a rough deep voice.

"Caleb no, Jace is dangerous, you need to stay away from him. Please... promise me you'll stay away from him." I look up at him; I can feel the worry etched on my face.

"Shit, you need to leave, what if he comes back? Shit, if he sees you here…I don't know what he will do. You need to go Caleb. Now." I say pushing against his chest. He shakes his head.

"You think I'm going to leave *my* girls here alone. I'm not leaving you alone, you either pack a bag and come home with me or I'm staying here to make sure he doesn't come back." He says seriously.

I hear little footsteps running down the wooden floors of my quiet apartment, before I can tell Caleb to get off me Willow comes running in.

"Mommy! Mommy can I also play?" she says running up to the bed with a big smile on her face and looking from Caleb to me. Caleb jumps up and leans against the head board. I start laughing at my little innocent girl. She tries climbing up onto my bed but can't quite make it; she definitely got her height and size from me, she's really tiny.

Caleb's deep chuckles soon join my laughs as he helps Willow onto my big bed. "There you go baby girl." He says smiling at her.

Willow comes up to my face as I lie on my back, and she plays with my hair. "Can I also tickle, Mommy? Tickle tickle." She says, tickling under my chin with her small hands. I start laughing at my cute child, listening to Caleb's chuckles as he watches us. I wrap my arms around her and bring her to my chest as she continues to giggle. I sit up next to Caleb and pull Willow to my lap. She cuddles up to my chest, and then she raises her head and wraps her arms around my neck and hugs me.

"I love you." She says with a big yawn and I swallow the tears forming in my throat.

"I love you too big girl. Come cuddle Mommy." She smiles and rests her head on my chest with her feet resting on Caleb's leg. After a few minutes of just staring at my beautiful sleeping daughter I look over to Caleb and see him staring at Willow's little foot resting on his lap. I look up to his face and notice his teary eyes.

"I want her to know me Harley." He says softly.

I give him a small smile; I've been dreaming about him saying these words to me for so long. "I want that too." He looks up to me as if my comment surprises him.

"You're fine with that?" he asks blinking away the tears.

"Yeah, I want her to have a relationship with her father, that's all I ever wanted. I don't care that we won't have one…" I look down at Willow. "I just want what's best for her. I'd do anything for her."

"You're incredible." I look up as he says this in his deep sexy voice. "You both are… she's perfect Harley. I want to be here for you guys, I want to be in your life and be there when you need me."

"I… I don't know what to say to that Caleb. I want you to be part of her life but… I don't know about us being together again. I don't think I'm ready for that, let's start slow. I know she's a very happy and playful child but I don't ever want to let her down. If you really want to be part of her life then we need to slowly ease her into it. I don't want her to feel overwhelmed. I also want to talk about other girls... I'd prefer if she wasn't around any of your girlfriends, unless you're in a serious relationship, then I guess it would be okay. I just don't want people coming in and out of her life. I want stability for her." I look from Willow to him. I know he mentioned he isn't with Ashley but that doesn't mean he doesn't have other girls. The thought hurts a little.

"I want to be part of *both* your lives Harley. There's no girlfriends. " He whispers as he leans against me to look at Willow in my arms. Willow's little hand holds onto my finger just like she did when she was a baby.

"I don't want to rush into anything Caleb..." I whisper.

He leans closer to me using his index finger to touch her little hand. Her little finger opens and I move my hand away so that Caleb's finger can replace mine. Caleb leans his chin on my shoulder as he strokes our daughter's little hand and she holds onto his finger with dear life.

Chapter 22

I hear giggling down the hall. I open my eyes slowly as I recall the night before. I remember Caleb arriving after Jace… Oh fuck Jace… he hit me. I touch my lip and flinch when I feel the little cut. I don't remember falling asleep, I don't recall getting under the covers either, but the blankets are tucked tightly around me. I stretch my legs and eventually get up to look for my little girl. I look at the clock and realize its already after ten, I need to start packing if I want to make it to my mother's anytime soon.

I walk down the passage and I smell something burning.

I start laughing when I see Caleb over the stove trying to flip pancakes; the pancake flies out of the pan and lands on the stove. Willow is sitting in the little chair by the table giggling and watching him. The little scene makes me smile and my heart clench.

"Mommy! Help him." Willow giggles as she spots me. I pick her up and give her a kiss and hug. Caleb turns to look at me and he has flour on his face and in his hair. I start laughing with Willow.

"Are you burning down my kitchen?" I laugh at him and he chuckles.

"I'm sorry Harlz, I really tried…" he says pouting. Harley jumps up in my arms, her arms opening wide for Caleb. Caleb smiles at her then me as if he's asking for permission. I smile and nod and Caleb takes her from me and I take the pan off the stove.

Caleb flips her over and acts as if he is going to bite her tummy. Willow squeals and giggles; the father/daughter moment makes my eyes water. I quickly turn my head to the stove so they don't see the tears threatening to spill over.

I make a couple pancakes before Caleb steps back into the kitchen after putting cartoons on for Willow. He sits on the counter next to where I'm cooking and eats a pancake.

He moans. "You always knew how to make the best pancakes."

I laugh. "And you always were a crappy cook."

"I like that." he says smiling at me.

"What?" I asked confused.

"You… laughing… I missed it." he looks down at the pancake in his hand. I smile and shake my head.

"You can use the shower if you like?" I say motioning to the flour in his hair.

He jumps off the table and reaches for his keys.

"Where you going?" I can't hide the fact that my voice sounds unsteady. I panicked there for a second at the thought of him already wanting to leave.

He smiles then walks up to me and lifts up my chin with one finger.

"I'm not leaving Harley. I have extra clothes in my car; I'm gonna go fetch them and come back. I'll be two minutes." He quickly runs out of the apartment and quick as a flash he's back locking the door behind him.

While Caleb is showering I get Willow ready and sit her at the counter ready to eat. Caleb comes out looking all fresh and walks over to sit next to Willow. I dish them out the pancakes and Caleb instantly reaches for the chocolate syrup; as does Willow. He smiles and I laugh. I hate chocolate syrup but Willow loves it so I buy it for her. I remember Caleb used to love that stuff too. I walk past him picking up toys and mumble. "Definitely yours..." he turns around and gives me the biggest grin.

"Love hearing that..." he says, showing me his dimples.

I hear a knock at the door and my smile immediately fades. Caleb gets up quickly and comes over to me; I don't realize I'm standing there frozen staring at the door until Caleb is right in front of me looking down at me. "I won't let him hurt you baby. Not anymore..."

"Harley? Babe? Open please. It's cold out here." I hear Brent's voice and immediately relax. Caleb however tenses, especially when Willow runs for the door yelling for "*Bent*".

"What's he doing here so early?" Caleb asks sounding angry.

Caleb moves around Willow and opens the door for Brent. Brent's eyes widen as he sees Caleb in my doorway.

"Hey dude, locking me in the closet? Not cool!" Brent says, walking past Caleb and immediately picking up a squealing Willow.

"You locked him in the closet?" I ask, gently smacking Caleb's arm. Caleb doesn't answer and I notice his eyes are fixed on Brent and Willow. I feel bad that he isn't as close to his daughter as Brent is. I put my hand in his and he immediately looks down at me. "Let's go finish breakfast." I smile and tug him along.

I dish out food for Brent. "Thanks babe." Brent says. I notice Caleb's jaw tense as he speaks through his teeth. "Dude don't call her that!" Caleb says before taking a sip of his orange juice.

"Yes I told you Bent, Mommy isn't a piggy!" Willow says wiggling her index finger at Brent as if reprimanding a child. Caleb is the first to burst out laughing.

He takes Willow from Brent, places her onto his lap and lets out a big smile.

"You are a very clever girl Willow. Don't let *Bent* ever call your mommy that. It's rude." Caleb looks up at me and winks. I look at Brent; funnily enough he too has a huge grin on his face as he watches Caleb holding his daughter on his lap while they share pancakes.

"So how long do you want me to look after her bab... uh... Harley." Brent says, looking from Caleb to me.

"Well I want to leave as soon as possible, so if you can just watch her until I get all her stuff packed. I also need to fetch some things from the pharmacy; I'll be able to do it faster if someone watches her." I say placing the dirty dishes into the dishwasher.

"Where're you two going?" Caleb asks.

"I'm going to stay with my mom for the weekend, I just need to get away for a little bit." I say wetting a cloth and walking over to Willow to wipe all the syrup from her face.

"I was thinking about that Harley, maybe I should go with you. It's a long drive and you know how easily she gets bored." Brent says, nodding in Willow's direction.

"No… not happening man." Caleb says, raising an eyebrow at Brent.

"Yeah it's okay Brent, I'll manage fine. I've got some toys and she was up late last night so she'll probably sleep the whole drive anyway." I say as I wipe down the table.

"No…not happening either. I'll take you both." Caleb says, looking down at Willow as she looks up and smiles.

"Can he? Please Mommy?" Brent and Caleb chuckle.

"Let's go play on the swings at the park so mom can get ready." Brent says. Caleb reluctantly lets Willow jump into Brent's open arms.

After they leave and I've picked up all Willow's toys, I turn to Caleb who's been watching me the entire time.

"You don't have to come with me. If you think Jace is going to come looking for me your wrong; I'm not that important to him besides… he doesn't even know where my mom lives."

"I'm going with because I want to spend more time with you and Willow; I have to go see my mother anyway. Think of it as killing two birds with one stone." He winks.

"Well you can go home and get your stuff if you like while I shower and pack our bags." I say as I walk back to my room; he just follows me.

"Sorry baby but I'm not going to leave you here alone knowing that Jace could come here any minute. I'll stay here until you're done, then we can go fetch my shit, whatever stuff you need from the pharmacy then finally we'll go fetch my baby." He smiles, lying down on my bed as if he owns the place.

I don't bother arguing with him; instead I fetch some clothes and make my way to the shower. After dressing, I walk back into an empty room. I quickly pack a bag for myself and make my way down the passage. I walk past Willow's room noticing Caleb sitting on her bed looking around her room.

I sit next to him on her tiny bed.

"You named her Willow… Why?" he says, looking down at me.

"I guess I still wanted you to have a say in it. I remembered the teddy you bought me, how you said you liked the name Willow and that we kind of both agreed. When I held her little body for the first time, I knew that was the perfect name for her. It was kinda like we picked it together... even though you weren't there." I mumble sadly.

"I love it baby; you chose the perfect name for our daughter." He says wrapping his one arm around me. Although I miss him and his embraces, I need to keep my distance. I trust Caleb fully with our daughter, I know he won't hurt her but I don't trust him with my heart. I'm not sure I can let him in just yet; even though it feels as if he never left me and that we weren't apart for all these years.

I move away from him and start packing a little bag for Willow.

After everything's packed and I've got a car seat for Willow, I lock up the apartment and make my way with Caleb to the parking. I don't look in the direction of the bar; I'll call my dad on the way, I just pray no one sees me leaving with Caleb.

Caleb walks toward a black Range Rover. "Where's your other car?" I ask him, remembering the old car that he'd saved up for because he didn't want to use his parent's money; I guess that's changed too.

"This is my new baby. The other one took its last breath a couple years ago so I decided to treat myself." He smiles at me as he tries to install the car seat.

"Fuck! Do these things come with user manuals?" he says seriously, struggling with where to put what latch. I laugh at him and push him aside.

"Here, look..." I explain what goes where and he listens intently to me.

We make our way to the pharmacy and Caleb steps out of the car with me.

"Where are you going?" I ask him.

"I'm coming with you. What do you need here anyway?" he asks coolly.

"Err... no... stay in the car, I'll be quick." I say as I open his door, motioning for him to climb back in.

"I'm coming in... let's go." He clasps my hand in his and pulls me towards the pharmacy.

I walk up to the counter and ask the lady for my pills. She hands me them but before I can turn Caleb snatches it from my hand. He looks at them and looks back at me raising an eyebrow. I know he's angry because he always works his jaw when he is; well he used to anyway.

I snatch it back and walk to the counter to pay.

Chapter 23

He drives into a gated community; the houses are mansions with sports cars in driveways and perfectly cut lawns.

"Where we going?" I ask, looking around at the beautiful houses.

"Home." He states.

I presume he's talking about his home. We stop in a driveway of a beautiful two story beach house; the beach lies to the front of the house. I follow him into the house; it's absolutely stunning, nothing like the apartment we planned on living in together all those years ago. The house doesn't seem very homely though, it's rather manly and it doesn't have that warm feel to it.

I watch as he walks up the stairs, I'm unsure of what to do so I just follow him. He leads me to a large bedroom, the bed is massive and the entire right side of his room is one massive window looking out onto the ocean. I walk up, place my hand to the glass and look out at the beautiful view.

"Wow... this is beautiful!" I whisper, now feeling embarrassed after having Caleb in my home. His house is so elegant, I don't feel like I belong here.

"I knew you'd like the view..." I hear him mumble. I turn around to see Caleb packing a bag; he closes it then stands next to me looking out.

"Why're you on the pill?" he spits out. I knew he'd react this way; that's why I didn't want him to go into the pharmacy with me.

"Why are you asking me that? You know what the pill is for; do you really need me to explain?" I walk away from him and sit on the side of his bed.

"Is it because of Jace? Are you fucking him?" he says with so much disgust laced in his words.

I would expect this from someone like Jace but Caleb has never spoken to me this way- ever.

"What? No! We aren't together anymore. I told you that Caleb."

He walks up to me. "Did you fuck him? Are you still fucking him? Is that why you're taking the pill?"

"Caleb stop this!" I yell as I get up and move around him, but he grabs me and pulls me to his bed underneath him. As his body crashes into mine, the air is smacked out my lungs.

"Just answer me!" he yells. I try and push against his chest; I've never seen Caleb like this before and it frightens me.

"I didn't Caleb... I didn't f... fuck him... stop... please... just get off me..." I say bursting into tears.

He immediately jumps off me and I curl up into a ball and cover my face as I cry. Caleb pulls me onto his lap so that I'm now straddling him.

"I'm sorry baby... I'm so sorry. I didn't mean to scare you, you know how jealous I get and when I saw the pills I just presumed." He whispers against my neck.

"Stop presuming Caleb! I haven't asked you who you've fucked and I'm guessing it's a whole lot more than me. You were single and had only been with one, *oh no I forgot...* two people. I didn't fucking ask you though! Did I?" I shout at him through the tears.

"No baby you didn't" He says sadly. "Harley, I've only ever been with two people. One of them I wish I could take back, the other was the love of my life; the best sex I've ever had was with her." I look at him and wipe my tears away confused.

"Bullshit." I say through snivels.

"It's the truth baby; I couldn't ever look at another girl the way I looked at you. I kept busy with... other stuff. I'm not going to lie to you babe, I have done other things with girls but I never fucked them... ever." he moves my hair out of my face.

I'm not sure whether to believe him or not. Deep down if I'm honest with myself, I admit that the thought of him not sleeping with any other girls makes me a little happy inside but that's if he's even telling the truth; I would never admit it out loud.

"Whatever Caleb, we don't have time for this, can we just go please." I say, pushing his chest gently and avoiding his eyes.

"I'm not going anywhere until you've done being angry with me baby." He doesn't let go but brings his head to my chest.

"I'm not angry Caleb, okay!" I let out a deep breath; I know struggling is not going to get him to release me so I rest my chin on his head. "Can we please go and get Willow?" I say softly.

He looks up at me and his eyes immediately go to my lips, he looks down my neck line then he stares at my boobs.

I push him, letting out a chuckle. "Caleb! Stop that."

"Sorry baby, I've just... missed you... every inch of you." His eyes now find mine again and they're filled with lust. I push him again and he releases me. *I can't get too close to him... I won't let him in just to break me again...*

I walk up to his bag that sits on the bed and zip it up completely. "You ready? Let's go!" I say. He jumps up and takes the bag from me.

Stopping by the park, I'm just about to get out the car when Caleb's hand stops me. He's staring into the park, I follow his gaze to see Brent pushing Willow on a swing; Willow is laughing and looks so happy. Looking back at Caleb, he looks nervous and sad.

"She ever ask about her father? Do you think she thinks Brent is her daddy?" he says this sadly, not looking at me. I feel so sorry for him because he thinks Brent has replaced him; I guess in a way he did, but Brent is more of a friend to Willow. On the other hand when Willow is with Hunter or Jace it's different. She seems to have a bond with them that's completely different to the connection she has with Brent. Brent is always about playing and fun, when Hunter or Jace come into the picture she always asks them to tuck her in or feed her. Things a parent would do. I'm not sure how Caleb will react when he eventually sees that.

"No… she's never asked about her father. I've seen her a couple times looking at other kids when they're with their daddy's but she's never openly asked me. I guess it's because she has so many male figures in her life, the fact that she didn't have a father hasn't ever crossed her mind." I say while looking out of the window at my little girl.

"She did have a father though… she does have a father." He says flatly.

"Yeah she does now…" I mumble.

We make our way over to Brent and Willow runs into my open arms. "Hey sweetie, you have fun?"

"Yeah Mommy we did." She turns to Caleb with open arms, his grin only widens as he takes his daughter from me; I smile at the scene.

We say our goodbyes to Brent and make our way to the car. I show Caleb how to put her in her car seat and we take off.

As suspected Willow sleeps most of the way and every now and then I catch Caleb stealing glances at his daughter in the back seat through the rearview mirror, I also catch him looking at me a couple times from the corner of my eye; I would be lying if I said I wasn't doing the same to him. We make small talk most of the way and stop a couple of times too.

We're half an hour away and Willow is wide awake looking out the window singing quietly to herself clutching the teddy bear Brent gave her to her chest. I'm listening to the news on the radio when Caleb speaks.

"You hungry, Willow?" Caleb says looking in the rearview mirror at her. She smiles and pats her tummy. "Yes, are you hungry Caleb?" she replies happily.

Caleb chuckles and shakes his head. "You wanna stop and get something to eat? There's a burger place nearby?" He asks me. Even though I want to get home so I don't have to deal with the good looking boy next to me, my adorable daughter begging me from the back seat convinces me otherwise. We don't eat much take out and it's usually a rare occasion that we do because I just don't have the money for it. I did however transfer extra money to my account for this trip but I don't want to overspend and regret it next week.

Caleb helps Willow out of her car seat once we reach our destination. We order our food and Caleb refuses to let me pay. I take Willow with me to the bathroom, picking her up onto the toilet. I laugh at how short she is, her feet don't touch the floor by a lot. I'm so thankful she's fully potty trained now, those days were so hard because she is just as stubborn as her father. She does have a few nights when she'll wet her bed but it hasn't been happening as often as it used to.

Walking out to find Caleb, I notice he's picked a table near the kiddies play room. He hands Willow her little kiddie's meal box and she immediately pulls out the toy. It's a little motor bike with some cartoon on it. I place her food neatly in front of her and watch her play with her toy, obviously more interested in it than her food.

"Look Mommy…just like Hunt Hunt's and Jacey's. Ooh and Grandpa's too!" she says enthusiastically, making bike noises as she moves the toy along the table as if riding it. I'm not surprised she picked this toy, she can be the most girly little girl one moment and the next she can be such a little Tom Boy.

"Hunt Hunt?" Caleb says looking at me but Willow answers.

"He's the best! He reads me stories before bed and tucks me in just like Jacey does. Hunt Hunt always takes me for ice-cream too and he bought me a bike but I can't ride it yet, my feet don't touch the ground. Hunt Hunt says it's okay though because when I'm bigger he'll show me how to ride it." she rambles on in an excited mess. Even though Caleb is smiling from ear to ear, I can see his hand holding tightly onto his leg just above his knee cap and his knuckles turning white with tension. I can already tell he's upset about Hunter and Jace spending so much time with *his* daughter.

"Eat up Willow, don't want your food to get cold." I say to her, attempting to change the conversation.

"Mommy?" she says after taking a big sip of her milkshake.

"Yeah baby?"

"I miss Hunt Hunt… when is he staying over again?" she says innocently. I know that Caleb's coughing means he's overthinking Willows statement.

Finally Caleb catches his breath and gives me a glare as if to say… *We will talk about this later….*

"He's away for work sweetie, how about I call him later and you can talk to him? Is that okay baby?" I say tucking a few loose strands behind her ear.

She smiles, nods then eats her food. After she's eaten she asks to go play in the kids room.

Sitting alone with Caleb is awkward, its quiet and I know he wants to say something and its killing me that he's not saying it.

"What's wrong Caleb?" I say with a deep sigh as I sit back in the chair.

"You know what's wrong Harley." He says seriously. "How can you let guys stay over while your daughter is sleeping down the hall?"

"What? Hunter rarely stays over, he's her Godfather and one of my best friends; he is really great with her. Don't turn this into something that it's not Caleb. He's just a good friend." I say digging into my bag looking for my phone that's now ringing.

I answer the phone as I read my father's name on the screen.

"Hey Daddy." I answer, avoiding Caleb's eyes.

"Hey Hun, where are you guys? Jace says he came there earlier and you weren't at the apartment?" he says sounding concerned.

"Yeah Daddy, Willow and I are going to stay with Momma for a little bit. I know you don't like the idea but I'm already on my way. It was kind of last minute, I was going to call you when I got there." I say hoping he doesn't get mad.

He's quiet for a second or two then he replies and I let out a sigh of relief that he's not mad. "Okay baby girl. You know how I feel about you two staying there, but if you want to spend time with your momma then I can't argue with that. Give my grandbaby a hug and kiss from me."

"Okay will do Daddy, love you." After ending the call I finally look up to Caleb.

"I don't want him teaching her to ride anything, I want to do that. I've missed out on four years already, I'm not going to miss anything else." He says, looking into my eyes directly. I feel guilty under those piercing green eyes.

"Okay Caleb." I say looking back to see where Willow is in the little jungle gym. She's playing with another little girl.

Turning back to Caleb I'm about to ask him if he's ready to leave but I'm interrupted.

"Hi, Sorry is that little girl yours?" I turn to see an older lady with long straight blond hair pointing to where Willow is.

"Hi, yeah she is." I say smiling at her. I can't help notice how this woman is looking at Caleb, licking her lips as if she hasn't even noticed me sitting right there.

"She is definitely your child, she looks just like her daddy… absolutely gorgeous, I just had to tell you." She says this to him. This makes him smile wider.

"Yeah she does look like me doesn't she?" he mumbles to himself. The lady smiles and continues to stand there.

"That's very sweet of you. Thanks." I say smiling; ignoring the fact that she is totally ogling Caleb right now.

After she finally says her goodbyes I pick up all the empty food containers and throw them in the bin. "She does look like me doesn't she?" Caleb repeats, smiling in Willow's direction.

"Yeah, it's pretty scary actually. She has your hair and eyes and sometimes when she laughs she looks a lot like you." I say smiling as I think about it.

"Never knew I would love someone so much after only spending a day with them. I love her so much Harley and she doesn't even know who I am to her…." He says quietly.

"I felt the exact same way the first time I held her in my arms. She already likes you Caleb and after you spend time with her and she gets used to you, she will love you too." I say looking back to him.

"Yeah… now that I know about her I just… I can't picture my life without her." he looks up to me sadly.

"Yeah… don't know what I would have done without her." I say softly giving him a sad smile.

The mood seems a lot less tense between Caleb and I as we drive the rest of the way to my mother's trailer. When we arrive, Caleb helps Willow out of her seat and grabs our bags.

"That's okay Caleb; I can carry in the bags. I don't think it's a good idea for my momma to see you." I say softly, only loud enough for him to hear.

"I'm taking your bags in, don't argue with me Harley." He says pushing past me.

"Granny!" Willow yells as my mother steps down the stairs. She looks up, her smile immediately faltering as she spots Caleb. She picks up Willow, spins her around then bends down and tells Willow to go and play with the toys that are in her room.

I knew this was going to happen…

As soon as Willow disappears inside the trailer my mother blurts out, "What is *he* doing here?"

"Mom-" I try to calm her down but Caleb interrupts me.

"Roxanne, I know you hate me and judging by your reaction when you saw me I know you know the story about what I did to Harley. You can't hate me more than I hate myself for what I did and there is no excuse for it. I didn't know about Willow until yesterday, Ashley never told me anything about it and I swear to you if I had known I would have fought harder for Harley to take me back. I gave up after a few months because she didn't want anything to do with me and I thought that it would be best for her. If I had known about Willow, I would have tried so much harder and I would have been in her life. She's *my* daughter too Roxanne and I want to be there for her. I've already missed four years of her life and I have no intentions on missing more." Caleb says sincerely to my mother.

My mother looks awestruck. She seems utterly speechless as if she's trying to find the words. She then does something I never expected;

She hugs him.

"I'm so sorry Caleb…. You know I was a terrible mother, but even as shitty as I was I couldn't bear not having Harley with me. Even though I wasn't around much, I dreaded every single time her father took her away from me. To find out that you have a child who's already four years old must be horrible. You've missed out on so much Caleb. I'm still upset about the whole Ashley situation but I could never hate you. You were so good to my Harley before all that happened and I never got to thank you for looking after her when I couldn't. I know you will be a great father my boy but you better treat my babies right! I do have to say though that you two made one gorgeous little girl; I can't wait for the day that you have to fight boys, just like you, to stay away from her." My mom says happily.

Now I'm the shocked one. I didn't expect all of that to come from her mouth, I especially didn't expect her to apologize to him and thank him for looking after me. That boy always had a way with women. I roll my eyes at their exchange.

Caleb chuckles. "There won't be any boys around Willow, especially no boys like me." They both laugh but I know Caleb is serious.

"Momma, Willow doesn't know who Caleb is yet. I'd like to keep it that way, just until I can figure out how I'm going to tell her." I say walking up the steps.

"Of course baby, anything you two decide. You staying over too Caleb?" My mother asks.

"No." I blurt out at the exactly the same time Caleb says, "Thanks…" he looks at me then gives me a naughty grin.

"Thanks Roxanne I would love that." He smirks at me as I glare back.

"Mom, where exactly is he going to sleep?" I say placing my hand on my hip with a raised brow.

"Don't be silly Harley, Willow can sleep by me and you two can stay in your old room. Don't act like you haven't shared a bed before. I know all about Caleb sneaking into your room when you two were younger." She walks right past me into the house calling out for Willow.

I look back to Caleb and find him laughing. "This is not happening… Your parents don't live far, I thought you came down to see them?" he immediately stops laughing.

"I'll see them later or tomorrow, I'd rather prefer to stay close to you and Willow. I want to spend as much time with her as I can. I'll sleep on the couch if I have to." His dimples are showing again.

I let out a deep sigh, walking right past him as he follows me. He places our bags on my bed then stands and looks around my room.

"It's still the same…" he says looking back at me.

"Yeah when I moved out I didn't take anything besides some clothes." I walk past him, blocking out the memory.

Chapter 24

My mother informs me while I'm bathing Willow that she's been unable to get someone to cover her shifts. I think it's just her attempt to get me and Caleb to spend time with Willow alone; as if playing house could solve all our problems. She leaves shortly afterwards.

I dress Willow in warm pajamas and she skips out my mother's room in search of Caleb. It's already dark outside and the weather has turned rather cold.

I walk out into the lounge to see Willow sitting in Caleb's lap facing him. She plays with his hair and he's smiling at her.

"We have the same hair." She says leaning her forehead against his.

Caleb smiles and says, "We sure do…"

I leave them chatting as I quickly take a shower. When I come back they are still sitting in the same position chatting away. I sit on the sofa opposite them as Willow tells him about how much she loves cartoons and which are her favorite. Much to Willow's surprise, Caleb loves cartoons too, he always has. After a few hours of watching cartoons, Willow is cuddled up to Caleb's chest fast asleep. I take my phone out and snap a picture because the moment is too special not too. Caleb doesn't even hear the sound my phone makes because he's so focused on the sleeping daughter he has in his arms. I get off the couch and walk towards them to see Willow holding onto his finger like she always does with me.

"I think I should take her to bed." I whisper.

He finally looks up and asks full of hope. "Can I? I'd really like to tuck her in."

"Sure." I smile.

He gently picks her up and follows me to my mother's room. I open the blanket and Caleb puts her down in the center of the bed. He pulls the blanket over her, I give her a kiss on her cheek and tell her I love her. She's fast asleep but I still tell her.

Caleb gives her a kiss on her forehead and I'm pretty sure he whispered, "Love you too baby girl." But it was too soft to tell for certain.

We leave Willow and I get out extra blankets and a pillow for him and place it on the sofa.

I fall asleep as soon as my head hits the pillow. After a few hours of dead sleep I'm awoken as I feel the bed behind me dip.

"What are you doing Caleb?" I whisper as I turn to look at him.

"That couch is fucking uncomfortable. I'll try to keep my hands to myself baby, don't stress." He says, getting comfortable in my bed.

He always used that as an excuse when he would stay over and sneak into my bed.

I lie on my back, looking up at the ceiling unable to fall asleep now that he's here lying next to me. It brings back so many memories.

"I missed this …" he says tenderly. I can feel his eyes on me.

I don't know what to say to that because I've missed it too. So I follow that up with, "Yeah…" Even if we aren't exactly touching… I enjoy his presence.

The silence in the room is killing me though.

"How's football going?" I ask knowing he got his scholarship because of how good he is at football.

"It's great… don't get around to playing with the guys that much nowadays but it's the one thing I'm good at… so I know I can't fuck that up." He says bluntly.

"And college? You graduate already?"

"Yeah last year; workload was crazy especially with football. What about you?"

okay I guess. I also graduated and now I manage my parents bar and Anna's Tattoo parlor; I enjoy it so I guess that's all that matters. Are you working for your dad now?" I ask, knowing he studied architecture to join a well-known Architecture firm owned by his parents.

"No definitely not my father's, but my mother's firm yeah…" He says.

"Oh, do they have different firms now? Since when?" I lean on my side waiting for his response.

"Since they got divorced." he says, leaving me in total shock. His parents seemed like the most loving couple I'd ever met. They were so kind to me and they loved me like their daughter.

"Oh gosh Caleb, I'm so sorry." I say resting my hand on his forearm.

He looks down at my hand, I see his lips twitch as if he's about to smile but he doesn't as he says. "Don't be, I'm not. The fucker cheated on my mother so she divorced his cheating ass." He spits it out with such disgust.

"How did she find out? Was it going on for long?"

"When I caught him fucking the tramp in his office; it was the same night as our graduation party. He said it was just the once but I don't believe one word out of his mouth." As much as I'm shocked and feel sorry for him, I can't believe how hypocritical he is.

"Like father, like son!" I blurt out before I can stop myself. His head whips around in shock.

"I'm nothing like him." he spits out harshly.

"You're not? Did I *not* catch you with Ashley? Yeah, I was lucky enough not to walk in but I heard everything and you're telling me you're nothing like him? Right…." I say this and watch as his face falls.

It's quiet for a few minutes, I can't even look at him any longer so I turn around. I feel the tears falling down the bridge of my nose until they reach the pillow; I didn't even realize I was crying. I don't want him to see me cry so I quickly make my way to the bathroom after peeking into my mother's room to make sure Willow's still asleep; she is.

Closing the door behind me, I turn the sink tap on to hide my sobs. Needing fresh air so I can catch my breath, I slide the window open and sit down leaning against the door because the door lock doesn't work.

I pull my knees up to my chest , fold my arms over my knees and rest my head in my arms as I attempt to hide my cries. There's a slight knock on the door. I quickly wipe away my tears and try to calm my breathing.

"Baby let me in… please." He pauses for a few seconds waiting for me to respond but I'm still trying to calm my breathing.

"You okay Harlz?" He says softly. I can tell he's bending down on the other side of the thin door. I hear him so clearly and he sounds close.

"Yeah, I'm good… just go back to bed." I say trying to sound normal, but it just comes out as a gruff mumble.

"Oh Harlz…" he definitely knows I've been crying now, him seeing how much he still affects me makes me weep harder. I try to cover my face and calm my breathing but I can't soften my snuffles.

I look up when I hear a noise coming from outside the window just in time to see Caleb jumping in.

He bends down in front of me and raises his hand to touch my face but I turn away from him to cover it.

"Please… please… don't look at me… just go away Caleb… go away." I cry.

He roughly pulls me to his chest and sits me on his lap so that my legs are on either side of him as he leans against the bath tub.

"I'm not going away Harley, I'm not going to let you leave either. I need you and I need… this." He tightens his arms around my waist. "I need you in my arms and with me. I can't let you go again, I can't…" he says softly in a coarse voice.

"How can I ever trust you again? How could you do that to me? I loved you so much…so fucking much Caleb! I never looked at any other guy or even thought about anyone besides you and you just threw that all away…" I cry into his neck; I realize my arms are wrapped tightly around his neck but I can't seem to let go and I'm not sure whether I want to.

"I'm so sorry baby… I didn't want anyone other than you, that night I was pissed and my head was so fucked up after seeing my dad. I just fucking lost it. I waited for you in one of the rooms but Ashley came in. I just needed to do something to clear my head and just stop thinking…I hate what I did Harlz. I don't even know why I thought it was a good idea, but for the five minutes it lasted all I could think about was how perfect you were, that I was doing the same thing to you that my father was doing to my mother. I fucked up I know! I love you so much Harley, I don't know how I'm ever going to make it up to you but I will, I promise you I will." His voice is muffled against my neck line and I can feel his body shaking underneath me; he's crying and it breaks my heart. I'm still stuck on him saying he loves me...present tense. The sorrow he projected as he spoke was too real. I've never seen someone look so regretful and it only makes me feel remorseful. Even when I thought he didn't want his child, I should have tried harder and maybe things would have been different. He's lost four years of his daughter's life because I was too afraid and stubborn to confront him face to face.

I loosen my grip and pull away from him. His head rises and his hand moves from my waist to wipe his tears but I stop him and he lets me. Looking down at his tear streaked face, I wipe his tears away from his eyes as he closes them and rests his head in my small hands almost as if he's content. I pull the messy hair out of his face and bed down to kiss her forehead.

"I'm sorry too Caleb." I whisper.

He seems shocked because he's looking up at me confused. I suddenly notice how close we are and I get butterflies in my stomach as I try to avoid looking at his lips.

"I was so scared to confront you about what Ashley said. I was afraid that what she said was true and I couldn't bear to hear it come out of your mouth. I wish I'd tried harder, I'm so sorry I didn't. I can't imagine missing one single day of Willow's life and you missed... so much time." I say finally looking down at his glossy green eyes.

"Baby, come here." He pulls my head so I'm nuzzling his neck. He runs his hands up and down my back just like he used to do. "I think we should start fresh, it's the only way to move forward and I want to move forward... with you and Willow. I don't want us to waste our time fighting over things that happened in the past. You're here, I'm here and our baby girl is here, let's just focus on us for now." I lift my head and he cups my cheeks with his big warm hands, he raises his eyebrows. "Okay?"

The thought of starting fresh sounds really good, even though I know there's too much shit in our pasts to just forget. A fresh start with Caleb at this moment sounds pretty darn good right now.

I give him a small smile and he returns it with an even bigger grin.

"Okay." I whisper.

After checking on Willow and climbing into bed, Caleb honors his promise and keeps his hands to himself and gives me some space.

Deep, deep down inside I'm a little disappointed because I miss his touch already.

I wake up in the morning to Willow's giggling once again; it brings a smile to my face. Looking at my bedside clock I see it's already ten. Willow sounds close by so I turn and watch her as she stands on Caleb's side of the bed and uses a piece of her long hair to tickle Caleb's nose; every now and then he scratches it in his sleepy state.

I totally forgot to close our door last night; I don't want her seeing me in bed with guys even if we are just sleeping. I always make sure to close the door when Jace occasionally sleeps beside me, making sure he was out of my bed before she got up.

I smile at her and she whispers. "Morning Mommy, look." She shows me what she's doing as Caleb scrunches up his nose as if that will help with the ticklish spot. Willow bursts out in giggles again clutching her tummy. She tip toes over to my side of the bed and I help her up, I turn my back to Caleb to cuddle her. I wrap my arms around her and whisper. "You sleep okay sweetie?"

She takes my hand, plays with my fingers and mumbles an *Mmhhmm*. She lets out a big yawn; as soon as she wraps her little hand around my finger I know she's going to fall asleep soon.

"I love you baby, go back to sleep." I whisper and kiss her forehead.

"Love you too Mommy." She whispers.

After a few minutes of watching Willow fall asleep in my arms I feel Caleb stir behind me. He moves closer behind me, moves my hair and then I feel his warm breath against the back of my neck. I feel him attempt to wrap his arms around me but he immediately freezes when he feels willow's little legs hanging over mine. I turn my head a little and he lifts his to look down at me. He smiles when he spots Willow sleeping cuddled up to me.

He whispers to me, "I'll be right back…" then quickly sneaks out of the bed and tiptoes to his jeans that are hanging on my chair. I watch as he takes his phone out and climbs back in bed.

"What are you doing?" I whisper confused.

"I need a photo of this." he says, lifting his camera taking a photo of Willow. Looking back at Willow, I smile as she stirs but doesn't wake; instead she cuddles closer to me. I hear the sound of his camera go off a couple times then I hear him place it on the bedside table.

Willow stirs in my arms again as Caleb rests his chin on my arm looking down at her. He leans down and places his hand over mine, the same one that holds onto Willow's as she holds my finger tight.

"She held my hand like that too." He whispers running his thumb over my hand gently.

"Yeah she always does that when she sleeps, even when she was a baby." I whisper and he smiles.

Willow's eyes start to open and she wiggles around; when she sees Caleb she giggles and Caleb laughs.

"You so funny Caleb…" she says. I laugh at Caleb's confused expression. I explain to him how Willow was tickling his face and what he was doing.

"Is that so missy?"

Willow sits up stretching and smiling. Caleb grabs her and she squeals as he starts tickling her. I leave them playing in the room as I quickly get dressed and make sure my mom made it home last night. After I make breakfast I walk back to find Caleb and Willow.

Caleb leaves for the rest of the day because he had some things to do. Willow and I spend the day playing in the garden while my mother slept, then Willow spent time with her granny while I went to the shops to get groceries for dinner. Caleb made it back for dinner, making sure he was there to watch cartoons with Willow and tuck her into bed that night. He didn't even bother setting up a bed on the couch; instead he climbed in bed with me straight away. My mother hasn't asked any questions but she has been passing smiles our way.

The next morning I wake up alone; I can hear Caleb and Willow chatting in the kitchen. I quickly shower and get ready for the day ahead. Walking into the kitchen I make myself some cereal then notice the house is too quiet. They're not in my room or in the house and I start to panic. Running outside, I hunch over and rest my hands on my knees trying to catch my breath. Willow and Caleb are playing with a ball outside.

Willow comes running up to me when she sees me. "What's wrong Mommy?" I pick her up and squeeze her tight.

I feel Caleb come up behind me. "You okay Harlz?" he asks concerned, placing his hands under my hair on the back of my neck.

I put Willow down and she runs off kicking a ball in the small back yard.

"I just panicked, couldn't find you guys, I thought..." I stutter running my hands through my hair.

"You thought I took her from you? I'm sorry... I didn't even think about that." he says giving me a hug.

"It's okay. You're her father, I need to trust that you will watch her; I just need to calm down." I say trying to brush it off.

I look over to Willow and notice she's no longer in pajamas but a cute little yellow dress with pink flats. "You dressed her?"

He smiles at me. "Yeah, she basically did it herself but I put her socks and shoes on. Hope you don't mind, it was good feeling needed."

"Thanks Caleb, of course it's okay." I smile to myself.

"So what have you got planned for today?" he asks me, sitting down on the step as he keeps an eye on Willow kicking around the ball.

"Well, this morning while Momma sleeps I wanna take Willow to the beach. She's never been and it's a bright sunny day today. Don't you have to go see your mom or something?" I ask him as I plant my ass on the step next to him.

"She's never been to the beach?" he asks ignoring my question; I shake my head.

"Well that's what we're going to do then! We can go over to my mom's place this afternoon." He says looking at Willow as she kicks the plastic ball around and giggles.

"We?" I ask.

"Yeah we, she bit my head off after I told her what I did to you. She misses you Harley, you were like a daughter to her you know." he says looking at me sadly.

"I miss your mom too." I admit.

Chapter 25

We pack a small lunch and spend most of the day at the beach. When Caleb takes off his shirt I nearly faint on the spot; not because his body has changed so much over the years or that he is so much more irresistible now. No, it's because of the ink that is displayed on his chest. There resting over his heart is a tattoo of a Harley, looking beautiful and shiny. Perfect.

Caleb doesn't even have to explain and I can't stop myself from reaching out to graze my hand over the ink on his pec. Willow watches the exchange quietly, not saying a word. He catches my hand and brings it up to his mouth, kissing it softly. Willow pats my leg and I look down at her and smile. She smiles at me then places a hand by her mouth as if she has a secret to tell. I bend down to her level and she puts her hand by my ear, whispering all too loudly. "I think Caleb likes you Mommy." I start laughing, unsure how a four year old can tell this about a person.

Caleb taps her shoulder, bends down to her level and moves his hands as if he's about to tell her a secret. Willow obliges and moves closer smiling wildly at him. He whispers, "I think you're right." Willow claps her hands and beams.

Willow is so fascinated with the sand and sea. At first she didn't like the feeling of the sand between her toes and kept saying it was "icky" but she soon got used to it.

Caleb has played so well with her and when she wanted to go into the ocean, he held onto her tightly and walked a little until it touched her feet. He's built sandcastles with her and I've taken a ton of photos of them together because this day is so special. Willow is getting along so well with him, it's even made me a little jealous when she keeps reaching out to him instead of me like she usually does. In the back of my mind I keep wondering if somehow she knows he's her father; I know the time is coming for me to tell her who he is.

She sits between me and Caleb as we all chat about how beautiful the sea looks today. Willow stops talking, so I look down at her to see why. She sits quietly watching another little girl calling her daddy; the girl's father comes up to her, picks her up then swings her around in the air as the little girl giggles. I look to Caleb who is also studying Willow. My little girl looks so sad. She must sense we're both looking at her because she looks up to me and climbs onto my lap; placing her hands onto my shoulders looking into my eyes.

"I want one…" she says softly.

"What do you want sweetie?" I asked her, but she returns to her seat in the middle of us in the sand, continuing to watch the little girl play with her father.

"I want a daddy. Why don't I have one Mommy?" she looks up to me with sad eyes and my heart hurts. I look at Caleb and see the question in his eyes so I smile and he nods.

I push the few stray pieces of hair that's fallen from her pigtails behind her ear.

"You already have a daddy baby girl." Caleb says next to me. Willow snaps her head around and smiles at me.

"Mommy, do I have one? Really?" She smiles, clapping her hands together in excitement.

"Yeah baby you most certainly do! Ask Caleb who he is?" I wink at Caleb and he mouths a thank you. She turns around so she's facing us as she waits in anticipation for Caleb to speak. Caleb moves closer to me and clasps his hands with mine.

"I'm your daddy Willow..." he tries to say more but Willow jumps up and almost tackles him. He starts chuckling and holds her tight; she kisses him on the cheek and looks into his eyes.

"I love you Daddy." Then she hugs him again tightly.

I wiped away the tears as Caleb grabs my hand again, lifting it to his mouth before kissing it; only then do I realize he has tears in his eyes too.

"I love you more than you know Willow." He says smiling at Willow who has the biggest smile on her face.

"Can we go swim again Daddy?" she asks as she stands up bouncing excitedly. Caleb smiles and nods then he turns to me.

"I will never get over that. I love being called Daddy. Love it!"

He smiles at his daughter then picks up Willow and throws her in the air, catching her as she giggles. I watch him walk into the water with her in his arms. I smile at how happy she looks and I feel my heart slowly starting to heal.

The beach is packed with locals; I don't know most of them but I recognize a few who were a few years younger and that went to the same high school. I sit under the umbrella watching my little girl and her daddy play in the water, Caleb keeping her tight against his chest. The beautiful moment is shattered when a football flies through the air into the sand right in front of me spraying sand all over my lap. I move my legs just in time but the fright I just got has my heart beating rapidly.

"Harlz is that you?"

I look up when I hear a familiar voice. I turn to look as a boy runs up to me then freezes when he catches my eyes.

There's another voice behind me. "Joey...you totally threw the ball at that babe on purpose."

I look up to see Josh.

"Holy shit it is you!" Joey says, pulling me up from the ground for a hug.

"How are you guys? I haven't seen you in ages, you both look so old and... mature." I say giving Josh a hug, then looking them over; they've both grown into gorgeous young men.

"We're great, haven't seen you in what? Over four years? My brother is a fucking asshole, can't believe the shit he did to you babe. Don't worry, we sure gave him shit about it, so did our parents. You were way too good for him anyway." Joey says. I can't help but notice his voice breaking at the mention of his parents.

"I swear if I wasn't stuck in high school, I would've come after you. I had the biggest fucking crush on you." Josh admits, making me laugh when Joey playfully pushes him.

"Stop flirting with her dude, I'm right here and if I remember correctly you weren't the only one with a crush." Joey blushes.

"What are you guys doing here?" I say trying to change the topic.

"We're just visiting mom for the weekend, you should come for dinner. You don't know how much she missed you after you did that disappearing act. " Josh says.

"Where were you by the way? We all tried to call you, even Connor had his stuck up nose pulled out of joint worrying about where you were. Caleb wasn't himself babe; we thought maybe bringing you home might sort him out but yeah..." Joey says interrupting his brother.

"I'm sorry you guys were so worried about me. Thing was, I didn't have a phone for a few days and when I got my number transferred I didn't really wanna answer my phone. I was humiliated and going through so much. As for the dinner, Caleb's already asked me to go with him to your mother's house." I smile at their confused expressions when I mention Caleb.

"Caleb?" Joey asks with raised eyebrows.

"What do you mean Caleb? You guys back together?" Josh asks with an angry edge to his voice.

"We're not together no, but he did come down with me." I look past them into the water where Caleb is and smile.

Their eyes follow mine and I watch them both frown.

"He's really here? Haven't seen that tool in a couple months..." Joey mumbles to my left.

"Whose kid is that?" Josh asks looking at me; I watch as his eyes widen then he turns back to look at the water and realization hits.

"Wait... she looks just like..." Josh says looking back and forth between Willow and I.

"You have a daughter? She's Caleb's right?" Joey asks in disbelief.

I bend as Josh smacks Joey over the head. "Can't you see the resemblance dumbass? She looks just like Caleb, us too since the Carter features are so damn prominent." Josh says. He's right, the Carter boy's features are all very similar. They all have their mother's looks. Connor the oldest brother has more of his father's face, but all of the boys have their father's height. These boys are a tall bunch.

The two are still arguing over my head not realizing Willow and Caleb are already out the water and on their way towards us. Caleb looks at his younger twin brothers and shakes his head smiling.

"You two never stop bickering; you're like two old women I swear!" Caleb says laughing, handing Willow over to me as she opens her arms.

The twins immediately pause, their eyes travelling over Willow as she shyly hides her head in my neck.

"Who are they?" she asks into my neck.

She looks at me then looks between the twins and Caleb. "Since when are you shy sweetie?" I giggle. "These are your uncle's." The smile is back on her face as she looks over at Caleb happily.

"Wow Mommy! I have so many uncle's." she giggles.

"Are you my uncle too?" She looks at Josh and he immediately picks her up and holds her.

"Can you name them for me?" he says in a softer voice; one that's completely opposite to his usual rowdy one.

"Uncle Hunt Hunt, Uncle Bent, Uncle Jesse and Uncle Jacey but I thought Jacey was my dad-" she rambles. Caleb's deep voice interrupts her.

"No Willow, Jace is not your daddy, I am." Caleb says possessively.

"I didn't know you had brothers?" Joey asks, looking confused.

"I don't; the boys are my friends, they've been in my life since before she was born. They're her uncles even if they aren't blood. You know?" I say looking at Willow as she touches Josh's face; he smiles and tries to catch her fingers in his mouth making her squeal.

"She's too darn cute Harlz." Josh mutters as he continues to act as if he's going to bite Willow's fingers.

"You may have many uncles sweetie pie but Uncle Joey and I *are* your blood. We are family and if you ever need something we will be there; always." Josh says sweetly before handing her over to Joey.

Joey smiles at her, but Willow looks confused as she whips her head around to look at Josh.

"You look like him and my daddy." She says to Joey, reaching for his black messy hair making him laugh.

"Uncle Josh is my twin cutie and your daddy is our brother. You look a lot like us too you know. Your mommy is gonna have a hard time when you grow older. The boys are going to drive your daddy mad." Joey chuckles to himself.

"It's getting late guys, how about we head over to Mom's house?" Caleb asks his brothers and I. I smile and nod. The boys ask to ride with us and

Caleb agrees.

I jump into the backseat with Willow and let Joey sit in the front with Caleb. Josh sits next to me, wrapping his arm around me. I watch Caleb glaring at his brother in the rearview mirror making both of us laugh.

Willow falls asleep as soon as she gets comfortable in her car seat.

Josh whispers in my ear. "Willow is amazing Harlz." He smiles at me and winks. I laugh knowing exactly what game he's trying to play.

I whisper in his ear, avoiding the sound of Caleb clearing his throat. "I know you're trying to piss Caleb off." I pull away and we both laugh.

"Little brother, better get your hands off Harley." Caleb says in a flat voice soft enough not to wake Willow.

"I think I like where my hands are; I'm quite comfortable actually. You knew I always had a crush on her but back then you two were together so I couldn't do much, but... now that you two *aren't* together I don't think I'm going to keep my mouth shut anymore." He says casually causing Caleb to almost growl. I can't see Joey's face but his body is shaking as he silently laughs. Caleb punches his arm.

"Wait till we get outta this car." Caleb threatens his brothers as Josh looks down and winks at me.

Twenty minutes later we arrive at their house; it's the same house Caleb grew up in. As we make our way up the long driveway many memories resurface; I used to spend more time here than at my own house.

Caleb carries Willow as we make our way through the house in search for his mom.

"I'm back here..." We hear her call out.

Walking toward the backyard patio we find her sitting on one of the garden chairs reading a magazine and drinking wine. She is still as beautiful as ever. Her blond hair is long and falls over her one shoulder in a neat braid. She looks older than the last time I saw her but it only adds to her beauty. She's dressed in a floral dress with wedges on. She smiles at the twins and stands up to give them a hug; she hasn't spotted me yet. I'm so nervous as I stand there thinking about what her reaction will be to seeing me and when she finds out she has a grandchild that I've kept from her for four years.

She spots me over Joey's shoulder and freezes. Her eyes are fixed on me; she doesn't even see Caleb holding Willow. Joey steps away from her and she stands frozen with her hands clasped to her chest then she whispers my name. Next thing I know I'm being pulled into her arms as she holds me tight. I wrap my arms around her waist soaking in the comfort I always felt whenever we would spend time together. She still wears the same perfume and it eases my nerves.

"Oh Sweetie, I've missed you so much!" She sounds as if she's crying and I can't help but hold her tighter as I try to take her pain away.

"I've missed you too." I watch over Holly's shoulder as Josh takes Willow from Caleb.

Holly steps away from me and looks me over smiling. She pushes the hair out of my face and turns me around as if she's inspecting me.

"You're still as beautiful as ever my darling. Where have you been? We were so worried about you." She sounds sad.

"I've been staying with my father, I'm so sorry. I should have called and let you know I was ok but at the time I was so upset and I didn't want anything to do with everything that reminded me of Caleb. It was stupid of me, I know... but I was so hurt at the time." I say looking down at the ground. I feel bigger warmer hands over my shoulder as Caleb brings me to his chest and rubs my back. I hear Holly's gasp realizing her son is here and that we're in the same room together. Caleb drops his head to the crook of my neck. "I'm so sorry for everything baby. I'm so sorry for keeping you from my family, they were yours too..." he says on a broken whisper. I squeeze him tighter against me then turn my mouth to his ear.

"No more apologizing okay? Remember, we're focusing on the future. No more lingering on the past. We need to be able to work together for Willow. We can do this." He holds me tighter and I feel him nod.

"I'm definitely missing something..." I hear Holly mumble. I move away from Caleb to see her standing there staring at the two of us. Willow is beginning to stir in Josh's arm. She wipes her eyes with balled fists and looks around confused.

"Mom, there's someone we want you to meet." Caleb says, walking toward Josh and Willow who are standing behind Holly. Holly turns to follow Caleb's movements and lets out a loud gasp when Willow opens her arms for Caleb. Holly practically collapses into the chair trying to catch her breath; her hand rests over her chest and I watch as tears fall down her cheeks. Willow makes a noise and wiggles in Caleb's arms, he lets her down and we all watch as she runs up to Holly.

"Don't cry." Willow says in a sad voice as she touches Holly's long braid. Holly smiles brightly.

"Here." Willow says lifting the long sleeve of the jacket she's wearing to Holly's face.

Holly looks up confused and I start laughing. "It's to wipe your tears away. I wipe away her tears with my shirt sleeve whenever she cries." The boys let out deep laughs and Holly chuckles too.

"No baby you keep your sleeve, these aren't sad tears my love. These are happy ones." Holly says looking down as she takes Willow's little hand in her own.

"Happy ones?" Willow asks confused.

"Yes, want to know why I'm happy?" Holly asks, using her other hand to wipe away her remaining tears.

Willow nods eagerly. "I just met my granddaughter and she's perfect."

"Huh?" Willow looks back and forth between Caleb and I evidently confused.

Caleb bends down to Willow's level, wiping the hair from her face. "This is my mom sweetie which means this is your granny."

"Another one?" Willow asks baffled, making all of us erupt in laughter once again.

"Yes sweetie, another one! You are a very special girl who has one *big* family." Holly says lifting Willow onto her lap.

Chapter 26

We leave Holly and Willow chatting on the patio while I help the boy's prepare the meat for the barbeque.

"Stay here tonight." Caleb says, coming up behind me as I wipe the table down in the kitchen. His hands rest on the granite counter tops on either side of me. He leans in and whispers in my ear. "Let them spend some time with her so I can spend more time with you. Please Harlz…"

I turn to look him in his eyes; he's so beautiful, his black hair is still messy from swimming and the smell of the beach still lingers on his skin. He pushes against me harder with one of his legs between mine and my lower back against the counter ledge.

He brings his head to mine again, this time running his lips against the curve of my neck until his lips stop at the base of my ear. A shiver makes its way down my body as I lean into his touch making him chuckle against me. He knows how weak I am against his touch and he's enjoying every minute of it. If I'm honest with myself, I'm enjoying whatever is between us too.

He whispers again. "Please?" I feel his lips latch onto my neck under my ear; I moan when he starts sucking. When he finally breaks away and looks down at me, I nod.

"Have you asked your mom about this?" I ask.

"She's the one who suggested it."

"I have to go to my mother's to fetch some clothes." I say, looking out of the window at the twins playing with Willow in the garden.

"I'll take you." He says picking up his keys off the counter.

"No, you need to stay here with Willow; she's just met your family and I'm not sure if she'll panic when she notices that we're not around. I'll be quick and I'll take your car, if you don't mind?" I smile at him.

I know the possession he has over his cars and if he allows me to use it, he must *really* trust me.

He runs his hands through his hair then lets out a smile and those damn dimples appear.

"On one condition…"

"Anything." I blurt, excited to drive his car.

He steps closer to me again, placing both his hands on my jaw cupping my face and forcing me to look into his eyes. He kisses my forehead, moves to each cheek then my nose and finally leaves a soft kiss on my lips.

"I know we haven't had a lot of time together but we've lost too many years already. I don't want to lose any more time and I want to be with you and my daughter. I want us to be a family Harley. That's all I've ever wanted with you. I love you so much baby. Please promise me that we'll try to work on us. I know you still feel something for me. I just need you to tell me that you'll at least try." The mood has done a one eighty and is totally serious now; the playful banter over. I know we have missed four years of each other's lives and that we have so much to catch up on. Caleb will always be in my life and I wouldn't have it any other way because we made our beautiful Willow together. I don't think I ever stopped loving him and even though we have a lot of issues to work through, I know deep down that I can do this as long as he is by my side. I guess you can never really let go of your soul mate. Maybe it's time for me to work on forgiveness.

"Okay Caleb, I'll try." I smile up at him just in time to see his shoulders loosen as he lets out a deep breath. He pulls me in for another hug then steps away, handing me his keys.

I quickly sneak out before Willow can see me leaving. Caleb's car still has that brand-new-car smell and it's so comfortable to drive; it's rather large and I have to squeeze my way in when I reach the parking in front of my mother's house.

My mother should be at work already but her car is sitting in the driveway. I look at my watch and double check the time. "Yeah, five thirty...wonder what she's doing home?" I question out loud as I make my way up the porch steps. I open the door and call out. "Mom, I thought you had wor-" As I close the door and turn around I scream. My mother is tied to a chair with a gag in her mouth. Her head hangs down, eyes closed as blood drips from a wound on her right temple.

"Ahhh... just in time baby; been waiting all day for you while you've been out playing fucking house." Jace saunters in with a beer in his hand. My heart is pounding and my fingers are shaking. Jace's eyes are blood shot and he doesn't look like himself at all.

"Jace..." I say on a whisper. "What are you doing?"

"Came to get you baby." He downs the bottle of beer and strains his neck to the side as if stretching.

"I'm not going anywhere with you." I start shaking my head as he runs his hands through his hair and lets out a frustrated sigh.

"That's what I thought you'd say; that's why I had to find a way to convince you." He plants his beer down on the coffee table and moves in my direction. I look over to where my mother sits out cold. I want to run to her and see if she's okay but I don't want to go near Jace. I look back at the door. Maybe if I can get out and shout for help he won't have time to hurt her anymore.

"Don't even think about it." Jace says through gritted teeth. I quickly turn to the door and open it only for him to slam it closed. I bend under his arms and run in the direction of my mother; I have to make sure she's okay.

I only get a chance to pull the scarf that is tied around her mouth out before he yanks my hair back and I'm smacked hard into his chest. He wraps an arm around my waist.

"Jace stop this! Please. Let us go. Why are you doing this?" I thrash and kick my legs about trying to get free, but his grasp is too strong.

"You're coming with me either way Harley." He turns me forcefully to face him. His eyes are dark and the veins in his neck are sticking out.

He looks down at my face lovingly, then his eyes freeze on my neck and his grip on me tightens.

"What the fuck is that?" He screams and shoves me. I stumble back and cover the spot on my neck where Caleb gave me a love bite. I hear mumbling to my side and see my mother attempting to move her head but her eyes are still closed.

"Answer me!" He roars making me wince. "You allow that piece of shit to touch you? You fucked him didn't you?" His hand is too quick, he backhands me with such force that I land on the little coffee table where his beer stood. It all crashes underneath me knocking the wind out of me. I let out the first of my sobs, it's just the beginning because now as I sit on the floor I'm covering my bloody face and weeping in my hands begging him not to hurt me.

"Fuck..." I hear him mutter. "I'm sorry baby!"

"When her daddy finds out, you're dead boy." I hear my mother's husky broken voice.

I lift my eyes to see Jace freeze and turn to look at her; Raven's back.

"You think I give a shit? Besides, there won't be any witnesses."

My mother spits in his face; I watch as he wipes his face, pulls out a gun from the back of his jeans and points it in her face.

"No!" I scream as I crawl up to his feet, looking up to him begging. "I'll come with you, I'll do whatever you want just don't kill her. Please!" I beg for her life with tears running down my face; I can taste the blood and salt from my tears on my lips.

I watch as he lowers the gun and places it back in his jeans. He yanks my arm up making me hiss out in pain. "I'm doing this because I love you, you know that right?" I don't reply which only makes him angrier.

"Answer me!" he shakes me but loses his grip as I go flying through the air. I feel the wall as my back and head hit it. I fall face first to the ground. I feel the moisture in my hair as I slowly raise my hand to the back of my head until I feel the wet spot, bringing my fingers to my line of vision.

Blood.

My vision starts to blur and the noises around me muffle as I lay on the floor. All I can think about is how I snuck out of Holly's house without telling Willow I loved her and how much I miss Caleb right now. My mother's muffled screams can be heard in the distance and I can feel the vibration off the floor boards under my cheek as Jace walks up toward me.

I wake up as Jace gently lies me down in the trunk of a car. I'm vaguely aware of him caressing my cheek.

"Can't live without you, I don't want to be alone in the dark. It's so dark without you my Harley. I need you."

Then he moves away, slams the trunk closed and I'm left in darkness... alone.

To be continued....

A Broken Beautiful Beginning – available now in both eBook and Paperback version.

About

Sophie Summers

I live in a small town off the South Coast of KwaZulu Natal. I am a 22 year old South African. I kept writing my dirty little secret for a couple of years before I decided to come clean and share my stories. When I'm not working I'm studying, writing or reading. I released my first book in 2013 which was a supernatural/werewolf based novel called Alexia Eden (Fairy Tales Don't Exist #1).

Although my life is busy as ever, I will never complain or regret the path I've taken that directed me to where I am today. The lessons I've learnt and the people I've met are my reasons for this. I work hard and write harder. Look me up sometime, even if it's just for a chat. I love receiving emails and reviews of my books so please email me and send me links of your reviews. I may not have responded to your emails but please note that I really do appreciate all of you who have taken the time to email me with words of encouragement and advice. Since I'm new to this writing world I still have a lot to learn.

You can find me on Goodreads and my blog
http://sophiesummers.weebly.com/.
Please feel free to comment, I'm always available to chat.
You can also follow me on twitter https://twitter.com/A_SophieSummers and even friend me on Facebook to keep up to date with release dates and upcoming works. https://www.facebook.com/sophie.summers.1048
   If you just want to chat? Email me on star.sophiesummers@gmail.com

Printed in Great Britain
by Amazon.co.uk, Ltd.,
Marston Gate.